SCOUTS

I0555613

ISBN: 978-1905091-68-3
Paperback version

© 2010 Nobilis Reed
Published by Logical-Lust Publications
www.logical-lust.com
57 Blair Avenue
Hurlford
Scotland
KA1 5AZ

Edited by Rachel McIntyre
Book layout and typesetting by jimandzetta.com
Cover art & design © 2010 Gypsy Thornton
gypsy@theinkgypsy.com

Printed in the UK and the USA

SCOUTS

BY NOBILIS REED

Norma Arm

Scutum-Crux Arm

Limit of Settlement   Sagittarius Arm

Coreward Reach

Old Stars

Rimward Reach

Perseus Arm

Chapter One

I stepped off the lift and froze. Two huge men sat at one of the tables across the mess deck, scanning the small crowd. They weren't wearing space armor, but I knew who they were. Marines. One had a long scar running from his temple down to the corner of his mouth, pulling it into a permanent sneer. The other had a nose crushed flat to his face, and lacked one finger on his left hand. Long, bulky weapons hung from straps on their shoulders, ready for use at a moment's notice.

Steaming cups of tea sat between them, but they weren't drinking. They were watching.

Valka squeezed my hand. "Challers . . ."

"Yes, I see them," I whispered. "Just act casual. Don't raise their suspicions. We don't know what they're here for."

"Nonsense. You know exactly what they're here for."

We walked slowly to the counter to pick up our trays of vedgepacks, teabulbs, and bean-curd cubes. I tried not to look at them, but my eyes kept darting in their direction. They were watching *us*.

I led Valka over to a table on the opposite side of the room. They were still watching with half-amused interest.

"They know," she whispered.

"Of course they do. The station's personnel roster is available to anyone." I growled and bit off the end of the teabulb. "Why don't they just do it? Why are they stretching it out?"

"Maybe they don't need anyone right now."

"They always need people. They're Marines." I munched on the sticks of carrots and celery, saving the bland bean curd for last. I knew from experience that I would feel fuller if I left it. "Valka, I can't live like this anymore—hiding whenever there are Marines around, or Merchants? Stakroya Station is a trade hub. There's a ship here more often than not, and with the station overpop, they can take one of us any time they want."

"What are you going to do, just throw yourself at them? Demand they take you, make you into one of them?" There was an edge of sarcasm in her voice, but I deserved it.

"Sometimes I think it would be better than this terrible waiting, and it would keep you from getting taken by the Merchants. Why did the Jacksons have to go and have twins?"

"It doesn't matter why." She reached across the table and gripped my hand. "They did and we're the ones who'll pay for it if we can't get off the station by joining the Scouts. We can get away. We can do it."

I nodded. "We have to."

The Fleet and the Merchants transformed their recruits, shaping their bodies to be more useful to the service. Marines became hugely muscled, thick-skinned giants, built for perpetual combat. Rumors held that they engaged in gladiatorial games on their ships. Merchant crews were clumsy blobs of flesh, fat on the profits of interstellar trade. I shuddered to think of what Valka would look like if they got her, but worse would be the separation from the only woman I had ever loved.

I picked up the lettuce-leaf full of bean curd and crammed it into my mouth. It was more than a mouthful, but I wanted this meal to be over as soon as possible. Once I choked it down, I glanced at Valka's tray. She had finished her meal quickly as well.

I held out my hand. "Come on. Let's get back to work."

The lift doors opened and we hurried to our console. I glanced at the doors. The Marines shouldn't have any business in the comm center, but they could go where they pleased. Nowhere was safe. I squeezed Valka's hand, as much to reassure myself as her.

Valka sat at a console and unlocked it with her thumbprint and passcode.

I sat at the console next to hers and linked it so I could skim the same mountain of information she was sifting through, but I didn't feel any more inspiration than before. "So we've established that the Scouts have certain minimums for academic achievement, health, et cetera."

"Which we meet."

"Which we meet," I agreed. "And they always pick up couples."

"Which we are."

"And that they will pass up hundreds of other likely candidates to pick up kids on some station out in the middle of nowhere."

"Right. The only question is why." She tapped out some more commands, reshuffling the data for the hundredth time. "The answer has to be in here somewhere."

"Maybe finding it is part of the test."

"I don't know, maybe it is the test, and if we find the answer we'll be in." She looked hopeful.

"Well, this data did come from the Scouts, we know that much. What else was in the data squirt besides all the statistics?"

"News articles, thousands of them, indexed and cross-referenced. Each one of them mentions, somewhere, at least one of the people recruited by the Scouts within the last five years. I already worked that out."

I brought up the main index, yet again. "What's this folder at the bottom, labeled 'Miscellaneous?'"

"Personal diaries and journals, mostly. Just like the news stories, all of them mention the people who got picked up by the Scouts."

"Anything good in there?" I tapped the data and scrolled through the titles. They didn't make much sense by themselves, just names and datestamps.

"I haven't looked. It seemed like, I don't know, an invasion."

I opened one at random and skimmed the first few entries. "They gave us this stuff for a reason, Valka. What if the answer we're looking for is in there?"

Valka slapped her forehead. "How could I have been so stupid? We have to read these now."

"There are hundreds of them."

"Wait." She tapped a query into the console. "Forty-two of them were written by people who were chosen to join the Scouts themselves. Let's start with the last few entries in each one. There might be clues in there."

We got down to work, reading the thoughts and feelings of folks so much like ourselves. It wasn't easy reading.

Personal Journal, date 2398.109:

I can't stand another night apart from Shopara. Just being near her makes my pulse race. And after today . . .

We went to the zero gravity training hub today, to practice for our EVA finals. She suggested that we share the changing room to get into our suits. She said it would save time, but that was just an excuse. Her body is incredible. Her breasts are round and full, with little pink nipples that stood out like buttons. She turned away from me to slide her coverall down. She heard me groan at the sight of her ass and giggled. I told her how beautiful she was.

She slipped her feet out of her coverall and turned around, one hand covering her crotch. "Really?"

Her eyes shifted from my face down to my cock. It was getting really hard. She believed me then.

She reached out and touched it, then pulled back like she'd gotten a shock. I told her it was okay, she could touch it. She blushed and I could hear her breathing. I wanted to tell her to grab it, squeeze it, do whatever she liked, but I couldn't. I moved closer and put my hand on her boob. It was as soft and warm as I imagined. She said we better stop, someone might find out.

I know the station is already overpop. I know what would happen if she gets pregnant, if she has a baby. We won't go that far. But I have to see her again. Maybe I can get my brother to let me use his quarters? I'm sure I could get Shopara to come with me.

I looked up at Valka. Her face was flushed, and she stroked her thigh idly with one hand.

My mouth seemed thick. "This is pretty strong stuff."

"Yeah." She swallowed hard and gave me an embarrassed smile. "I guess they really were a lot like us."

I opened another file.

Diary Entry, date 2397-045:

Dear Diary,

> *I dreamed of Cosar again last night. I was in my bed, just listening to the ventilators, and the door opened. He came in and sat on the bed next to me, and put his hand on my leg. He said something, I don't remember what it was, then he leaned down and kissed me. It wasn't tense and scared, like the kisses we stole in the docking bay. It was long and warm and passionate.*
>
> *I undid my covers and pulled them back. I was naked underneath. I let him touch me everywhere. After he touched my boobs and my cootie, he wanted to climb on top of me, like I saw in that holo the other day, but I said he couldn't, and that was fine. He stood up, and he was naked. I touched him, and felt it, but nothing more than that. That's when I woke up.*
>
> *I want to be with him so badly. We're meant to be together, I know it. I hope the Scouts will take us, but even if they don't, we'll be together working in the sensor array.*

I slid my chair closer to Valka's and took her hand. "I can't read any more, not feeling like this."

"Challers, we can't! What if someone comes in?"

I leaned close and breathed the scent coming up from the skin of her neck. "I don't care," I whispered. "I can't stand it anymore."

"We only have to wait." Her fingers ran through my short hair. "Somewhere we can be alone together."

I kissed her neck. "We're alone now." I put my hand on her stomach and let it move slowly towards her chest.

"Challers, no." She put her hand over mine, holding it in place. "Listen. Those diary entries. Were any of them about a couple who had . . . done it?"

"No. Well, not the one I read, anyways."

"Read some more. I think that may be the key."

Reluctantly, I went back to my tablet and skimmed a dozen more diaries. She was right. While all of them were in deep romantic relationships, none of them had taken the step we were going to take that night. Not a one.

"Oh, vack! Val, do you realize what this means? We can't do it. We can't do it."

She put her arms around me and kissed the top of my head. "Yes, but now we know why those other couples, the ones the Scouts passed up, weren't picked."

"It also means we have to cancel our night together." I groaned and dropped my head in my hands, elbows propped on my knees. Our plans for our first time had been in the works for months. We had rented a room at the station hotel. We had even talked to our parents. If we were going to get dragged from the station by the Fleet or the Merchants, we would at least have that time together first.

"I'll cancel the reservation." Her voice held as much disappointment as mine. "Don't worry. We'll have our night together. It won't be right away, that's all." She stood behind me and rubbed my shoulders.

"I don't get it," I groaned. "What's so important about virginity?"

Val sat down next to me and put her arm around my shoulder. "If we're right, and if we're lucky, we'll find out."

I turned to kiss her. "I want you so badly I could scream." My voice grated with desire and frustration. Our lips met, full of hunger.

"We're just going to have to control ourselves, at least until the next Scout ship comes along. Then, one day, we'll be one of those couples, and we can be together for the rest of our lives."

"I hope so."

We didn't have to wait long. Val and I were kissing in the oxygen gardens when the call arrived. I pulled the buzzing comm-unit from my belt and answered it.

My brother-in-law's voice was calm. "They're here, Challers. Arriving in Docking Bay Two in four minutes. Better hurry if you want to meet them."

I jumped from my chair, taking Val by the hand. "Thanks, Partik. We owe you."

"Good luck." The signal cut and my comm-unit went silent.

We ran full out through the hallways and down the tube to the docking bay and got there just as the vacuum alarm was starting to sound. We watched through the observation windows as the massive outer doors of the hangar yawned wide.

Val put her hand in mine and gave me a nervous smile.

I leaned in and kissed her. "It'll be all right. They'll take us."

"Challers . . ."

I was putting on a brave face, but inside I was as nervous as she.

"Are you sure it's Scouts coming in? If it's a Fleet shuttle we need to hide."

"I got the word from Partik up in Orbital Control. They're Scouts."

A subtle vibration in the deck plates stopped as the doors stopped moving. Twenty breaths passed before the nose appeared at the doors, hovering slowly forward. The holos we had found didn't do it justice. Silver, sleek, and graceful, it extended slim landing gear and set down so lightly I couldn't tell exactly which second it happened.

It sat for several minutes as the doors closed and the air flowed back into the hangar. Val and I stood watching until a voice startled us from behind.

"Quite an impressive ship, isn't it?"

I looked up to see Captain Shaunson emerging from the passageway. "Uh, yes, sir."

I wasn't sure what to say. We weren't in an actual restricted area, but we didn't have a good reason to be there, either.

He stopped next to us and stood looking into the hangar. He wasn't particularly large, but the air around him hummed with authority.

Inside the hangar, a hatch opened in the bottom of the ship and a woman dropped to her feet on the deck. She had the biggest boobs I'd ever seen on anyone but a Merchant, more curves than anyone on the station. She turned to help a broad-chested man down behind her. They were older folks, but not as old as Captain Shaunson. The male Scout seemed to be in his late twenties. She seemed a bit older, with just a hint of gray speckling her hair. They wore plain, white, skin-tight clothes that showed off their perfect physiques. Her sleeveless uniform was cut high on her shoulders, showing off perfectly sculpted arms.

Captain Shaunson clapped me on the shoulder with a familiarity he had never shown me before. "Would you two do me a favor and wait here for a few minutes? I'd like to speak with our guests in private."

"Of course, sir."

"Good. Be seeing you."

He activated the airlock and stepped through into the hangar. When it closed, all sound was cut off from inside. Captain Shaunson walked over, shook their hands, and chatted.

"They're beautiful," breathed Val.

The Scouts looked at each other and smiled. I couldn't hear the chuckle, but the mirth on their faces was infectious. I couldn't help laughing a bit myself.

Captain Shaunson led the Scouts back to the airlock.

Val grabbed my sleeve. "They're coming! Vack, Challers, what are we going to say?"

I didn't know. The Scouts inspired no less awe at close range. To my boundless relief, Captain Shaunson spared me the turmoil of having to introduce myself.

"Challers Dizen, Valka Parl, meet Captain Shirley Smith and Pilot Masters Pale."

She was the one in charge on that ship. It surprised me for a moment—women rarely took positions of leadership on the station—but the moment passed, and it made perfect sense. She would have to be in charge.

Val poked me in the ribs.

"P-pleased to meet you, captain."

She smiled and took my hand. "The same, I'm sure." Instead of shaking my hand, she kissed my palm. "I understand you want to be a Scout."

"Yes, ma'am."

"Please, Challers . . . we don't use honorifics like that in the Scouts. Just call me Shirley."

Captain Shaunson took out his comm-unit and took a brief call. "If you will all follow me, we have a small reception planned. There's a shuttle coming in and we need to clear the passageway."

"Of course," said Shirley, "lead the way."

Shirley walked beside me, a few steps behind Captain Shaunson. I looked behind me, briefly, to see Val beside Shirley's partner, Masters. She gave me a stunned smile. It was actually happening—or was it?

I turned back to Shirley. "Are we being recruited?"

"We're considering it. You've passed the first test. You've got the drive and curiosity to determine the basic job requirements, and the restraint to make sure you met them. Your investigations and data requests caught our attention, so we're here to begin your evaluation and training. But that comes later. For now, we celebrate."

Captain Shaunson's outer office had been transformed into a tiny banquet hall. Our parents stood there, more pleased and proud than I had ever seen. I sat with Shirley on one side, my mother on the other, and Val across the table. Everywhere I looked, there was loving, smiling appreciation.

The meal went by in a blur. Captain Shaunson made a toast. I think I ate some of the food.

Finally, Shirley touched my hand. "Get a good night's sleep, Challers. We leave in the morning."

I took Val aside as people began taking their leave. Tears sparkled in her eyes.

"I can't believe it. We're going on a Scout ship!" She wrapped her arms around me and nuzzled my chin, a gesture we had shared a thousand times before.

As always, my body responded to her touch. It happened whenever we got close.

"I love you too," she said, and kissed my neck.

Fingers to her chin, I raised her mouth to mine to kiss her. "Meet me tonight," I whispered.

Shirley put her hand on my shoulder. "I meant what I said. Get a good night's sleep."

I blushed. We kissed once more, just a peck, and separated. I took her hands in mine and looked into her eyes. "Until tomorrow."

I thought I wouldn't be able to sleep, but the stress of the afternoon, as welcome as it was, took its toll. I slept, and dreamed of Valka.

CHAPTER TWO

I woke to find my mother packing a small duffel. The months since we had discovered that the station was over the population limit had been tough on her, and it was good to see the weight off her shoulders.

"Good morning, Scout," she said with a smile. "They're only giving you a ten milliLowell mass allowance, so I'm making it count. I hope you don't mind that I let you sleep."

I climbed out of bed and kissed her temple. "No, Ma. I don't mind. Thanks."

"Captain Smith said that all your clothing and equipment would be provided, so I'm just packing some mementos. There's a holo with some pictures of the family, and a data chip with your journals and records. You're going to want things to remember your life here. Scouts live a very different life than station people."

"How?"

She had never spoken of Scouts before, and the thought that she might have been holding some information back troubled me.

She shook her head. "Don't worry. I'm sure you'll do just fine." She put the duffel on my dresser. "Go ahead and get ready."

I showered and shaved, and picked an outfit of pure white to match Shirley's. I had pretty good shoulders, too, though I hadn't had nearly as much time to sculpt them. From the look of Masters, the Scouts didn't lack for workout facilities.

I hurried through breakfast. I didn't want to be late, even though we didn't really have a firm departure time. My mother cried as she waved to me from the hatch of our quarters, and then I was on my way.

Val met me at the intersection at the end of our corridor. She hugged me, pressing her lithe body to mine. I could feel her heart hammering in her chest. "I still can't believe it's real. I dreamed last night, of you and I on a Scout ship of our own, out among the stars. And when I woke up, I almost believed it was all just a dream."

"It's real," I said, stroking her hair, "but we still have to pass their evaluation—whatever that is." I pulled away and took her hand. "Come on. The stars are waiting."

All along the way, people took us aside to congratulate us.

"You remember us when you're out there," they said. "Remember where you came from."

I started to wonder whether Scouts ever came back. They weren't giving congratulations, they were saying goodbye, and the elation I felt ran with streaks of sadness. It occurred to me that I had never met an ex-Scout, but then I hadn't met an active Scout until the day before, either.

As we came to the end of the gallery, those emotions froze in a block of terror. Three huge Marines stood in front of the door to the docking bay. Even without their space armor, they were terrifying beings. Two and a half meters tall and massing at least six of me, all of it muscle, there was no denying their immediate power. The fact that the station folk had disappeared from this end of the gallery only added to the Marines' authority. One leaned forward and stared at me. His eyes were entirely black.

"Challers Dizen?" His question was no question.

Valka took my hand. "There must be a mistake! We've been recruited by the Scouts."

"You're a citizen of Stakroya Station. Stakroya Station is overpop. In the interest of maintaining life support integrity, I am relieving the station of excess burden."

The words felt ritualized, as if he had to say them before they could drag me away. I wanted to run, but where? The only way to the Scout ship was past them. I backed away, pulling out my comm-unit. I hit the emergency button. Nothing happened.

Faster than I could have imagined such a creature moving, the Marine's massive hand shot out and grabbed my forearm. Valka screamed and batted at them, but they ignored her, dragging me towards their ship. I thrashed in their grip, but kicking them was like kicking a bulkhead wall. I had no more chance of getting away than a baby.

"Valka!" I shouted over my shoulder. "Call Shirley!"

"That won't be necessary." Shirley stood in the passageway in front of them, arms crossed. "Did you think I wouldn't know, lieutenant? Did you think I would just let this slip by?"

He leaned down and glared. "We're within our rights," he growled.

She stood her ground. "That man is a Scout, lieutenant, and you are *not* within your rights. Put him down, or there will be consequences."

I was close enough to hear the buzz coming from the comm-unit clipped to the Marine's ear. He stood at attention and put his hand to the side of his head. "Yes, sir." He turned to the men holding me. "Put him down."

They obeyed, setting me down lightly on my feet.

The Marines stepped back away from me and Valka squeezed past them to wrap herself around me.

Shirley didn't hesitate. "No time for that now. They can still change their minds."

She took my hand, I took Valka's, and we hurried down to the hangar.

The interior of their ship was no less wonderful than the exterior. The hatch led to a long, narrow passageway that opened into a circular chamber, with a soft, spongy floor, about as big as my family's main room. Wide, padded benches ringed it with breaks fore and aft for the passageways leading to the rest of the ship. The dark walls beyond the benches glowed with status displays and programmable controls in between access panels and lockers. The air felt warmer than the station.

Shirley popped open a panel, revealing a set of cubbyholes. Two were stuffed with rolls of fabric and the other two were empty. "Put your things in here, and we'll be on our way."

Masters left us, taking the other passageway towards the nose of the ship, and Shirley took a seat on a bench, facing the center of the room. She stuck her legs out and crossed them, leaning back on her hands.

When our things were stowed and the panel secured again, she waved her hands at the benches. "Sit, sit, and I'll give you the talk while Masters takes us out."

Val and I sat together, our hands touching on the padded seat.

"Welcome to the Scout Service. You are now provisional cadets. This means you do as I say—or as Masters says, or any other Scout you're likely to meet, for that matter. Don't worry, we're a very informal service. No salutes, no honorifics. It's actually more like a family than a military service. There are some rules, though.

"One: Take care of your body. It is your greatest possession as a Scout. No unapproved drugs, no alcohol, no caffeine. Of course, it'll be hard to violate that rule when you're on a Scout craft, but it's a rule you should always follow.

"Two: Take care of your mind. I've already seen your academic records and you two have solid foundations. You still have much to learn to be full-fledged Scouts. Astrophysics, engineering, xenobiology, economics, history, politics, diplomacy—you're going to study it all. Scouts get sent on a wide variety of missions, and your most efficient tools are the ones you carry around in your heads.

"Three: No orgasms without my express permission, under any circumstances. The ship is highly sensitive to releases of orgone energy. It shouldn't be an issue since there's no privacy on this ship, but there have been accidents."

I looked at Val. Her brow furrowed.

"I know," said Shirley, "you're young, and you need release. I'll make sure you get the opportunities you need, but they must be under controlled conditions. Don't worry. The last thing I want is to cause you trauma."

Masters's voice broke in, transmitted from the bridge. "We're away, Shirley. Ready for jump."

Shirley nodded. "Thank you, Masters. Meet us in the chamber." She addressed Val and I again. "Looks like it's time for your first engineering lesson. Faster-than-light travel is dependent upon orgone energy. Merchant ships use basal orgone, the ordinary everyday energy of life. Warships need to be able to generate bursts of speed, so their engines can also accept crisis orgone from rage, fear, and pain. It's a horrific life, but as long as there are Pirates preying on Merchant ships, we need the Fleet."

"And then there's us. Scout ships can travel across the galaxy in a moment, powered by transcendent orgone. Some of the great adepts have learned to release it at will, but most of us use orgasm."

"Orgasm?" The implications of this secret burst upon me like a bomb.

"You are familiar with the concept?" She smiled. "I've read your medical report; everything seemed to be all right, but if there's a problem . . ."

"No, no." I shook my head. "No problem."

"Good." She glanced around the room. "This chamber is surrounded by collectors that channel the orgone into field generators set in the hull. If the field generators are properly primed, and the navigation computer set to trigger? Pop! We're there."

Masters emerged from the passageway and stood in the center of the room.

Shirley stood and moved next to him. "Ready to give a demonstration?"

"As always," he said, and pulled his shirt up over his head.

I scratched the back of my neck and looked away. "Don't you want us to, um . . ."

"Of course not," said Shirley. "How else are you going to learn? Station folk have different ways of looking at sex."

Masters chuckled.

Shirley shot him a look. "So to speak. You need to shed your inhibitions, and this is your first step in doing that."

I looked up to see her tossing her top behind a bench. Her full, round breasts bounced with her movements.

"Should I take off my clothes, too?" I didn't know what I was supposed to do. It felt strange to just sit there, watching.

She rolled her pants down, revealing full hips and thighs. The naked cleft of her pussy held my fascinated attention.

"No, keep your clothes on, and don't touch yourself, either. You need to learn control and now is the time to start."

I looked over at Val. Her lips were pursed and one hand nervously picked at the neck of her shirt. She caught my eye and gave me a fleeting smile. This would test her as much as it would me.

Now completely naked, Shirley and Masters kissed, their left hands laid gently on each other's waist, their right hands roaming over each other's body. Their kisses were quick, rhythmic, but open-mouthed and full of passionate promise. They sank down onto the floor as one, performing a dance they obviously knew well from long practice. She lay on her back, her hands caressing his shoulders, neck, and ears. His lips traveled over her body, kissing and nuzzling her skin as he gradually approached her breast.

I adjusted my pants so my cock could slip into a more comfortable position. How could they possibly expect me to watch this and not have an orgasm? I had never seen anything so arousing in my life. Some of my friends had exchanged sex holos on the station, but my parents never allowed any such things in our quarters. I longed to touch myself, to relieve the pressure I felt building within me, but Shirley had given specific orders. I crossed my legs and focused my attention on her face.

Shirley's eyelids fluttered closed, and her mouth curled into a gentle smile. As Masters's attentions moved gradually lower, her mouth opened, letting out small gasps.

Even this second-hand pleasure was difficult to bear. My erection pushed against my pants, begging for attention. If I didn't attend to it soon, I would wind up with a serious case of blue-balls.

I glanced over at Val. She had crossed her legs too and shoved her hands under her butt, and I could barely sense her trembling. I didn't dare say anything.

A soft cry of ecstasy drew my attention back to Shirley and Masters. He knelt between her legs, his arms under her thighs to lift her plump, shaved pussy to his mouth. I couldn't see exactly what he was doing from my angle, but Shirley showed every sign of enjoying it. Her hands squeezed her breasts, and her mouth gaped open as her body writhed beneath him.

As if responding to an unheard command, they parted and Masters lay on his back. Shirley stroked his cock a few times with her hand, then engulfed it in her mouth. It took only a matter of seconds to bring him to full erection. She threw a leg over his abdomen and mounted him, impaling herself on his rigid member.

Valka whimpered. I glanced her way again. She had closed her eyes, shutting out the passionate vision in front of her. I didn't blame her. I was fascinated, certainly, but if I kept watching, I was going to come whether I wanted to or not. I closed my eyes too.

The sounds they made aroused me just as much, though. The wet movements of skin on skin combined with their grunts and moans, and my imagination filled in the blanks. The chaotic music of their lovemaking filled my head as it grew louder and more insistent. The end finally arrived, punctuated by Shirley's shriek of bliss and Masters's drawn-out groan.

The ship shuddered as if it, too, had had an orgasm. A drum-like thudding came from the wall behind me and the hair on the back of my neck stood up. Valka, suddenly, had her arms around me and I held her. Had she broken the rule and let the orgasm take her? Had I? My confusion ran so deep I couldn't tell.

CHAPTER THREE

When things quieted down, I opened my eyes. Valka sighed and sat next to me. Her hand, still holding mine, did not clutch so tightly.

Masters sat, still naked, working on a console folded out from the wall. Shirley stood before us, wiping her body with a small towel.

"We didn't quite make it," said Masters. "I'm plotting another course. We need about, hmm, a half a parsec."

Shirley shrugged. "This happens when Scouts have been together too long. Things become routine and the ship doesn't perform as well." She looked at me. "Challers, let's see if you can finish the job. Even alone, a half a parsec is possible."

"What? Alone? You want me to masturbate for you?"

Sitting and watching Shirley and Masters having sex right in front of me was enough of a shock; now she wanted me to jack off for her? I looked over at Valka. She was dumbstruck.

"You're more than ready, Challers." She nodded in the direction of my crotch. "Come on, lie down. Show me you've got what it takes to be a Scout." She took my hand and pulled me to the center of the room. "I want to see what you do when you masturbate, see what makes you come. Show me, Challers."

Valka's face was flushed. Her eyes fixed on mine. There was fear there, but I also saw curiosity and desire. She nodded. I had her permission.

Shirley helped me off with my clothes. My fingers trembled so much I almost needed it.

"Get comfortable," she said, and sat down on the bench next to Valka. "Position yourself there, in the center of the chamber. That's where the collectors are focused."

I decided to kneel. It wasn't my usual position, but it would allow me to watch Valka and Shirley. I knelt down, knees slightly apart.

"Don't worry about making a mess," said Shirley. "The floor is designed to handle it. Self-cleaning."

I saw no trace of the session they had just had in the same spot.

I took my cock in my hand. I was still incredibly aroused, hard as a rock. With my eyes locked on Valka's, I imagined what it would be like when it was our turn to lie down together, to propel a ship between the stars with our passion. How far would we go? I squeezed and stroked, my hand dropping into a familiar pattern.

Valka looked worried. She still had her hands jammed under her butt, and while she was watching me with an intensity I had never seen before, there was a painful cast to her face. If she was in as much need to come as I was, watching me must have been torture. A knot of guilt tightened in my stomach that I would find relief and she would not. I tried to push the thought away, to focus on the sensation, but it wouldn't go.

"Will Valka have a turn?" I asked between gasping breaths.

"Yes," said Shirley. "Even if you take us the whole way, she will have a turn."

The relief of that one nagging thought was all I needed. All the pent-up desire from watching my mentors fucking the ship across the stars crystallized in my spine and shot down into my cock. My throat locked, my balls clenched, and I sent thick strands of cum onto the floor between us. Again, the ship throbbed and whined, but even in my erotic haze I could tell that it lasted only a few seconds. I felt a strange prickling sensation on my skin that hadn't been there before. It wasn't uncomfortable. I fell backwards, all the tension draining from my body.

"Not bad," said Masters, from behind me. "You're about ten percent over baseline, Challers; you're going to make a fine Scout."

Shirley helped me to my feet, handed me a towel, and turned towards Masters. "Was that enough to get us there?"

Masters shook his head. "Not quite. Still about point-two parsecs to go."

Shirley nodded to Valka. "Your turn."

I wiped myself down and switched places with Valka, while Shirley took Masters's place.

He let Valka take off her own clothes, watching with a calm, welcoming smile. "Just relax. Bring us in, Valka. Bring us home."

He sat down where Shirley had been and leaned back comfortably. I wanted to ask him if he needed to be there, but Shirley seemed to be handling the job of monitoring the ship during the jump. The look in Valka's eyes told me everything; she was embarrassed, she was afraid, but she was determined not to foul up our chances of being accepted by the Scouts.

She knelt down where I had been and ran her hands slowly up and down her body. I couldn't help making comparisons. Her breasts weren't as big as Shirley's, nor her hips as generous, but her smooth skin shone. Her fingers toyed with her pink nipples, making them stand up from the curve of her breast like little pyramids. She pinched them lightly, and twirled them between her fingertips. I imagined what it would be like to kiss them, to suck them—what they would feel like under my fingers.

As her hands moved down, my gaze followed them to the triangle of bushy hair. It grew thick enough to conceal all but a vague outline of her sex. I heard her breathing change as she massaged the area, pushing and pulling at her lips. When I looked up, our eyes met, and all thought of watching what her hands were doing disappeared. The need in her eyes drew me in.

"You're beautiful," I whispered, more on instinct than anything else.

A quick smile flitted across her mouth, followed by a gasp of pleasure. I could feel my cock rising again, responding to the erotic vision before me, but I felt no great need to deal with it. My eyes could not leave hers.

Her orgasm built slowly. Her jaw twitched, opening slightly as she drew in each escalating breath. I could hear wet sounds coming from her fingers. The gasps turned to whimpers, and the whimpers to cries. When she closed her eyes and let her head fall back, my eyes shifted to her hands. Both were jammed between her wide-spread thighs, slowly rubbing her sex.

"Challers," she moaned. "Oh, Challers . . ."

I knew I wasn't allowed to touch her. I glanced at Masters long enough to see that his cock wasn't responding to the display much, if at all. I hoped I never became so jaded.

Masters leaned over to whisper close. "Tell her to imagine you."

"I'm here, Val. I'm with you. Imagine my hands on your body." I fought down a stammer. What was I supposed to say? I glanced over at Masters.

He gave me a smile and a wink, and mouthed the word *more*.

"Imagine me between your legs. I'm, ah, kissing you. Kissing your breasts."

She gasped, a small shudder passing through her body. I felt a thrumming sound, too low to hear, in the air, in the ship. She was close.

"Kissing your, um . . ."

"Sex," whispered Masters.

"Kissing your sex."

Sweat broke out on her body, and her face and breasts flushed. "Oh, Challers!"

Her thighs squeezed shut around her hand and the engines roared to life. The ship pulsed so hard it nearly shook me from my seat, the sound drowning out Valka's quiet cries. The sound and vibration seemed to go on forever.

When it finally stopped, Shirley was whooping and slapping the seat next to her with her open palm. "Almost four hundred percent over baseline, Valka! That's incredible! If you perform that well under operating conditions, you'll be able to go to the Norma arm and back!"

Masters helped Valka to her feet, took her shoulders, and shook her gently, a broad grin splitting his face. Valka looked stunned. She took Shirley's offered towel and dabbed at her moist body. Then her eyes met mine, and she smiled. "We did it."

I nodded. "We did it."

She pulled me into a hug and squeezed so tight I thought she'd crush me. My cock poked her side and she pulled away, blushing.

Shirley clapped her hands. "Okay, cadets. Clean yourselves up. You'll find a fresher just aft of the bridge. Put your towels in the recycler when you're done. Remember, no orgasms. Masters, bring us in."

Valka went to the fresher. The tiny room was cramped with a shower, toilet, and sink. She climbed into the tiny shower cubicle, making room for me in front of the vanity. "Can you believe it? We're really doing it!"

I smiled, trying not to let the insecurities that brewed in my head escape into my voice. "It's incredible. Powering a starship, just with an orgasm."

"I know, and soon, it will be us!"

I took a tube from a small shelf near the sink and idly rolled it in my hand. Would it be? We had assumed that we would stay together, but Shirley's comment about what happens to Scout couples after they've been together too long implied that they would separate. What would happen then?

Valka finished her shower, and I switched places with her, enjoying the closeness of the tiny bathroom and trying not to get turned on. I welcomed the spray of cold water and let it calm my overactive hormones.

She took a towel from a rack near the hatch and dried herself. "I wonder if they'll let us have a ship like this."

"There's got to be a lot of training first." I turned off the water and followed her, drying myself as I went.

We put our towels in the recycler, as we had been instructed, and stepped out into the main passageway stark naked.

Shirley met us dressed in her plain white clothes. She handed us small bundles of fabric. "These are your new uniforms. The black color identifies you as cadets; you'll get whites once you've graduated to full Scout status."

They turned out to be thin, stretchy shorts and tops that left little to the imagination. The fabric clung closely to Valka's body, making the shape of her nipples and pussy lips clearly visible.

"This is it?" I said, pulling them on. "This doesn't seem like much more than underwear." My cock was outlined so clearly you could see every ridge and vein. "I might as well be naked."

"That's part of your training, cadet." She crossed past me, patting my butt on the way. "Go on up to the bridge. Headquarters should be coming into view."

Valka and I watched from the bridge, huddled behind the control chair. Scout headquarters turned out to be a station totally unlike my home. Instead of a globe of a hundred meters or so, a ring a kilometer in diameter grew before us. Its main structure, a ribbon of green and blue, gleamed in the light of an orange star. The only word that could even come close to expressing my feelings at that moment was "Wow."

Masters made a minor course adjustment. "Ten thousand people, an entirely self-sufficient community. We grow our own food, manufacture our own parts and supplies."

"And that's allowed?"

"We're the Scouts," said Masters. "Those rules don't apply to us. No mandated trade routes, no manufacturing prohibitions. This way, we never have Merchant ships docking at the headquarters. No Merchants, no Pirates; no Pirates, no Fleet. We're part of the galaxy, but apart from it. They need us more than we need them, and we like it that way."

Growing up, the Scouts had been agents of mystery, ghostly ships that would appear, hang mysteriously in the sky for a day or so transmitting and receiving data, and then vanish again. This revelation served only to enhance their cachet. Separate from the Merchants? Separate from the Fleet?

"So your kids don't get recruited by the Fleet or the Merchants."

"That's right."

The metal walls of a small docking bay enveloped us, close around the ship. I heard and felt lock-downs clunk into place on the hull. Green indicator lights on the console flipped over to yellow, and Masters stood up and nodded to us. "Cadets, welcome to Scout headquarters."

CHAPTER FOUR

The belly hatch connected to a short access tube, which in turn came out into the center of a circular gallery. A woman met us there, dressed in a sarong of red and blue. She smiled broadly as we filed out and arranged ourselves.

Shirley provided introductions. "Cadets, this is Academy Director Anna Kal. We'll be reporting to her during your academy training."

"We? You mean, you're staying with us?"

The director nodded. "The Scouts operate on a close apprenticeship system. Since Shirley and Masters are the ones who located and recruited you, they have the first opportunity to be your teachers. If that doesn't work out for some reason, we'll find you someone else to learn from until you earn your full status."

Valka was bouncing on her toes. "What are we waiting for?"

Director Kal gave Valka a nod of appreciation. "Indeed. If you'll follow me, we'll start with a tour of the academy."

The academy consisted of a few docking bays on the outer rim of the station and a couple of levels on the side of the main ring. There were classrooms, a dormitory, a gymnasium, a few simulator tanks, and a large data processing center. Here and there we came across groups of people, just two Scouts and two cadets, or sometimes just one of each.

The five of us had a meal in the cafeteria. I'm not sure whether it was breakfast or lunch, but I hadn't eaten since leaving Stakroya and I was starved. I couldn't believe the variety of foods available there. There were the usual hydroponics, of course, but in addition, there was bread, cheese, milk, butter, and eggs cooked any way we liked.

I heaped my tray until Shirley laughed and stopped me from taking a second piece of cake. "Okay, hold on, cadet. We're not fattening you up for the slaughter here."

"Do you always eat this well?"

"On the ship, things are more controlled, but here at headquarters we like to enjoy our luxuries. You'll probably gain some weight in basic training, but we'll make sure it's mostly muscle, in your case."

At the end of the buffet line, she put a couple of foil-wrapped squares on my tray.

"What are these?"

"You'll see. Have them after you've eaten everything else."

It was something called chocolate. It was wonderful, smooth and just sweet enough, with an aftertaste that was bitter rather than metallic or chemical.

Valka liked it too. She liked it a lot, judging from the noises she made.

After seeing the facilities, we entered a large display hall showing some of the accomplishments of the Scout Service in its long history. Images of star systems mapped by the Scouts hung from the walls. There were hundreds of them. In the center of the room, display cases held artifacts and other memorabilia from notable Scout missions. Each one had a holographic display where the Scouts involved described the circumstances and details of their discovery. In every case, the couple was a man and a woman, dressed in simple white uniforms, and always with affection and respect for each other in their eyes. I followed Valka from display to display as she listened to every single one.

The tour wound up at the entrance to an auditorium big enough for maybe three hundred people. Shirley took me aside. "This is the big moment. Challers, I want to know if you have any second thoughts, any reason you might not want to join us. If you think that this life isn't for you, then you need to speak up now. If there's a problem, we'll fly you right back home to Stakroya Station. This is a big step; if you decide to stay, we'll be asking you to pledge yourself—heart, mind, and body—to the Service."

I struggled with my misgivings. I felt vulnerable and scared, sitting there in underwear that wasn't even mine. How long would it be before Valka and I would be allowed to have a ship together? I didn't want to seem impatient, but that was what we had come all this way for, wasn't it? It wasn't just to escape the Merchants and the Fleet, but to be together. With all their hopeful faces turned in my direction, I just couldn't say it. How ungrateful would that be? They had saved me from the Fleet, saved me from being carried off bodily to become one of those huge, muscle-bound monsters. I felt a black pit opening in my stomach. I couldn't go back. It would be too humiliating. People would think I couldn't take it. People would think I had failed.

"I'm worried," I said. "I want to be with Valka. Are we going to be able to stay together?"

Shirley smiled and nodded. "Your relationship with Valka is one of the reasons we chose you. Of course you want to be with her. Your capacity for love is one of the things that will make you a capable Scout. The Service respects that. You'll be training here together. Once you've become full Scouts, though, you'll need to be strong. Your first cruise will be on a different ship than hers. Most of the time, you'll be apart. But there's a lot of play in the schedules for those cruises, and there will be opportunities for you to be together. After that, things will get better."

I took a deep breath. I knew Valka wanted this. Her reactions to the museum confirmed it, and if she wanted it, then I wanted it. Going home would mean leaving her here.

"Yes. Okay, I'll do it."

The pit in my stomach yawned wider. I swallowed it back down, and tried to pretend that I knew I had made the right decision. Shirley brought me into the auditorium. All together, everyone I had seen on the tour would fit in it with room to spare. It felt empty with just the five of us.

The director stood us up. We repeated an oath that sounded as old as the ages, and she congratulated us.

We were Scouts.

The rest of the day we spent getting settled in. First, there was a medical workup. It was much more thorough than anything I had experienced at Stakroya Station. In addition to taking blood, a cheek scrape, and poking and prodding just about every part of my body, there were measurements of every sort. Bicep circumference, thigh circumference, chest, abdomen, and waist measurements. They reviewed the medical records from the station hospital and we filled in a few gaps from my own memory. When that was all done, they put an implant in my palm that would activate the academy facilities for me. It would allow me to use the mess hall, information terminals, everything.

After that, we got our personal supplies and uniforms, and were shown to our rooms.

They were bigger than the dormitory cubes back on Stakroya Station. The space was about five meters square, with a big round pad in the center about three meters in diameter. I knelt down and touched it.

"This is just like the chamber in the ship," I said.

Shirley smiled and stepped inside. "You're observant. I can see already that we made the right choice in picking you." She put her hand on my shoulder. "Go ahead, lie down. It's for sleeping, too."

I did. It felt soft without being bouncy or yielding. "Comfortable," I said.

She lay down next to me, folding her arms behind her head. "If you want a pillow or a prop under your knees, you can program it to provide that."

"Eh. We never had that kind of thing on Stakroya. A pillow is just another thing to wash." I rolled onto my side, facing her. "Where's, ah, your room?"

"Right here." She shook her head in amusement. "You really are sharp, you know that? Catching onto these things so fast and with the tact to phrase them without making accusations." She rolled up to a kneeling position and took my hand. "Challers, you're going to learn a lot of things while you're here at the academy, but one of the most important is going to be sexual discipline. Ultimately, sex is what we do, what we are here for, and we need to make it work for us, not the other way around. You're young, and you have a powerful sex drive. It's going to take some effort on your part to learn to control it. I'm here to help you with that."

I sat up. "And who says I need your help? I grew up on a station where an evening's privacy has to be requested a month in advance and paid for with a week's wages. I know how to control my urges."

"You know how to suppress them," she said. "I'm going to show you how to harness them, how to hold back without suffocating them, and then let loose without restraint." She put her hand on my cheek. "Don't be afraid. I'm not going to traumatize you. I went through this once myself; I know how scary it all can be." She leaned back onto her arms. "I remember when I was in your place. I was rescued, like you were, from a station that was overpop, and not just by two. We were up by eleven. Our life support really was overburdened. The captain was calling for passing Merchant ships to come take his excess.

"Who did you get picked with?"

She smiled and looked up at the ceiling. "His name is Robert. He had silky blond hair that felt amazing to touch." Her tongue briefly licked the corner of her mouth.

"Do you still see him?"

"Oh, sure, whenever our paths cross. I have a flag set to tell me when there's a possibility of a meeting. We leave mail for each other all the time. In fact, chances are good that he'll be on-station two or three times while we're in training. Would you like to meet him?"

"Yes, I would." I wanted to see what the separation of the Service had done to their relationship. To see what separation might do to Valka and me.

Shirley got up and went to the little dressing-table by the door, fished around in her little duffel of belongings, and produced a personal holo. It clicked on, producing an animated face glowing in the air over her hand, and a soft tenor voice. He sang in a language I didn't understand.

I stood up to get a better look. He was older too, with a few wrinkles around his eyes. I could see something very human, very loving in those blue eyes. He knew he was singing for Shirley.

"Does it make you sad that he's so far away?"

"I'm never lonely," she said. "I love him, and I miss him, but I've had Masters close by."

"Do you love Masters?"

"You can't have sex as many times as we have and not develop feelings, Challers. He's been my friend and my confidante, as well as my partner, for a long time now. Yes, yes, I love him too, but in a different way than Robert." She turned off the holo and put it back in its place.

"I'm going to replace Masters, aren't I."

"You'll take his position, if you do well here at the academy, but you won't replace him. I'll always have feelings for Masters, just as I'll have feelings for you, and as I hope you'll have feelings for me."

I shook my head. This was all going so fast I could hardly absorb it all. I was confused and angry. It seemed like I would never have the kind of life with Valka that I wanted to have. I ran my fingers through my hair. Why couldn't we just be together? I felt the walls closing around me, and there was nothing I could do about it.

Shirley took my hand between hers. I yanked it away.

"Challers," she said quietly, "talk to me. You've asked a lot of questions, and I've given you honest answers. Tell me what's on your mind."

"I want to see Valka." I sounded petulant and immature and I wanted to kick myself for it.

"Are you sure you want to see her in the state you're in? You're likely to upset her."

She was right. I didn't want to see Valka in that kind of state. I tried to calm myself down.

"Now tell me what's on your mind."

I forced myself to stay calm. "I've made a terrible mistake. The whole reason I left Stakroya was to be with Valka, and you're not going to let us be together."

"That's a bit of an overstatement," she said. "Let me lay things out for you, to the best of my knowledge. You're going to be in training here for about two hundred days. Through that time, you will have many opportunities to continue to develop your relationship with Valka. After that, you'll both be going on a training cruise. You'll be separated for that time. It'll probably be three or four years long, though there will almost certainly be times when you can see each other during that period. When you both have completed your training cruise, you'll be eligible to pick your next cruise partner. Depending on how well you perform on your training cruises, you may well be able to pick each other."

"Three or four years," I said. It seemed like forever.

"You'll be able to leave mail for each other on a regular basis, and like I said, there will be times when you can see each other, either here at headquarters or at other rendezvous points around the galaxy. Now, are we done with the panicked flights to conclusion?"

I sighed, ashamed that I had made such a big deal. Three years still seemed like a very long time, but I would find some way to endure it. What other options did I have?

"This training cruise," I said, tentatively. "Would we be powering the ship, ourselves?"

"Yes. Unless something happens to change the assignment, you and I would be having sex in our own ship, to drive it. Likewise for Masters and Valka. That's how it works."

I clenched my teeth and turned my back. The very idea of Masters and Valka fucking was enough to make my blood boil. My stomach heaved. I ground my teeth, and was about to say something hateful when Shirley grabbed my shoulder. She spun me around with a surprising strength.

"Jealousy will not be tolerated, Challers. You do not own Valka. A Scout does not act like this. You are torturing yourself and if she sees you like this, you'll be making it more difficult on her as well." She spoke in a measured tone, but it was clear that I had made a very grave error.

"I can't help my feelings," I growled. "I love her."

"Love her, Challers. She's a lovable woman. But you need to accept that you won't be the only one in her life. Not as long as she's a Scout. What you're feeling right now isn't love, Challers. It's jealousy. It's ugly and it's evil and it will eat you up if you don't let it go."

"How?" I was nearly screaming, nearly crying, with the emotions churning inside me. "How do I just let it go? It's not that simple!"

"Lie down," she commanded.

I flopped down in the middle of the bed, legs sprawled.

"No, legs together. Like this." She lay down next me, relaxed, hands by her sides. "This was going to be part of your physicality training, but you need it now."

I pulled my legs in. I couldn't help clenching my fists.

"Emotions are as much a part of the body as they are of the mind. They can become a cycle, where the tension in your body tells your mind to be tense, and the tension in your mind tells your body to be tense. It's a spiral that can work for you, or against you. Right now, you need to bring it to a halt. Now breathe evenly and focus your attention on your toes. Let the tension just flow out of them, relax them, feel them melt into the floor. Focus on your feet." She named off body parts, her voice low and calm, gradually working her way up my body.

Guided this way, I could feel the knots in my stomach unclench, the hold of my resentment weakening. I closed my eyes and let it happen. I didn't want to be angry. I didn't want to be hurt.

Coming to the end, she was nearly whispering. "How do you feel?"

"Relaxed and jealous."

"You love Valka," she said. "Focus on that. Keep that at the center of your attention. Imagine her face in your mind's eye, and feel all the positive, affectionate emotions you hold for her." I felt her weight shift on the bed, and her hands on my shoulders and neck. She massaged the muscles gently through my shirt. It was easy to keep Valka's smiling, beautiful face in front of me, and love suffused my mind and body with warmth.

Shirley's hands gradually moved down. I could feel the warmth of her body on my face. She stroked my chest, not so much massaging as just running her hands over my body. I opened my eyes. She was kneeling just above my head, leaning over me to stroke my chest. Her breasts hung just inches away. They were magnificent. Fuller than Valka's, maybe a little droopy, but that didn't matter. They were marvelous.

"Feeling better?" She moved her hands down to my ribs and abdomen, still stroking lightly over me. My cock twitched. "Mmm, I guess you are." One hand brushed over my cock. She had touched me. Deliberately.

"Wait," I said, tensing up again. My head bumped her tits as I tried to reorient myself.

She shushed me and pushed my shoulders back down on the mat. "Just relax. Imagine Valka. Do you remember how beautiful she was, sitting in the middle of the chamber, stroking herself for you?"

"Yes," I gasped. It hadn't been just for me, it was to run the ship, but I wasn't in a position to argue. It was finding it hard to breathe.

Shirley's hands massaged my cock through the thin material of my shorts. It grew. "Remember that moment. Remember how much she loves you, and how much she wants you to be happy."

I couldn't believe what was happening to me. Shirley was playing with me, squeezing my cock, encouraging me to think of Valka. My ability to think ebbed away as my hard cock pushed at the material of my shorts.

Shirley slipped her hand underneath the fabric and her massage turned into strokes. "Hold that image in your mind," she said.

I tried, but my mind kept straying to what her hand was doing to me. Part of me, horrified at what was happening, shrank from it, but I couldn't deny that I wanted this, too. Ever since I had first seen her with Masters, a part of me wondered what it would be like to be in his place.

In a way, I was in his place. I was in the place he had occupied with Shirley.

She flipped the material of my shorts down under my balls, freeing my cock. "You can touch me, if you like," she said. "And you may have an orgasm when you feel the urge."

I raised my hands and found them shaking, almost too badly to get a grip on her shirt. I pulled it up, releasing the breasts that hung tantalizingly close above my head. Her nipples, mere inches from my face, begged to be kissed.

"Use only your hands."

Could she read my mind?

I obeyed. Her breasts were warm and soft and full. I held them, trying to emulate the gentle touch she had used with me. I was dizzy and weak, out of control, a slave to drives and emotions that I didn't understand. All I could do was squeeze and caress, too distracted by the very thought that this vision was stroking me this way. After only a minute or so, I cried out and arched my back, releasing powerful jets of cum across my chest.

"There now," said Shirley, adjusting her top and lying down next to me again. "Don't you feel better?"

I was too stunned to speak. I just lay there, breathing.

"Tell me, Challers. Do you love Valka any less now than you did before I gave you that orgasm?"

"No," I said. "Not at all."

"You see? And it will be the same with Valka. Just because she has sex with someone else doesn't mean she loves you any less." She helped me to my feet. "Now let's get you cleaned up. We don't want to go to the mess hall like this."

CHAPTER FIVE

Dinner was just as generous as lunch had been. Vegetables, beans, eggs, cheese, potatoes, and butter—not a teabulb or vedgepack in sight. At the end of the line, I waved my implanted hand over the sensor and a screen popped up with, "Recommendation: Two squares chocolate." Shirley explained that while I had a lot of leeway in what foods I ate, the computers would make sure I got everything I needed "for best performance."

I added two squares of chocolate to my plate from the dispenser. Who was I to argue? The stuff was delicious. If it would help with "performance," that was fine with me.

The four of us sat together in the mostly empty mess hall. I kissed Valka on the cheek. "I missed you."

She turned and kissed me on the lips. "I missed you too." She took my hand in hers. It felt wonderful. I squeezed. It was good to see her smile.

I dug into the food. Even after the huge lunch, I still felt ravenous.

"So, how was your afternoon?" asked Valka.

"Uh." What was I going to say? "Pretty, uh, good. And yours?"

"Masters and I just sat and talked."

"About what?"

"Oh, stuff about being a Scout—the things he's seen, the places he's gone. Challers, I can't wait to get out there and do things. What did you do?"

"Shirley and I, ah, talked." I nodded to Shirley, trying to act nonchalant.

She nodded back. "And then I gave him an orgasm with my hand."

I sputtered, trying to think of what to say to salvage the situation. I couldn't believe Shirley had done that to me—just said it, just like that. How could she just blurt it out like it was nothing? We had practically had sex, and she was waving it around under Valka's nose!

But Valka just giggled. "Ooh, lucky you! I haven't had one since the ship."

"I didn't know you were in any need," said Masters. "You should have said something."

"Oh, no, I'm good," said Valka with a nod.

"Okay, well, just speak up if you get uncomfortable."

I looked from face to face around the table. I couldn't believe what was happening.

Shirley reached across the table and took my hand. "It's all right, Challers. Scouts talk about this kind of thing all the time. It's our business. You understand? If you panic whenever anyone talks about sex, you're going to have a very difficult time."

I shook my head. "It doesn't bother you?" I asked Valka.

"No, why should it? In another year, you'll be having sex with her—full-on real sex—all the time. It'd be pretty silly for me to get upset about that now." She squeezed my hand again. "It's okay. Shirley's a good person. And besides. It's not like you love me any less, right?"

"I think I love you even more." It was a big relief for me that Valka was being so mature about this, but it made me feel even more childish for my earlier outburst. I kissed her again.

After dinner, we set up our curriculum, matching what we already had against the requirements for graduation. The topics were diverse, but all understandable as must-haves for Scouts. There was Astronavigation, Technology, First Aid and Basic Medical Care, History, and a subject called "Physicality." Shirley explained that it was the general study of how to use one's body effectively, for a variety of purposes. We would be training in meditation, exercise, sexual stimulation and arousal, orgasm control, and self-defense. This was a significant part of our studies; we'd have Physicality sessions three times a day, once before each meal. Valka and I were able to skip the data-handling course because we had gotten most of it in our education at

Stakroya Station. What little we were missing we could pick up on the job.

On the way back to our quarters, Shirley and I encountered a pair of cadets speaking in hushed tones. They stopped when they caught sight of us and quickly went their separate ways.

Shirley chuckled.

"What's funny?"

She shook her head. "Oh, just the things cadets will get up to. Come on. You're probably getting pretty tired. There's a busy day ahead, and you're going to need to get used to sleeping in the chamber."

While I cleaned my teeth, Shirley stripped out of her shirt and pants. The sight of her naked body set my heart thudding again, and I had to adjust my cock.

Looking up, she caught me and smiled. I looked away. She stepped over to the door of the fresher, put her finger under my chin, and moved my head to face her.

"You're allowed to look," she said. "I like it that you appreciate my body. I'm proud of it."

"I just didn't want to need another orgasm, that's all."

"Ah, I see." Her hand drifted slowly down my chest. "Why is that?"

"I'm supposed to be learning control?"

"Just because you have an erection, doesn't mean you have to have an orgasm, but I understand if you'd rather not get worked up before bed. So I'll give you the choice." Her hand reached my crotch and she squeezed my cock through the thin material. "An orgasm before bed, or I just get dressed now."

"It's a little late to keep from getting worked up now," I said, my voice already husky. My cock swelled in her hand.

She chuckled low in her throat. "I thought you'd see it my way." She pulled my shorts down, turning them inside out on my thighs. My cock bounced out into her hand. Shirley squirted some lotion onto it and spread it around. Her hot breath played over my ear. "Do it for me. Real quick. Just let it go; don't hold back even the slightest bit. You're young. So strong. I bet you splatter all over the sink." Her arm snaked around my back, holding me.

No one had ever talked to me like that. My hips jerked. I put my hands out against the mirror-bright wall in front of me. Her hand made slick, wet sounds against my cock. I watched in the mirror, watching her hand move, watching her smiling into my ear. She saw me watching and looked into my eyes.

"Do it," she said. "Do it now."

Spasms ran through me, closing my eyes involuntarily. A sharp breath blew out through my gritted teeth.

"Yes," she whispered. "Yes. More."

My body tensed under her skilled caress, ecstasy thundering in my ears. White and black warred behind my eyelids. My knees trembled, but with her shoulder behind me, supporting me, I didn't collapse.

As I finally returned to my senses, I felt a warm, wet washcloth running over my skin. She cleaned me meticulously. Her reflection smiled back at me. "You are going to make one incredible Scout, Challers. I can tell."

I smiled weakly, still breathless. I didn't know what to say.

She went back out into the bedroom and tossed me a clean uniform. "Get dressed," she said, "and come to bed. I still need to show you how to operate the controls."

Still trembling, I changed into the clean uniform.

Using the circular Scout's bed turned out to be a fairly simple matter. A set of controls at one end controlled firmness and temperature, and with the firmness set low, it could be pushed and spread to make little hills and valleys. I smoothed out a shallow depression—something vaguely shaped like my old sagging mattress.

"Do you move around much in your sleep?" asked Shirley.

She had changed into an outfit much like mine, except white instead of black. It left little to the imagination, but I managed not to let it get to me much.

"I don't know. I suppose I don't, because I would have fallen out of bed if I did. It wasn't very big."

"All right. Then we'll deal with that if it comes up." Shirley just made herself a soft pillow-like lump and a fairly firm sleeping area.

A white sheet came from a set of low shelves. I ran the fabric through my hands. As alien as everything else in this trip had been, the sheet felt familiar.

Shirley caught my thoughtful expression. "What's on your mind, Challers?"

"Just remembering the way my mom tucked me in. The sheet felt just like this." I pulled it to my nose. "Doesn't smell like home, though."

"In time, the chamber will come to be your home." She touched a switch by the bed and the room lights went dark. Only a dim outline around the doorways remained illuminated.

I felt tears coming to my eyes. I didn't want to cry, but I missed the familiar sounds of the station, the sounds and smells of people moving in the chambers around me. The academy felt empty and cold, no matter the air temperature. I swallowed hard, clamped my jaw shut, and lay down, wrapping myself in the sheet.

Shirley put a hand on my shoulder. "Feeling a little homesick?" She got up, retrieved a container from a cabinet near the bed, and pulled a tab on it as she handed it to me. Fragrant steam wafted from the open top. It smelled of milk and chocolate.

"More than a little. Am I ever going to see them again?"

"It's possible. It happens. You might have an assignment that takes you back there, but I can't make any promises."

I sipped from the bottle and set it aside. "Have you ever gone back home?"

"Once. Things had changed. It wasn't home anymore." She patted my shoulder, then went back to her side of the circle.

"Will you just hold my hand? I feel alone."

"Of course, Challers. I'm always here for you."

I stretched out my hand and she took it gently in hers. She didn't speak, didn't touch more than just that. She wasn't my mother, she'd never be my mother, but it did feel better just having her there. She threw the sheet over the both of us, and I closed my eyes.

After a time, I slept.

The melancholy stayed with me through the night, and into the morning. Shirley climbed to her feet and leaned down to offer me her hand. She pulled me up with surprising grace.

"You're strong," I said.

"It's part of our regimen," she said. "You'll gain a lot of strength in the academy, too. Come on, we have Physicality before breakfast."

For the morning routine, we met Masters and Valka in the gymnasium. We each had a workout routine created for us—a combination of stretching, resistance training, and something they called "partner movement." This last part was something like a couple's dance performed in slow motion with an emphasis on grace, fluidity, and harmony. After Masters and Shirley demonstrated, Valka and I tried it. It would have been easier with music. It also would have been easier if Valka could have kept a straight face. We kept breaking up giggling.

The whole time, I couldn't help admiring her body. It was there, right in front of me, flexing and moving. Up close, her nipples stood out against her pale skin, clearly visible through the sheer black fabric of her uniform. Her stiff, curly pubic hair was similarly apparent. I tried to maintain my concentration and avoid an erection, but I could only manage somewhat.

After a while, we caught the gist of it and, at Masters's instruction, we gradually sped up our movements. With sweat starting to soak into our uniforms, Shirley called a halt and told us to cool down with a walk around the gym.

Once we were a few steps away from our tutors, Valka turned to me. "How was your night?"

"It was rough," I said. "Missed my bed back home."

She nodded and made a small sound.

"You?" I asked.

"I slept pretty well, actually. That bed is a marvel, isn't it?"

"Yeah. What do you think of Masters?" I tried not to let the feelings that still lurked in the pit of my stomach color my voice.

She shrugged, made a noncommittal sound, and leaned in and kissed my cheek. "Looking forward to Astronavigation class?"

I pulled her close and shuddered in anticipation. "I can't tell you. I want to know everything. I want to know how the ships work, how those drives work, how far they can go and why. I want to crawl inside a ship and just look at the engines. I want to open the panels and see how the computers are wired up."

Too soon, Shirley's voice cut our moment short. "Hey, lovers! Come clean up. Breakfast in ten minutes."

The showers off the gym were a collective system, a set of nozzles pointing into one waterproofed space. I expected the exercise to leave my libido at something of a lull. After all, back on the station, that was always the best way to work out my frustrations. Seeing Shirley and Valka stripped down, however, started getting me excited again. Valka noticed and smiled, blushing as I watched her wash her body. Too soon, she rinsed off and stepped into the warm air vent to blow herself dry.

"Are you going to be all right?" asked Shirley, coming up behind me as I had my turn under the vent.

"No, I'll be fine," I said. I was a little hard, but not enough to be painful. I stepped into the dressing area beyond and walked up behind Valka as she dressed. I put an arm around her belly and nuzzled her neck.

She laid a hand on my cheek, and then patted it gently. "Come on, I'm hungry."

Chapter Six

Breakfast wasn't quite the feast that the previous night's dinner had been, but there was plenty of food available: eggs, yogurt, breads, and fruit. The four of us ate together, again, in a mostly empty mess hall.

Valka found a moment between bites to ask whether Shirley and Masters would be teaching the academic classes as well as Physicality.

"Yes and no," she said. "There will be prepared material, like lectures and readings, but we'll be there to answer questions and make sure you're absorbing the information. It will be just the four of us in most of your classes."

"Most?" I asked.

"You're not the only cadets in the academy, as you've seen. Some of your classes may have other cadets, and their mentors. If another ship comes in with recruits, you could have more classmates for your entire run here."

We finished breakfast and headed to the classrooms. Each one had desk space for eight students, arranged in an arc around a lectern. Above and behind the desks was an observation area where our mentors could keep track of our work. Waiting for us, at each desk, was a slab of dark gray plastic with our names glowing on the surface in orange letters above an orange outline of a hand. Each sat on a black pouch, clearly fitted to allow it to be carried over the shoulder.

I placed my hand where it was indicated. The handprint flared and disappeared, replaced by a standard tablet operations screen. A hologram flared up in the center of the room as we took our places behind our desks. The image portrayed an old woman, my grandmother's age, dressed in a Scout's white uniform.

"Welcome to Technology class, cadets," said a recorded voice, synchronized with the hologram's movements. "These are your new tablets. They contain all of your reference materials for your classes, basic simulators, and a link to the academy datastores. These will be your primary information tools throughout your careers as Scouts."

I poked tentatively at the interface. It used the same basic protocols as the machines back on the station, but far more advanced and responsive.

Valka shook her head in open-mouthed wonder. She had the technical specifications readout for her machine displayed on the screen.

"Challers, do you see this? This thing has more processing power in it than all the machines on Stakroya combined!"

"Now if you'll settle down," said the hologram, "we'll get down to today's lessons concerning the efficient use and proper care of your new equipment."

An hour and a half wasn't enough to even scratch the surface of what our new toys could do. They had their own holographic projectors, as well as holographic and audio recording functions, and could interface with any piece of Scout equipment via line-of-sight infrared beacon.

That class ended, and after a short fresher break, the next one started. History hadn't been taught on Stakroya Station, so this was entirely new material for me. The closest we had gotten were tales some of the older folks told around the banquet table during celebrations.

Here, we started with the founding of the Scout Service at the end of a time known as the "Planetary Era," when all of humanity's settlements were located in one system. The discovery of orgone drives scattered them to the stars. We saw how the basic geography of the known galaxy traced all the way back to that event.

No one was exactly sure where the first system was, though various experts had their theories on the subject. It had to have been in the high-density region between the Sagittarius Arm and the Perseus Arm of the galaxy, but there were dozens of stars in that area that could have been the origin star. Within fifty years, every star system in the area had been visited, if not colonized.

The area between this high-density region and the Perseus Arm came to be known as the Rimward Reach, and the area towards the Sagittarius Arm came to be known as the Coreward Reach. Between them was known as Old Stars. Each of these three bands of stars had an "upstream" and "downstream" section.

The main things most stations needed for long-term habitation in a colony were volatiles like water and hydrocarbons, and metals like iron and aluminum. Most star systems have at least some of these resources, but the stations that found them in fairly dense, easily harvested asteroid fields did better than those that had to scavenge over wider areas of space, so that became the standard practice.

After History, we returned to the gym for another hour of Physicality. This hour was quieter than the first hour had been. We spent the hour in stillness, learning more of the meditation techniques Shirley had introduced me to the night before. There were a few minutes of meditation, followed by a discussion of situations where this kind of control would be useful, and then a few more minutes of meditation.

I had never really paid that much attention to my body. It was always just there, often just taking care of itself while I engaged in some kind of activity. After just an hour of focusing my attention on, for example, the sensations in my resting hands, I felt things I had never felt before. Even with something as simple as my body, the Scouts were going to show me amazing things.

By the end, I was more than ready for lunch. We ate, chatting about the morning's studies, and how they fit into the life and work of a Scout.

After lunch, we had a free hour before our next class.

I gave Shirley a hopeful smile as soon as I finished eating. "Could Valka and I just take a walk together? We haven't had any time alone since we got here, and . . ."

"Certainly," said Shirley. "You know where the main entrance is. Through there is a promenade that leads out to the oxygen deck. Don't wander too far, but I doubt you'll get lost. Your tablet has your schedule; it'll signal you if you're in danger of being late. And remember—no orgasms."

"Why not?" I asked.

"Discipline, Challers. Discipline."

I loved walking with Valka. She took my left hand in hers, wrapped my arm around her back, and held me close. I shortened my stride a little for her as we walked. When we started, I felt some slight worry that the intimacies I had shared with Shirley would get in the way, but we fell into our accustomed places with ease. It felt good to do something so familiar, even if the place we were doing it was not.

The promenade was lined with little bars and eateries, but having just finished lunch, neither of us was interested. We looked them over, sampling the music that wafted from open doors, drawing a few interested looks from passersby. Having spent the whole morning in our cadet uniforms, I'd forgotten how revealing they were. I felt suddenly self-conscious.

"Maybe we should go back," I said. "I don't see any other cadets out here."

"How many other opportunities like this are we going to get? If there aren't many other cadets out here, that must mean they don't get away often. Let's just walk."

We continued down the promenade. It wasn't crowded, but the wide corridor had plenty of traffic, both white-clad Scouts and those in more colorful garb. We figured out soon enough that only active-duty Scouts wore the white outfits. Everyone else was either a native of the station who had never served, or retired. Even off-duty Scouts seemed to dress in white.

At the end of the promenade, a wide gate led out onto the oxygen deck. It was like nothing I had seen before. Wonder upon wonder had been presented to me that day, but they all paled in comparison.

This wasn't just an oxygen garden. We were in the main ring of the station, standing on the edge of that ribbon of blue and green we had glimpsed when we docked. The blue was water, an impossible amount of it, flowing in a wide stream. The green was grass and trees and plants, artfully arranged and jubilantly healthy. Just from where we stood, we could see dozens of robots working in the fields and orchards, tending to the marvelous greenery.

Still, I hesitated. It didn't feel safe to be out in the open like that. The enclosure above us, holding in the air, seemed impossibly far away, and too transparent. My skin felt itchy, my breath tight. I wanted a spacesuit.

"Is this safe?"

"Come on," said Valka. "It has to be."

Slowly, the promenade shrank behind us and we made our way down to the water. There were voices, shouting and laughing. As we got closer, we could see that there were people in the water. Valka and I stared.

"Are they supposed to be there?" I asked. Valka just shrugged.

As we got closer still, the figures bobbing about in the water saw us and shouted, "Look! Cadets!"

They waved and smiled, inviting us down to the water's edge in musical, gentle voices. There were four of them, paddling about in the clear water. When we finally reached the shore, I couldn't help but stare. They seemed to be women, but there was something odd about their faces.

"Hi, I'm Challers," I said.

They introduced themselves as Trey, Shar, Jo, and Hom. They climbed out of the water, and my eyes nearly popped out of their sockets. Their bodies were slim and mostly hairless, and while each one had a modestly feminine pair of breasts, each also had a set of male genitalia.

They noticed my amazement and laughed. As they picked up their towels and began drying off, Trey asked, "Have you never seen our kind before, then?"

"We only arrived yesterday," said Valka, recovering quicker than I did.

"Where are you from?"

"Stakroya Station," I said.

Shar nodded. "I've heard of it. It's a trade hub, out in the Rimward Reach. They're mostly puregens out that way."

"Puregens?" I hoped it wasn't an insult. It didn't seem that way, but one could never tell.

"Yes, you've still got the same basic body shape from the Original Seed." Shar finished drying off and wrapped up in the towel. "You're puregens, and we're newgens. Chevalier newgens, specifically. I'm sure you'll learn all about it in the academy."

"I'll be sure to ask about it if we don't." My tablet bipped. I checked it, and gave the foursome a bow. "We need to be getting back now. Class will be starting soon."

On the way back, after we were well out of earshot of the hermaphrodites, I leaned in close to Valka. "I'm glad it wasn't those kind that picked us up."

She squeezed my arm and gave me a disapproving look. "Challers, don't be like that. They're just people."

"Okay, but where would I, you know, put it?"

"You didn't see Jo bending over? There's a vulva there too."

I tried to imagine how that would work. That piece of information made things a little better, but the image still disturbed me more than it intrigued me.

"I'm still glad it was Shirley and Masters that found us."

"She is beautiful," said Valka.

"Not as beautiful as you," I said and kissed her cheek. I paused. It seemed the right time to ask a question that had been on my mind whenever I had an idle moment to think. "Have you, uh, done anything, with Masters yet?"

She nodded. "Yeah. And you?"

"Before bed last night. With her hand."

"Masters used his hand too."

I swallowed hard, trying not to let the queasy feeling in my stomach show. I was beginning to think that the Scouts were the lesser of three evils, but saying that to Valka would only create a rift between us. I just squeezed her tighter and kept my doubts to myself. She was far happier than she had ever been on Stakroya Station. I wouldn't spoil it for her.

Any pain was worth it, to make her happy.

CHAPTER SEVEN

As we got closer to the academy, I remembered that our next class would be Astronavigation. I broke into a jog, and the two of us ran the rest of the way back. We sat down at our places in the lecture hall and I eagerly activated my tablet.

To my horror, we wouldn't be starting with any of the stuff I wanted to learn. Before we would get to the stars and engines and computers, there was a lot of basic, foundation information to go through that hadn't been covered back on Stakroya Station. Galactic coordinate systems. Stellar coordinate systems. Time-shift vectors. Synchronization schema. The first forty days, at least, would be mathematics.

Vacking math.

My headache started just a few minutes in, bad enough to make me groan and rub my temples. We hadn't gotten any further than skimming the syllabus. The holo paused mid-sentence.

"Are you all right, Challers?" It was Shirley, above and behind me.

"Headache," I said. "It'll pass."

Valka ran her hand over my shoulder. Her sympathy helped, some.

I heard Shirley come down and stand behind me. She put her hands on my head, working on the knots in my temples. "Breathe deep," she said. "Relax. Use what you learned in Physicality today. Let the tension go."

"Math always gets him like this," said Valka. "I helped him through it, back on Stakroya Station."

The truth was she had practically taken my tests for me. Even with her coaching me every step of the way, I had barely passed.

Crippling headaches are no way to go through a class. Math was the only blemish on my academic career, and the thought that it might get me sent back to Stakroya Station, never to see Valka again, gave my stomach fits.

Shirley gave me a good five minutes with her strong hands. She knew exactly where to put her fingers. Within a few minutes, the headache had faded a good deal and, with it, the queasiness in my gut.

When I sighed, she patted me on the back. "Good job, Challers. Are you ready to restart the lesson?"

"Yes. Thank you, Shirley."

She returned to her place, and the lecture continued. Keeping the calm centeredness as much as I could, I managed to fend off the headache at the cost of some of my attention. Still, the result was better than before, and when the class was over, Shirley bent over her desk to ruffle my hair.

"You did a good job there, Challers. I'm proud of you."

I smiled back at her. "Thanks for helping."

After a short break, we started on the next class. Valka and I were both certified for basic first aid, as was everyone on Stakroya, so we would be starting with more advanced material. Once again, the technology available to the Scouts surpassed what we had back on Stakroya by a huge margin. Since travel of any great distance, for a Scout ship, required two healthy bodies on board, they went to great lengths to make that a certainty. Every ship carried a "gentank" underneath the main passageway. If a Scout could make it into that tank, the robotic systems there could repair any damage short of brain failure. For this reason, our methods focused on ways to stabilize and transport people to the gentank.

"Excuse me," I said, "during the free hour, Valka and I met some people who called themselves 'newgens.' Does that have anything to do with the gentank?" I turned to look up at Shirley.

"It comes from the same technology," she said. "Gentanks can alter, as well as repair, all the way down to the cellular level. We'll get into more detail about newgens in our other classes."

My curiosity was momentarily satisfied and the lecture continued. I had trouble paying attention. I didn't much like the idea of being altered, especially as radically as the hermaphrodites I had met down by the water.

"Pay attention, Challers." Shirley tapped me on top of the head. "If you've got something else, make a note and move on."

I nodded and focused. This lecture was actually quite interesting. There was an "excursion kit" onboard the ship, with gear for treating any number of problems that might occur. This implied that Scouts didn't spend their time cooped up on a ship day after day, and that prospect interested me. What kind of dangerous situations did Scouts find themselves in? Before Shirley could tap me on the head again, I let the question pass and went back to the lesson. The answers would come in due time.

After Medical, our day would be rounded out with the third hour of Physicality. Instead of leading us to the gym, however, Shirley brought us into a circular room focused on a raised Scout-ship bed.

"During this hour," said Shirley, "we'll continue our study of sexual response. Sex is the fundamental act at the center of your duties as a Scout. You will finish this training understanding it under a wide variety of conditions. For now, we will be studying each other. This may be a little uncomfortable, but I want you both to stay with me. It's important not only to understand the anatomy of the opposite sex, but also your own. So let's start with the erogenous zones."

Gradually, Shirley went on a tour of her body, talking about each part and its general level of sensitivity, both for women in general and for her in specific. First, her head and neck, then her hands and arms, then feet and legs.

Then she pulled up her shirt and laid it on the edge of the bed. "Now. Breasts."

After the things that had happened that day, it wasn't as shocking as it could have been, but I still found myself blushing. I took a breath, centered myself, and tried to enter a more receptive frame of mind. It wasn't easy, and in spite of everything I did, my cock swelled, and the room seemed to be getting warmer.

"Women vary widely about how they like their breasts treated," she said. "For me, you can squeeze and pinch and suck as hard as you like."

I glanced over at Valka. She looked a little pale and was shaking her head slightly. I guessed she didn't like that kind of treatment.

Shirley went on to talk about ribs, navel, armpits, gradually working her way down, and then removed her pants. There was no hiding my erection. In spite of the clinical language and her matter-of-fact attitude, I found myself getting turned on.

"For this part, you're going to want to get closer, Challers." She sat on the edge of the bed and crooked her finger, inviting me closer. "I doubt you've seen a woman's body up close like this before. Come and see."

She spread her thighs, and I knelt in front of her. My breathing felt a little tight and I swallowed, trying to control it.

She pulled her outer lips apart, naming them and explaining them to me, and then pointed out what I was looking at: outer labia, inner labia, clitoral hood, clitoris, vagina, urethra. Again, she described what most women liked in terms of stimulation before going on to her own personal levels of arousal.

"I like being rubbed right here," she said, demonstrating with two fingers on either side of her clitoris. "You can go ahead and be just as boring and repetitive as you like, because that's my trigger."

"You said the clitoris was the most sensitive spot," I observed.

"Yes, too sensitive to touch directly for most women, at least with your fingers. Now, a tongue, or lips, that's another matter, but we'll talk more about that when we get to techniques." She rolled her hips back a bit. "Down here, in between the vaginal opening and the anus, is the perineum. Mostly it's sensitive because it's around everything else."

I felt a little dubious as she went on to describe the nerves and sensations around the anus, but when I glanced over at Valka, she had one lip pulled between her teeth. Maybe she would like that? I realized that I really didn't know very much at all about what Valka liked. The few times we had been more physically intimate than a deep kiss were so hurried that there wasn't time to explore.

Shirley got up and slipped back into her clothes while Masters began the exercise himself, for Valka's benefit. I hung back near the door, breathing deeply and trying to let go of the jealousy that was, once again, making itself felt.

Shirley saw the sour look on my face and stood next to me, leaning my way to speak quietly with me. "Look at it this way," she said. "When you do get together, she'll be better prepared to do what feels good to you, more understanding of your body."

"Yeah. Fine. It could be me doing the demonstration," I whispered.

"There'll be other times."

"Will there? Will there really? It seems like you and Masters are taking every opportunity to keep a wall between us. We barely even get to touch each other here!"

Shirley hissed in my ear. "This is not the time, Challers. You're interrupting. Stop it right now. Get yourself under control. Act like a Scout. Act like an adult."

I closed my eyes and tried to remember my relaxation training. One day didn't seem like nearly enough. I was frustrated and angry. "Will we talk about this later?"

"Yes."

I let the anger subside, not really gone but held quiet. With my eyes closed and concentrating on my breathing, Masters's voice became just waves in the background, cresting now and again to bring words into my consciousness. I endured it in silence, half meditating, half sulking, until the demonstration ended.

"Dinnertime," said Shirley.

Valka gave me a sour look as we all filed out of the room. I blushed and looked away. She had every reason to be mad at me. I was acting childish again; the same as I had before, but this time it was in front of her. I walked behind the three of them down the corridor to the mess hall. Solitude felt better than enduring Valka's scowl.

"Psst. Hey."

I stopped and looked up.

A young woman, a cadet from her clothes, beckoned to me from a doorway. "C'mere."

She was short, and plump without being overweight or misshapen, with her black hair in a long ponytail hanging down over her shoulder.

I glanced ahead at the others. They were chatting and walking well ahead of me. They wouldn't notice. I stepped quickly into the room, and she slid the door closed behind me.

"Quick, did you bring a personal holo? From home?"

"Yes, why?"

She grabbed my hand and shoved a thumbnail-sized data wafer into it. "Hide this. Plug it in when you're alone. After your keeper is asleep. Watch the neck. Now go, before you're missed."

She opened the door again and shoved me out. I tucked the sliver of plastic into the waistband of my shorts and hoped it wouldn't be too visible. Luckily, Masters and Shirley were nowhere in sight.

Watch the neck? What could that mean?

Clearly, there was some kind of conspiracy going on. I wasn't sure if I even wanted to get involved. I didn't know this girl. I had no reason to trust her. Still, the fact that I wasn't the only one keeping secrets felt good. Someone, somewhere, didn't like the system, didn't like the Scouts, enough to take the risk of contacting me. The knowledge felt warm, but prickly and dangerous. I treasured it. I would find a way to read whatever message was on that chip.

Chapter Eight

I hurried to the mess hall, grabbed my food, and sat down next to Valka. No one said anything, but Shirley gave me an eyebrows-up expectant glance.

"I'm sorry, everyone," I said, "that was a childish thing to do."

"And?" said Shirley.

"And I'll try not to let it happen again," I said haltingly. "I can't guarantee anything about my feelings, but I'll try not to let them get in the way of our studies."

Shirley gave me a nod.

Valka put her hand on my knee and kissed my cheek. "Apology accepted."

I couldn't help the smile creeping back onto my face. I put my arm around her and squeezed. My appetite, which had gone missing a half-hour or so before, came back with a growl and I dug into my food.

When Valka finished eating, she set her hands in her lap. "Why is it that there aren't any newgens in the academy? Everyone I've seen has looked perfectly human."

"Newgens are still a minority in the galaxy," said Shirley. "Not only that, any man and woman from puregen stock are almost certain to be physically compatible. Not always true with newgens. So it's harder for them to get in."

Something clicked together inside my head. "The Fleet is all newgens, though, aren't they? That's how they make recruits into Marines."

"Yes, that's true. Many Merchant ships are also crewed by newgens. I suppose that kind of balances out, if you're looking at it in an us-them kind of way. Probably best to just see us all as different kinds of humans, though. No matter what we look like on the outside, we're all just people."

"I'll get to that right after figuring out this jealousy thing," I muttered.

"Speaking of which," said Shirley, tapping the table, "finish up your dinner. We need to have another talk tonight, I think."

I took a deep breath and let it out.

"Not punishment," she said. "I think you're doing a good enough job of that on yourself. You're forgiven, but this isn't forgotten, and you're going to need some help getting through this."

Perhaps so, but I still found myself dragging dinner out. Masters and Valka put their trays in the recycler and left. Shirley sat patiently, waiting for me to finish.

It's amazing how quickly a healthy appetite can vanish when you're waiting for an unpleasant encounter.

After I picked at my food for a few minutes, Shirley put her hand on mine. "I'm not angry with you, Challers. Like I said, all is forgiven, but we do need to work on your jealous feelings. The sooner you deal with them, the better."

I sighed. "All right."

I stood, put the tray in the recycler, and I trudged solemnly back to our quarters with Shirley's arm around my waist.

We entered our quarters, and Shirley sat down cross-legged on her side of the bed, gesturing for me to join her. Under the cover of putting my tablet on the dressing table by the door, I slipped the mysterious data wafer from my shorts and dropped it into the bottom of the tablet's carry-pouch.

"All right, Challers," she said when I joined her, "this is getting worse instead of better. Let's take another crack at this, hmm?"

"I'm sorry," I said. "I . . . just . . ."

"No, no." She put a hand on my knee. "Stop. What's past is past. Let's dig a little deeper this time, okay? What you're feeling isn't uncommon. You're just having trouble fitting some of your expectations and preconceptions into the Scout way of life. The thing is, they don't fit. And you need to let go of them."

I nodded.

She put her fingers gently under my chin and lifted my face to look into my eyes. "Now, Challers. Tell me honestly, are you afraid you will lose Valka?"

"No, no, it's not that. I realize that doesn't really make any sense. I never really had her in the first place, so thinking I'd lose her is kind of silly."

"Good. You got that lesson. I'm glad we don't have to go over it again. Back in the classroom, you seemed resentful that Masters was doing something that you could have done. Were you feeling envious that he was enjoying her attention?"

"Isn't that the same as jealous?"

"Not exactly. Instead of feeling afraid that you're going to lose something you think you own, envy is when you wish you had something someone else is enjoying. It's like going to a friend's quarters and he's got his own bedroom, all on his own, where you're sleeping in a fold-out in your father's workspace. You wish you could have that, but you can't, and you feel angry and hurt that you don't have it. So, envy?"

"Yeah, yeah. Envy."

"What do you think we might do about it?"

"Hunh? You're not going to jump all over me again?"

"Would an orgasm help?" She cocked her head to the side with a small smile.

"No. It just gets me even more confused."

"Then what?"

"Shirley, I've been with Valka for a long time. Almost a year, I think, and we've been really close ever since we decided to try to get into the Scouts. We tell each other everything. There's no one else I care for like her in the whole galaxy. I want her attention, and when I see her giving it to Masters . . . yeah, I'm envious. Is that so wrong?"

"It's an understandable reaction, Challers, given where you come from. Think back about what I've already told you. I respect your relationship with Valka, and so does the Service. But I want you to make room in your heart for more. These feelings, they're not limited to just one person." She took my hand in hers.

This time I didn't pull away. I wanted to be mature about this. A Scout.

"A Scout must learn to broaden his heart. Make room for more than just one person. You love Valka, and so of course you're going to value her attention over mine. But we're together in this, and it's in our best interest to develop our own relationship. I don't want to replace Valka. I don't want to diminish her in any way. I want both of you to grow as people in your capacity to love."

"So, what do you want me to do?"

"I want you to try to see your time here at the academy as an opportunity to not just get closer to Valka, but to get closer to me, too. To give our way of life a chance. To accept the things we're offering you."

"This is all just going a little too fast for me, you know?"

"It's an abrupt change, Challers, but it really is for the best. You're leaving your old life behind, your old ways of thinking and feeling. It's understandable that you'd cling to it, that you'd have some difficult times, but you will be better off to let it go. You do want to be a part of us, don't you? Think of the life you would have had back on Stakroya Station—hungry, cramped, and under the constant threat of being taken away. Even if you had evaded the Fleet and the Merchants, you would have been stuck there for the rest of your life. Now think of all the things you've seen since coming here."

She was right, of course. The Scouts had shown me some wonderful things. Rationally speaking, having to give up a little attention from Valka to get them wasn't that bad a trade-off.

But it still hurt.

"So we've got a few hours before bedtime," she continued. "What do you say we work on your math?"

I groaned and rolled my eyes.

"Come on. Get your tablet. If we get a head start, you'll be able to sail through tomorrow's lesson. Wouldn't Valka be surprised?"

I reluctantly retrieved my tablet from where I had left it by the door and we started. I wanted to sulk. I wanted to lie there and let my weakness for math just end things, and if it had been Valka tutoring me, that's exactly what would have happened.

Shirley surprised me. For one thing, we never sat down the whole time. She had me set my tablet down in the middle of the bed, activate the holographic display, and made the entire room into our workspace. The transformations and demonstrations didn't sit in the tiny box of the tablet, but they were all around us, as big as life. Whenever there was any kind of obstacle, she found another way to put the concept, and another, and another. Mathematics, to her, wasn't a collection of cold transformations and sterile equations to memorize. For Shirley, it was a dance of art and science binding the galaxy together in pure, shining threads, and she wanted to teach me the steps.

When we finally noticed the time, she shook her head and sent me to the shower. I talked through my shower about what I had learned, then through Shirley's as well. Finally, as we lay side by side in the bed, she had to put her finger over my lips and shush me. I tried to relax, certain that the new revelations bursting in my mind would keep me up all night long.

And then I remembered the data wafer, sitting in the bottom of my carry-pouch. I tried to stay awake until I knew Shirley was asleep, but there was no way. I fell asleep as soon as I stopped moving.

The next morning, we overslept a bit and had to rush to make Physicality on time. The class went pretty much the same as the previous day's, though Valka and I had an easier time working into the partner movement exercises. I pushed hard, trying to wear us out, so we could have some more time to talk privately. Shirley noticed, though, and held me back, forcing me to maintain the correct forms. When we completed the program, there wasn't time for a walk together, and the four of us went directly to the showers.

In the showers, I noticed a change. "Valka, your pubic hair is gone."

She looked down and ran her hand over the smooth skin above her cleft. "Yeah, it really shows in the cadet uniform. I thought it would look better."

I wanted to ask whether Masters had suggested it. He probably had. I glanced over at Shirley and Masters. Both were hairless below the neck.

I felt another knot of jealousy forming in my stomach, but I ignored it. "So how do I join the club?"

Shirley took a tube from a shelf of toiletries on the wall. "You can shave it, just like you do your face, but I recommend this stuff. It's a nice depilatory—leaves your skin smooth, and lasts a long time before getting stubble."

I squeezed some out onto my fingertips. "Can I use it on my face, too? I'd like to be able to skip shaving there."

"I wouldn't recommend it," said Masters. "If you get any on your head, you'd lose hair in strange patches."

I grunted an acknowledgment and rubbed the thick paste into my pubic hair. Gradually, the hair disintegrated, and when I turned my body back under the shower, it rinsed away and down the drain. The skin was smooth and sensitive where the hair had been. It would certainly make everything feel different with the hair gone.

When I finished, Masters and Valka had already finished their showers.

Shirley stepped over and ran her hand over my naked skin. "Nice, isn't it?"

My cock responded instantly, twitching just below her hand.

"You're teasing me," I said. "You know we can't just do it here."

"Oh, we can, but we don't have time. Later, maybe." She gave my cock a squeeze and headed for the warm air vents, giving me a smile over her shoulder. "I imagine you're hungry."

In the dressing area, Valka spotted my erection and flashed Shirley a little smile. I couldn't help checking to see what Valka's body looked like in the sheer cadet uniform, making my erection even worse. I pulled on my shirt and shorts, but that only served to make it more prominent.

By keeping my mind occupied with some of the equations I learned the night before, I managed to get myself distracted enough for it to subside before we sat down for breakfast, but that just left me with a mild ache in my testicles.

It wouldn't be the last.

CHAPTER NINE

The morning passed roughly the same as it had the day before, except that I felt a bit more comfortable with the routine. By lunchtime, the pain in my groin from Shirley's teasing had eased. I asked if Valka and I could go for another walk together during our free hour. Since our studies had gone well through the morning, Shirley and Masters gave their permission.

I stayed quiet until we were out of the academy, in the long corridor leading out to the oxygen deck, then took a moment to prepare. "You're doing so much better than me at this."

"What do you mean?"

"It's like a kick in the stomach every time I think of you and Masters being together, but you seem to be taking everything that happens with a smile and a nod." It sounded like an accusation, but I couldn't think of any other way to put it.

She shrugged. "Just the way I am, I guess. I've never been real jealous. Do you remember when you had that thing for Sindra Colpey?"

"What thing?"

"Oh, I saw the way you looked at her. I could tell what was going on in your mind, but I know you, Challers." She went up on her tiptoes to kiss me on the cheek. "We're in love, right?"

"I don't know, Valka, I feel like this whole thing is changing us."

"Yes, we're growing, becoming Scouts. But love is more important than that."

I pulled her close. "We have to hold onto it, Valka. We have to hold onto it hard. I feel it, I don't know, slipping away." I bent down to give her a kiss, a kiss that would seal us together, a kiss like we had never had before.

When I opened my mouth, probing with a tentative tongue, she pulled back. "Challers . . ."

"What?" I held on. I couldn't let her go, not like this, not now.

She stiffened. "I don't think we should take our relationship down that road right now. It'll be a long time before we can really do anything about it, and I'd really just rather not start."

Reflexively, my hands gripped tighter. "What are you talking about? Valka, I love you. You don't want to kiss me?"

"Mmm, not like that." She smiled. "I want us to be like we were back on the station."

She pushed out of my grip, took my hand in hers, and wrapped my arm around her waist to walk with me. Just like always.

I yanked my arm away from her. "Not like what? Not like having sex? Not like Masters?"

"Oh, don't be like that, Challers. You don't have anything to be jealous about. I have a completely different relationship with Masters. It's business, you know?"

"No, I don't know! You can't have sex with someone without having feelings for them. Look at Masters and Shirley!"

"I did look at them. If you might recall, we saw them having sex, and there was no passion there at all. They were just going through the motions. You didn't see that?" She shook her head. "I can't believe you didn't see that."

"Shirley said . . ."

"Oh, please," said Valka, sneering. "You have to look at what she does, not what she says."

"Are you saying she's lying to me?"

"Shirley and Masters are not in love. Not even close. It's just business between them, the same as between Masters and me. People say things they don't mean all the time."

"Oh, does that include you, too? Because what I'm hearing is that you're putting Masters—who you say you don't love—ahead of me. In less than a year, you're going to be having sex with him, probably every day, and you won't even kiss me! Do you love me, Valka? Do you really? Because you're not acting like it."

"Vacuum take him!" She gestured wildly with the foul curse on her lips. "No, I don't love Masters, and I shouldn't have to prove it to you by having sex with you!"

"I don't want to have sex with you! I just want a vacking kiss! Is that so much to ask? I love you, Valka!"

She set her jaw, lip trembling, as if about to burst into tears.

"What? What did I say? People who love each other kiss! What's the big problem?"

"You go on your walk, Challers," she said, voice trembling. "I don't want to come this time."

She turned her back on me, and slowly made her way back into the academy.

I stood there, blinking, throat tight and cramped. I wanted to stop her, I wanted to scream at her to come back, but the words just wouldn't come.

What had happened to her? What had I said to upset her like that?

I watched her until tears blurred my vision and I had to wipe them away. I stumbled out to the oxygen deck, down the path between the fields and orchards, until I came to the water.

The newgens weren't there. I was glad of the solitude. I didn't want anyone to see me right then. I sat down on the bank, letting my thoughts slide by like the slow-moving current.

After a time, my tablet bipped. I ignored it. It bipped again. I took it out and silenced it. I wanted to throw the stupid thing into the water.

I wanted to throw myself in.

Shirley sat down next to me. She didn't say anything, didn't do anything, just sat.

"I guess you know what happened," I said.

"A little of it. You and Valka had a fight."

The tears threatened to start flowing again. "She doesn't want me anymore." The effort of holding back the emotions made it hard to talk.

"You want to have Astronavigation class out here? We can just lay out your tablet and listen to the lecture. You already know today's material. It'll be easy."

I shrugged. "Sure. Whatever." Everything I had been fighting for had evaporated.

Shirley took my tablet and laid it on the grass between us. "Just access the classroom feed, there."

"I know." I tabbed through the menus and pulled up the Astronavigation class for day two, and routed it to the tablet's projector. The semi-transparent form of the lecturer appeared and immediately began the day's material.

I tried to lose myself in it, but the image of Valka's snarling face kept coming back to me. I shut it off and collapsed onto the grass. Too tired to hold it back any longer, I let the tears out, let the sobs out, let everything just pour out of me.

Shirley put her hand on my back.

I felt empty. I felt like my only reason for being there, at the academy, was gone. Why should I bother with the classes? What was there for me? I was alone. If I just disappeared right there, no one would miss me. My parents would think I was safely cruising the stars, among the galaxy's elites. To everyone else, I was just a resource. A resource that could be replaced.

Even to Valka.

Then a thought occurred to me: she had used me. She had never been sincere about her feelings. It was all a lie to get me to help her get off the station. She told me she loved me, because she knew that would make me want to help her, to save her. I had been shamelessly manipulated. Or at least . . .

No. It was easier to believe she had no feelings at all for me, easier to believe it was all a lie.

"We really shouldn't skip two classes, Challers. We need to get back for Medical. It's not a holographic lecture; this is hands-on equipment training."

"I don't think I want to be in the same room with her right now."

"We'll find another room. Come on."

She helped me to my feet and picked up my tablet. As I put it in the carry-pouch, I heard a little *tic* of plastic on plastic. The little data wafer was still down there, the one that had been handed to me by the mysterious cadet the day before.

As we walked up the path, I found my thoughts drifting back to it. A part of me wanted to put those thoughts out of my head. It was too dangerous. If she felt a need to be secretive about it, then there must be some penalty. I could feel a hungry curiosity building, though, and I knew it would not be sated without reading that wafer.

Back at the academy, Shirley opened a supply closet with her palm implant and took out an excursion kit. She brought it to a nearby classroom and laid it out on the desk, and then went up to her place behind me. The lecture started. Each item in the kit was named. I repeated the names. The items were named, and I presented them. Items were presented, and I named them. Each item's function was described. Each item in the kit was named, and I described their functions. The functions were described, and I named the items and presented them. The rote memorization of these isolated bits of information made an uncomplicated drone of my consciousness that I found strangely comforting, like a hot shower. Steady. Mindless.

When it was done, Shirley complimented me on my focus.

I nodded.

"Are you ready for what's next?" she asked.

"Physicality," I said.

We walked down the hall. I watched, hoping and dreading that Valka would come out of her session in Medical, that we would be face to face again. She didn't. Shirley opened a door. I went in. Shirley and I were alone.

"Yesterday, I gave you a tour of the female body," she said, stripping off her clothes. "Now it's your turn to explore. I want you to touch every part of me and pay attention to how I react. It's not necessary that you give me an orgasm today, though I certainly wouldn't complain if you did."

She lay down in the middle of the bed, legs slightly parted.

The sight didn't look inviting at first, but a little beat of curiosity pulsed behind my breastbone. This would be a welcome distraction. Maybe if I did this, really pushed through and put myself into it, I could forget about Valka, at least for a time. I crawled onto the bed and knelt by her side. She offered me her hand. I pushed away the thought that Valka would be doing something very similar with Masters, right then. I closed my eyes and focused, putting the rogue thought out of my head. If she didn't want me, then fine. I didn't want her.

At least, that's what I told myself.

I took Shirley's hand between mine. I brought it up to my face. She smelled faintly of the cleanser we all used, but there was something unique about her scent, as well. I held her hand lightly in mine while I ran the other hand up her arm, feeling the firm muscles under her skin.

"Your arms were the first part of you I noticed," I said.

She gave me an amused half-smile. "Really."

"No lie."

She flinched a little as my hand moved closer to her armpit.

"And ticklish too," she said.

I could feel the ache inside me dissipate a little. Her shoulders were firm and strong.

"You don't have to go in any particular order," she said. "Explore anywhere and in any way you like. Just pay attention; you're learning not just about my body, but about the way it reacts to your touch."

Another deep breath. My fingers moved slowly to her neck, up to her jawline, and around her ear. I drew some of her soft hair between my fingers. From there, I trailed my fingers down to her breasts. I cupped one in my hand, squeezed and stroked, alternating between looking at what I was doing and looking at her face for a reaction.

"You can be a little rougher," she said. "They're not going to break."

I squeezed harder, exploring the pliable flesh, how it would move and stretch. Her nipples poked out from the round surface, begging for attention. I gave it to them, first stroking, then twirling, finally squeezing and pinching.

Shirley cooed contentedly.

I didn't want to merely make her contented, I realized. I wanted to see her orgasm. Even though it wasn't the aim of the lesson, I wanted to do it anyways. A secret, irrational part of my subconscious told me it would serve Valka right if Shirley was the first to orgasm by my hand. Another part wanted to see Shirley's face thrown into the same twisted luxury that I had shown her previously.

"I haven't had an orgasm since I was on the ship," she said. "It shouldn't be hard for me to have one. Go ahead. Give it a try."

I moved, seeking out the tender flesh below. She widened her legs a bit, and I shifted my position to make the reach easier. She was wet. I drew my fingers up to get the scent and taste of her. It wasn't unpleasant, nor was it particularly pleasant, but I did notice the Shirley-ness that I had sensed before.

Watching her face carefully, I moved my fingers among her folds, trying various combinations of rhythm and pressure. She didn't speak, but let her face and breathing speak for her. When I did something too rough, she flinched. I learned early on to be gentle. If I didn't find something good to touch, she pouted a little and looked up at me expectantly. Touching her clitoris directly was too much, she had said, so I kept my attention nearby, but not too close. Tapping and rubbing seemed to work well, and combining those motions worked even better.

I was too nervous to get very turned on. Seeing her lying there, offering her body to me, aroused me somewhat. Touching her certainly helped. I didn't feel too turned on to pay attention, however. I was still very much in control.

She closed her eyes and arched her back, almost offering her breasts to me. I put my other hand on her nipple, taking it between my thumb and forefinger. Little jolts of tension started running through her body—her hand, face, arm, leg—little spasms that grew and merged until her whole body was startlingly rigid.

"I'm going to . . . oh . . ." Her face contorted, lips pulled back, eyes clamped shut. "Faster," she gasped. "You can . . . harder . . ."

I increased the pace, even though I was getting cramps in my wrist, until suddenly she grabbed my hand, mashing it into her crotch, and let out a startling hiss. She shuddered in a slowing rhythm in between gasps for air.

When it finally passed, she let go of my hand and I swallowed nervously. "Was that . . . ?"

"Yes," she said with a smile. "It was. Congratulations, Challers. You just gave your first orgasm."

Chapter Ten

Valka and Masters got to the mess hall before us, and were already sitting and eating when Shirley and I arrived. After I got my dinner tray, I walked toward her, until she gave me a tight-lipped look.

I had told myself that she had been using me, but I was wrong. I didn't see contempt there, or disdain. She didn't look good. She had been crying. Her eyes were still red, and she was sniffling. She picked at her food. The same emotions that I spent the afternoon wrestling with were roiling inside her, as well.

I left my tray at a different table and started to walk in their direction, but Shirley put her hand on my shoulder. "Maybe you should give it a little time, Challers."

I patted her hand. "No, I need to talk to her. I have to try."

When I got there, Masters gave me a warning look and shook his head slightly, but I ignored him. "Valka. I never meant to hurt you. You know that, right?"

She gave me the tight-lipped look again.

I took a deep breath and leaned down. "Valka, I'm sorry. I don't know what I did, but whatever it was . . ."

"Just go away," she snapped. "I don't want to see you."

Masters shook his head when I opened my mouth. "You better go."

I returned to my table. Shirley gave me a look of sympathy.

"It happens sometimes," she said. "Couples come here, and the relationship just can't take the strain of adjusting."

I watched Valka. "She'll change her mind."

Masters said something, glanced over at me, then gave Valka a reassuring pat.

"Eat, Challers," said Shirley. "Come on."

My appetite wasn't as strong as usual and none of the food seemed to have any flavor. Even the chocolate tasted bitter. A cramp took hold in my stomach and twisted my guts from one end to the other. Each mouthful had to be choked down past a throat tight with misery. By the time I was done, I felt like I had been in a fight.

Shirley finished first and had a private word with Masters. He nodded. She came back and sat down across from me. "We're going to adjust the schedule a bit. We're going to take our classes a couple hours earlier."

I glanced over at Valka. She was getting a similar talk from Masters.

"Valka's going to be a couple hours later, then?"

She nodded. "It's for the best, at least right now, don't you think?"

Valka and I had been drifting apart, I realized, from the moment we arrived on the station. This separation had been inevitable. Still, it felt like a dagger through my chest to have it end like this, so quickly. Had we ever really been in love? It seemed unlikely.

"Yeah," I said. "It's best this way."

We took our trays to the recycler and returned to our room. Somehow, the thrill I had gotten from studying math with Shirley the day before was gone. We studied until Shirley called us off. I cleaned up, changed uniforms, and went to bed early. The day had left me emotionally and physically exhausted, and I fell asleep as soon as I lay down.

I woke up before Shirley. I stumbled to the fresher and splashed some water on my face, trying to dispel formless anxieties, the shadowy remains of a nightmare. Still a bit fuzzy with sleep, I took out my little bag of personal effects and found my holo viewer.

I turned it on, and my mother's face appeared over its projector. Her voice sounded thin in the darkness. "Challers, I can't tell you how proud I am that you were able to get into the Scouts. You're going to go and do many amazing things. Through it all, though, I want you to know that I love you, and I will never stop thinking about you." A ghostly holographic tear appeared in her eye. "Good luck, Challers."

My father's face appeared next, but I shut it off before it could make me any more homesick than I already was. I wanted to wake Shirley up right then, tell her to take me back home, but I knew it was a stupid idea. I swallowed back more tears.

I slid my tablet out of its pouch onto the table by the door. A flat black wafer fell out onto the desk.

The wafer the strange secretive girl had given me.

I put it into the reader slot on my holo. The projector came on and played soft music. A floating, semi-transparent head sang a lullaby. Her delicate face, framed with gossamer curls, seemed full of love and warmth, but it wasn't the round face of the woman who had approached me.

"Watch the neck," she had said. What did that mean?

The singing woman wore jewelry of some kind, almost too low to be in the frame. I looked closer.

Tiny letters, inscribed into the beads of her necklace, spelled out words.

MEET US NO KEEPERS 02 DECK GRAPE VINES OLD ROBOT 1 HOUR AFTER LIGHTS OUT

Some kind of secret society? A conspiracy? I shut the holo off and yanked out the wafer. I didn't want to get involved in anything that would jeopardize my position. Too much was at stake.

Or was it? What was the worst they could do? Send me home? Yeah, there'd be some danger, but the station would only be overpop by one. It wouldn't be fun, but I could survive it.

I turned on my tablet and checked the station chronometer. Lights out in the oxygen deck coincided more or less with my own sleep schedule. Shirley, clearly, slept heavily. She hadn't even budged when I crawled out of bed.

I could do this.

The day passed all too slowly, as any day would that was steeped in such anticipation. Shirley took Valka's place in the morning Physicality class, putting me through a grueling routine that put my troubles out of my head. Astronavigation was the only one that caught my attention, really, and only because I found myself doing better at it than I could've imagined. The headaches were a thing of the past.

During the last Physicality session of the day, my lesson covered the stages of arousal—specifically, mine—in what rapidly became excruciating detail.

"The goal is to become completely familiar with each stage, what it feels like to approach the borders of that stage, and what it takes to keep from crossing it." She said this while slowly stroking my erect phallus as I lay on my back in the middle of the classroom bed.

"It's just the two of us," I said. "We could do this in our quarters."

"Now Challers," she scolded, "class is class and bed is bed. There's a difference. Now then, if you are trying to hold yourself back from orgasm, you may be tempted to think about something else besides what is going on, but that's not helpful for a Scout. You need to be in the moment and aware of what your body is doing, and in control of it."

My breathing quickened and I could feel my balls clenching. I was close.

"Try to hold off your orgasm. Maintain your consciousness in the moment, and hold onto it for as long as you can. You have my permission, but delay it as long as you can."

I understood what she was saying on a rational level, but I had no idea how to put it into practice. "I don't know what you mean."

"Just try, Challers. Just hold that moment, just before you orgasm, and maintain it in stillness."

She spoke softly and her words faded into the background. My world shrank down to her hand, my cock, and the air shuddering in and out of my lungs. Soon, too soon, I felt the wave crest, and I fell down the far side. I groaned in ecstasy and felt warm splatters of cum land on my abdomen.

When I opened my eyes, she had already retrieved a warm cloth and was cleaning me off. "Not bad for your first time at this. Do you understand what it is you need to do?"

I shook my head. "Not really."

"I'm sure you'll get it. Would it help if I brought someone in to demonstrate?"

I rolled my eyes. That was the last thing I needed. "No, that won't be necessary."

"This is a challenging technique for some folks, but everyone eventually gets it."

I sat up and took the cloth to get the cum out of my navel. Her tone was really starting to get to me. "When we get out there, on our ship, we're going to be partners, right? I mean, you're the captain of the ship, but the whole reason I'm going through all this is so I can fulfill my responsibilities."

"Of course! And I'm sure you'll do just fine."

"And so am I." I stood up and crossed my arms, trying not to look petulant. "I know I'm having a little trouble fitting into the Scout culture, but I am getting tired of being treated like a child."

She sat back, kneeling, and regarded me with pursed lips. "That's a bit of an ironic thing to say right after wiping semen off your belly. I certainly wouldn't be teaching a child the things I am teaching you."

I tried to keep my voice level. "That's not what I'm talking about."

"Then what are you talking about?"

"The constant instructions to only orgasm when you tell me to. I know that rule. I know why I have it. I haven't broken it. You don't need to keep repeating it."

She nodded curtly. "All right, that's fair."

"That's not all, either. You're always right there, right on top of me. I need some time to myself."

"When we're out on a mission, we're not going to have that luxury," she observed. "The ship is a pretty small space. If you can't handle having me this close here, the ship will be even worse."

"It's not that I can't handle it. It's that I feel like you're always watching me, evaluating me, judging me. Shouldn't you be my friend, rather than trying to be my . . ." I stopped myself. I didn't want to say the word; it was too much, too weird, too wrong.

"It's my responsibility to make sure you learn what you're supposed to learn, Challers."

I sighed. She just didn't get it.

She stood and pulled off her shirt. "While we wait for you to recover, let's review yesterday's touch techniques, just on my breasts this time."

And that pretty much ended the conversation.

It was several days before I could make the mysterious rendezvous. For one reason or another, sometimes involving a bedtime orgasm, I found myself falling asleep before I could sneak away.

The time certainly wasn't wasted. My classes went well, even Astronavigation. The way Shirley taught math was almost enough for me to forgive everything else. I stopped seeing mathematics as an obstacle between me and the fun part, and found the beauty in it, all by itself. Not only that, Shirley took a genuine delight in my success, as well. For the first time, I actually understood the math—really got it, rather than just memorizing the rules for pushing numbers and letters around on a page.

The concept we were working on, synchronization schema, was interesting even without the math. When a ship uses an orgone drive, it's basically breaking down the fabric of the universe on a submicroscopic scale. The jump drives used by Scout ships use a highly focused spacewarp to "weave" the threads of local space into the fabric at the destination, and then travel along them to get there. After the jump, the threads return to their resting state.

In order for the jump to work properly, the vibrations in those threads have to be synchronized, and that's where the math comes in. Computers handle it in practice, of course, but in order to understand how to operate the computers most efficiently, it's good to know the math.

In History class, I was given my first research assignment. Using the tablet and the sources available to me through it, my job was to learn everything I could about the newgens, and their impact on the early Galactic Empire. My curiosity had already been peaked about these people, so I spent my free hours diving into the subject.

I learned that the gentank technology actually came before the orgone drives, so there were already newgens in the galaxy before the great scattering. Chevalier newgens were created in an attempt to construct a society free of gender discrimination by simply not having separate genders. Ovor newgens, who were a kind of egg-laying human, were intended to give women direct control of their fertility. There were dozens of others: people with four arms; people with armored, radiation-proof skin; people who only grew to a meter tall.

At the time of the scattering, each type of newgen was confined to one habitat, so when they built their warp drives and steered themselves out into the void, they brought all of the members of their type to one place in the galaxy to settle. Puregens, on the other hand, could be found all over. About half of the human stations could be found in the Old Stars, with a smaller number in the Coreward Reach and the Rimward Reach. Newgens were mostly moving coreward, where puregens moved mostly rimward.

For a long time after the scattering, the stations were fairly isolated from each other and developed different cultures and traditions. I particularly looked forward to learning about those cultures in detail, but first I was to produce an overview document, and I had to put off the more fascinating research until later.

The other classes weren't as interesting, but they weren't as challenging either, so in the end, they balanced out. Physicality reached a plateau very quickly, where the things I had learned in the first few days were drilled into me by constant practice. The sexual sessions, before dinner, didn't improve any. My body was filling out and, even though it had only been a few days, I felt stronger, fitter, and maybe even a little bigger.

Through it all, the idea that the mysterious cadet was waiting for me, out among the grape vines, kept me going. Eventually, I managed to fake sleep without actually falling asleep and slip out of bed.

I went into the fresher. If Shirley woke up, I could say I had a sudden need to empty my bladder, but when I came out, she was still asleep. I fiddled around in there for a few minutes, making a little noise, but she didn't wake up for that either. She was soundly asleep.

It was time to go.

CHAPTER ELEVEN

The academy was dark, lit only by the dim glowing outlines around the doorways. I encountered one or two Scouts, but I kept my focus and walked by them as if I belonged there, and they didn't question me. The promenade, in contrast, was busy and noisy. Crowds filled the passageway, spilling out from the clubs, amid a riot of music and lights. There weren't any cadets mixed in with the Scouts and locals, but in the noise and confusion, I had no problem slipping past them.

On the oxygen deck, I could hear the distant sounds of water, but I could hear nothing of the robots or other inhabitants of the gardens. There was enough light to see outlines, but no more. The vineyard lay on one side of the path leading down to the water. I stepped over a low hedge of plants, towards a tall, multi-legged machine standing immobile among the vines.

Something clanged. I looked up. A dim light shone from a hatch in its side, silhouetting a head and shoulders leaning out over one of the "shoulder" joints on a massive leg.

"Come on up," she said.

The rough, pitted surface of the robot's leg made for an easy climb. When I got to the shoulder, she took my hand and helped me inside. I found myself in a broad space about the size of a standard cargo container, illuminated by a utility light in the middle of the ceiling.

My hostess closed the hatch, then nodded her head at me with a wry smile. "Glad you could make it. I'm Trace."

I nodded back, trying to keep from staring at her enormous breasts. They were easily bigger than her head, tipped with nipples that poked out from her clingy cadet shirt. She didn't have those tits when she met me in the hallway. I had never seen boobs that big on any woman, much less a woman as small as her.

"And you are?"

Her question knocked me out of my breast-induced trance. "Oh, um, sorry. I'm Challers. Challers Dizen."

I collected my wits and glanced around the chamber.

At one end of the space, a desk had been created by setting a door panel across a broken robot chassis. On top, a tablet projected a holographic image of the grapevines below. That was how she had spotted me coming. In the middle, a group of chairs, clearly taken from the academy, stood in a circle around a low table. On the far end, some kind of vegetation lay on metal racks, apparently to dry.

"So, welcome to the hideout. You've probably got lots of questions. Like, why my boobs are twice as big as they were when you saw me last."

"I suppose."

"If you weren't going to say it, you at least were thinking it."

She went over to the drying rack and plucked a small cluster of leaves. Rubbing them between her hands, she let the dry dark-green shreds fall into a bowl. I watched this strange operation, only half listening to what she was saying.

"I'm shipping out soon, so my keeper put me through the tank. He says this will enhance our 'performance.' Me, I just think they look weird, like it's not me anymore."

She scooped the greenish-brown flakes into a strange little spoon, and then held the handle up to her lips. She sucked on it, briefly, then something inside the spoon flared red and a curl of smoke rose from the other end.

Smoke, for station folk, was a bad thing. Usually, it meant something had shorted out and was in the process of breaking. Worse yet was if a fire got out of control. There were two ways to fight a fire on a station; you could seal the section and let it use up the oxygen, or you could seal the section and evacuate the air. Either way, anyone trapped inside would likely die. No one ever started a fire on purpose. If they needed heat, it came from an electric element. The concept of making smoke on purpose, of starting a fire, was the worst sort of blasphemy.

She saw the alarm on my face and chuckled. "Here," she said, crossing the room to offer me the handle end. "It's just a pipe.

Have some smoke. Makes it easier to take all the vack-yack they hand you around here."

The little smoke-spoon didn't look like any pipe I had ever seen in the station's plumbing, but I decided that blasphemy was exactly what I was in the mood for. I took the "pipe" and tentatively sucked on the hollow handle end. It was metal, and just a little moist from her lips. An acrid scent filled my nose and I coughed, spewing the smoke into the air.

"You get used to that," she said, taking the implement back from me. She sat, leaning her chair back precariously, and propped her feet up on the table. She took more smoke.

"Why are you doing this?" I asked, taking the seat next to her. "Showing all this to me."

"Gotta show someone. I'm leaving soon, and if I don't pass it on, it'll all just go to waste."

"Do the Scouts know about this?"

She laughed so hard I was afraid she'd fall out of her chair. "That's the whole point, Challers! They don't. Or if they do, they don't care. No, this is a place to get away from the keepers and just be who you are, without having to worry about what anyone else thinks."

She passed the pipe back to me and I took just a little smoke, letting it fill my mouth the way I saw her do it. It helped keep me from coughing.

I passed it back again. "What happens if you get caught?"

"They'd probably take this old robot apart, or else fix it up or something, and rip out the plants. It would 'interfere with performance,' but I doubt we'd get punished. What are they going to do, send you home?" She gestured with the pipe, leaving trails of blue smoke in the air.

"That wouldn't be so bad, if they did."

"See? Nothing to worry about." She took more smoke and handed it back.

"So, after you go, I need to find someone else to pass this on to?"

"Yeah, but you have plenty of time, right? You only just arrived."

I breathed in some more smoke. I felt something strange happening behind my eyes. I wasn't exactly dizzy, but I definitely felt more comfortable. "Yeah, a few days ago."

"Don't rush it. The more people know about this place, the more likely it is to get discovered."

I looked over at the hatch. "How do I get in when there isn't someone to see me on the monitors and open the hatch?"

"Ah," she said, setting the pipe on the table. "I need to show you the secrets of the hideout. First, the Command Center." I followed her to the tablet and its holographic display. "This is hardwired into the robot's sensor array. The rest of the thing is junk, but the lenses still work, so you can keep an eye on what's going on outside. You don't need to do anything with it, just let it run."

"Who set all this up?"

"I don't know. It was all here when the guy before me showed it to me." She pointed to a cable that ran along the wall to a hole cut in the corner. "This cable is wired into the leg you climbed up. If you grab its middle toe and lift, it sends a signal up here." She pointed to another cable running to the hatch where we had entered. "The tablet will get the signal and open the hatch. If it doesn't work, that means someone has gotten in here and messed with the tablet."

"Clever."

"Right. Well, like I said, I didn't set it up." She pointed to a section of the holographic display of the surrounding area. "You see those plants there? The ones in between the road and the vines?"

"Yeah, I stepped over them coming here."

"Grab one whenever you come in. That way there's always some ready when you want it." She crossed the room, towards the drying racks. "Throw it up on the rack on this side, then turn each other plant over and move them to the right. When they get to the far end of the rack, they're usually dry enough to use."

"What are they? The plants, I mean."

"Don't know the name for them. Never really cared to look them up. Didn't want to throw any suspicion."

"What do you mean?"

"The Scouts keep track of what you look at on your tablet. If you were to start doing research on these plants, they'd know about it, and they might wonder how you knew to look them up."

"But they're growing right there, out where anyone can see them. I could just say I thought they looked interesting and wanted to look them up."

"Have you looked up anything else since you've been here? Anything they didn't specifically tell you to look up?"

"Well, no."

"That'd be enough. They'll get suspicious of anything like that."

"How careful do I need to be?"

"Well, no one has ever gotten in trouble just coming out here. Someone stopped me once, but I just said I was going out for a walk, and that was fine. You get a reputation for midnight walks on the oxygen deck, and they don't bother you. But they definitely wouldn't like the smoke, so don't draw any attention to that. Speaking of which, it's a good idea to take a shower when you get in. They might smell the smoke on your clothes."

"Good point, I'll remember that." I squinted up at the light in the ceiling. "So, that's it?"

"What do you mean?"

"No big conspiracy or anything?"

"Just a conspiracy to get out from under them once in a while. Do something against the rules, and get away with it."

"Sounds like my kind of conspiracy. Is there anyone else in on it beside us?"

"There's a couple of newgens who come in from the residential section once in a while, but you and I are the only cadets. Helps keep it secret if only a few people know about it."

I wondered what kind of newgens they would be. I wondered if they'd give me the same kind of uncomfortable feeling I'd had at the river.

"Thanks for picking me," I said.

"Oh, you were an easy one. You don't belong here any more than I do."

"What do you mean?" I asked.

"I'll tell you about it sometime, but I don't want to depress you. There's time for another round of smoke before we go." She scooped up the pipe and went back to the plants to fill it.

I took my seat at the table again. From the back, there was something odd about the way Trace stood there. I tried to put my finger on exactly what it was, but my thoughts wouldn't line up.

She looked uncomfortable somehow, as if her shoes didn't fit right.

She walked back to the table and plopped down again, leaning back with one foot on the table. Through the thin material of her cadet uniform I could clearly see the outline of her pussy.

"Uh-unh," she said, waggling the pipe at me. "None of that, Challers. I didn't bring you up here to let you have a go at me; you should be getting enough of that back at the academy."

"What?"

"I see where you're looking." She pointed the stem of the pipe at my crotch. "Little Challers, there, knows what you're looking at, too."

"Sorry," I said, adjusting my gaze back to her face. "I guess I just never met a woman who acts like you."

She handed the pipe back to me and I took another draw on it, this time with less coughing. I tried to keep my eyes on her face.

Trace laughed.

"What?"

"You're funny!"

I scowled and looked away. "I don't see what's so hilarious."

She laughed harder. "Look. Go ahead. I was just teasing! My finely sculpted body is fascinating to you. Of course you're going to look."

"It doesn't bother you?"

"I understand completely. In fact . . ."

She stood up from her chair and pulled the uniform shirt up over her head. The retreating fabric made her breasts bounce hypnotically.

I could only sit and watch, mouth agape.

"You can see better this way, eh?"

I silently thanked Shirley for advising me many times to arrange my shorts so that I didn't have to adjust them if I got an erection. "You're teasing me."

"Well, I have to admit that I'm enjoying watching you blush, but how could I be teasing you if I'm letting you look at me like this?" She tried a crude pirouette, winding up facing away from me. "Oh, forgive me. I'm only going halfway, aren't I?" She bent and pulled down her shorts, giving me a clear view of her pussy lips between her legs.

I put my hands over my face. My cock was becoming painfully hard, and if I didn't do something about it, I would suffer later. I could feel it pulsing against the thin fabric.

"Oh, Challers, I'm sorry."

I opened my eyes.

Trace stood with her arms across her chest and a contrite look on her face. "I didn't mean to do this to you."

I waved my hand. "It's all right, I'll . . ."

"No, it's not all right. I know how . . . I know you're going to be in pain. I'm a cadet, right? I've studied these things. It's okay if you need to relieve yourself."

My embarrassment took another leap. This whole scene was just too bizarre for words. Unfortunately, it had no effect on my cock. I slid my hand down under my waistband, covering my cock and giving it a little squeeze.

"That's it," she said. "Go ahead."

"Now whose eyes are wandering?" I asked.

"I'm sorry," she said, glancing down at the floor. "I like watching you. I know it's very strange, but could you do this for me?"

I let out a deep breath. "All right. But don't do this to me again, okay?"

"I promise."

I pulled my shorts down under my cock and stroked myself. There was something about Trace that seemed almost wrong, but I couldn't deny the feelings that looking at her huge breasts aroused in me. They didn't sag or droop; they were as firm and inviting as Valka's, just *bigger*.

It seemed like it only took a few seconds of stroking to bring myself to orgasm. It wasn't the most intense I had ever had, probably from the confused swirl of emotions growling in my gut, but it was enough to relieve the pressure.

Trace sighed. "I'm sorry I did that to you, Challers. I promise it won't happen again." She looked down at the stripes of cum splattered on the floor between us. "I'll clean up." There was a note of sadness in her voice.

"I can help." I looked around the hideout for a rag.

"No, no, I got it." She swallowed and there was something like a crack in her voice. "Just go."

"But . . ."

"Get out!" Her eyes were brimming with tears and I stepped back, confused and afraid.

"Okay, okay. I'm going."

What had I said? Had I done something wrong?

As I walked back to the academy, I went over the events of the evening in my head again and again, but nothing made any sense. Why had she reacted so badly? I had done everything she wanted. Nothing in my studies had prepared me for this kind of thing. Worse, I couldn't ask Shirley for help. I was on my own.

CHAPTER TWELVE

When I returned from the hideout, I slipped back into the academy, went to my room, and into my bed. As far as I could tell, Shirley hadn't moved. When we woke up, I was a little sleepy, but Shirley said nothing. I had gotten away with it.

The next day was the best since I had arrived. I felt liberated. I forgot all the indignities I had encountered and enjoyed myself. My secret brought a smile to my face whenever I thought of it. Even Math class went by without a twinge.

The food had always been good, but somehow it tasted better. The chocolate was smoother, the butter richer, the fruit sweeter. Shirley noted my appetite and warned that if I started gaining weight, she was going to put me on a diet. I just laughed.

Go ahead, I thought. *Put me on teabulbs and vedgepacks. I don't care.*

I returned to the hideout that night and did my duty in replenishing the supply of the unnamed plant. Trace wasn't there, but that was fine. I took some smoke, poked a bit at the camera tablet, and generally enjoyed my independence.

It actually felt easier to learn under those circumstances. The pressure was off. I had always liked learning, and without the toxic weight of jealousy and loss hanging over me, I could focus on doing just that.

The research project on the history of the Ovors was going particularly well. I had mapped out the region of the galaxy where they had settled after the Great Scattering, along with the founding dates of their various stations, and made notes on the interaction between their needs and the systems they colonized. They grew very quickly, about twice as fast as the puregens, because they could easily bear two or three children with each pregnancy, sometimes more—if they wanted to.

Ovor women could consciously hold back their eggs, keeping them suspended until they were needed. It struck me that if I had grown up on an Ovor station, I probably wouldn't be in this mess. Ovor stations would have no reason to go overpop.

Of course, if I had been born on an Ovor station, I'd also probably be female. Ovors gave birth to three or four females for every male. What would it have been like to grow up on one of those stations? The history sources I found were fairly vague on the day-to-day details.

A few nights later, I spotted Trace on the monitors shortly after I had arrived at the hideout. I helped her in the hatch with a big smile on my face.

"Welcome back," I said. I was proud of myself, having taken what I thought was good care of the place while she was gone.

As soon as the light from the overhead struck her face, though, I stopped cold. "What's wrong?"

She turned her scowl from me to the holograms floating above the monitor tablet. "What. Is. That?" She jabbed a finger at a spot near the path. "Do you see that?"

I looked close. There was a dark smudge along one side of the road.

"I don't . . ."

"It's an empty spot in the plants," she spat. "A great big hole where you've been pulling out the first plant that came to hand."

"But . . ."

"You're going to have to be more careful. You don't get your plant from the same place along the border every time you come by." She looked over at the drying rack, which was piled with the results of my harvesting. "Let me guess, you've been in every dark shift since I showed you the place?"

"Well . . ."

"Are you insane? You can't do that! You'll ruin everything!"

"What's all the yelling?" A calmer voice floated into the chamber, a sweet soprano.

I turned towards the entrance. A woman's face, framed by dark wavy hair, poked into the hatchway.

Trace spun and stalked over to the drying racks. "Vack-head, here, has been here the last five nights straight, near as I can tell, and left a bare patch out by the road. It's a wonder this place hasn't been found already."

"Hello, vack-head," she said, stepping fully into the hideout. She smiled broadly, deflating the insult.

I wish I could say I reacted with grace and decorum, but when I saw her four impressively rounded breasts, concealed only by a handful of brightly colored scarves, I was speechless.

Trace surveyed the drying racks with a growl. "And you burned up all the best leaves! Vack-head." She poked around in the stems and seeds for whatever leftovers she could locate.

The new woman bowed to me, smiling. "I am Suna. And you?"

"Challers," I croaked, finding my voice again. "You're a . . ."

"Newgen," said Trace. "I told you that a couple of newgens might come around."

She flopped into a chair, causing her breasts to roll and bounce on her chest. No woman I had known moved that way. She seemed almost careless with them.

"Challers, you can't come here every night. You'll burn up the plants before they can recover, and you'll get us discovered and spoil it for everyone." She took a huge lungful of smoke from the pipe and offered it to Suna.

Suna gave her a smile and waved it off. "No, I have eggs now; it would not be good for them." She patted her belly. "And do I not recall a certain cadet I know going a bit too far with the smoke her first few nights in here?"

Trace rolled her eyes and offered the pipe to me. "Right, very well. It doesn't change the fact that he can't keep acting this way."

I accepted the pipe. "You must be an Ovor newgen, then," I said, and took some smoke.

She smiled, nodding. "Yes, that is right. Ovor. You have not seen one before?"

"Just a few holos in my lessons. I'm writing an essay about your people. You've put together a very interesting culture."

"Well, not exactly," she said, quirking the corner of her mouth in a half-smile. "I was not born on an Ovor station. I became an Ovor here, at headquarters."

"What?"

Trace pulled the pipe out of my hand and took another big lungful of smoke. "The gentank isn't just for giving sweet kids gigantic mammaries, you know. They have all the old templates. They can turn anyone into an Ovor. Even you."

Out of politeness to Suna, I tried not to look too uncomfortable with the suggestion. "Why?"

She shrugged. "I thought I'd try it out. See whether it suits me."

"So you can just ask to be put into the gentank, and have them make you into whatever body you like?"

"Or whatever body your keeper likes," grumbled Trace.

"Oh, you." Suna shook her head. "I think your breasts look quite good on you."

Trace rolled her eyes.

"Don't you think?" asked Suna, looking at me.

I stammered. "They're, um, quite impressive. Yes."

Trace shoved the pipe back into my hand. "Here. Have some more smoke."

I took it and drew the smoke into my lungs. In the back of my head, I could feel the little hum start to build. It was taking effect.

"Honestly?" I said. "I like them smaller."

I thought of Valka, her breasts quivering as she stroked herself that first time in Shirley's ship, and I felt the need to clear my throat. I coughed smokily.

Trace caught my eye and her scowl softened. "What's her name?"

"Valka," I said. "We were together for a year before coming here. Two days after we arrived . . ." I snapped my fingers. "Pfft."

"I'm sorry," said Suna, leaning out to squeeze my hand.

"Happens to a lot of folks," said Trace.

I squeezed Suna's hand and she dropped her gentle grasp. "Did you break up after coming here?"

Trace shook her head. "Nah, we weren't really a couple. I figured out what it took to get into the Scouts on my own and just went and found someone to get picked up with. No big breakup, no big drama."

"Where is he now?"

Trace shook her head and waved away the question. "No, no, you don't get that answer yet. I barely know you." She handed me the pipe. "The smoke isn't doing me any good. I'll see you next time." At the hatch, she turned back to us. "My last night on the station is four nights from now. Will you . . .?"

For just a moment, the look on her face flashed vulnerability.

"Of course we will," said Suna. "I'll make sure Zun knows to come, too."

It didn't seem like it would be a happy occasion.

When the hatch closed, Suna sighed and shook her head. "Trace is a good person, but she can be a bit closed off. She needs to open up more."

I took some more smoke. "I think we all could do with being more open. Too many secrets. Too many things left unsaid."

I stared at the curl of vapor drifting up from the spoon and wondered whether there had been anything I could have said to keep Valka from throwing me away.

"Truth," said Suna. "So, tell me honestly, then, you do not like large breasts?"

She arched her back, thrusting her chest forward. The thin material of the scarves pulled tight against her body, revealing every contour. Next to Trace's huge rack, Suna's weren't that large, but the comparison was unfair.

"Oh, I, ah, wouldn't say that." Somehow I managed to keep the stuttering to a minimum. "I just like one particular pair of breasts better."

"I thought you said you had broken up." Suna stood up and moved closer. "Surely that isn't coloring your preferences, anymore."

"Suna, um, you know that I'm not supposed to have orgasms without permission, right?"

"You're also not supposed to use any drugs without permission." She nodded in the direction of the smoke curling from my hand.

I looked down at it. The buzzing in the back of my skull told me she was right. I hadn't injected anything or taken any pills, but this smoke was a drug. I looked up and again found my vision filled by Suna's chest. With her standing, they were right at eye level.

She pulled the scarves down from her lower pair of breasts, exposing hard pink nipples. "Scouts have such educated hands, such skilled mouths. Are you sure you don't want to break any more rules?"

I swallowed hard. Coming out here in the middle of the night wasn't against the rules—at least, no one had ever told me I couldn't—but by taking this smoke I had broken one of the first rules Shirley had given me. No, not one of the first. The first.

I was never a troublemaker back on the station. I was a good kid, a good student, a good son.

I put the smoke-spoon down on the makeshift table. It rolled onto its side and went out.

Suna stepped in front of me, lifting her breasts toward my face. "Go ahead."

In that moment, what else could I do? I smiled up at her.

Chapter Thirteen

My hands floated up to Suna's breasts. I stroked the soft skin, felt the gentle weight in my palms. She pulled the scarves free of her body and cast them aside. Her marvelous breasts gave more resistance than Shirley's. They felt taut.

I liked it.

She took an upper breast in her hand and offered its tip to my open mouth. I hadn't studied much of this sort of stimulation with Shirley, but I found a raw confidence and licked it anyway. Suna rewarded me with a coo of pleasure.

"What do you like?" I asked. "Are they sensitive?"

"Yes," she said. "Be gentle."

Between the smoke drifting around in my brain, Suna's exotic body, and the heady rush of knowing I was about to break the second of Shirley's Cardinal Rules, I was completely intoxicated. I eagerly squeezed and stroked, licked and kissed and sucked. For a moment, I wished I had another hand to apply to the last of Suna's four breasts, but when I looked up, she was taking care of that herself. I drew back and enjoyed the sight of four hands, two mine and two hers, caressing her four beautiful breasts.

I knew from my research that she would not have to worry about getting pregnant. The eggs she was carrying would only be fertilized if she chose it, and even then they would not develop until she decided she wanted them to.

She eased herself back onto the table. "Give me your mouth, Challers."

She hitched one foot up onto a chair, revealing that the colorful skirt she wore was the only garment left on her body. Her plump, moist vulva parted as she spread her legs, releasing a musky scent that only added to my desire. I could feel my cock straining against the fabric of my shorts.

I spread her lips with my fingers and explored with my tongue. Her clitoris was larger than Shirley's, as big as the last joint of my little finger, and it thickened as I directed my attentions to it.

"Do you like this?" I asked, between flicks of my tongue.

"Yes," she breathed. "Don't stop. Please don't stop."

I hadn't done anything like this with Shirley. She had always just had me use my hands. The feel of Suna's delicate flesh on my lips, on my tongue, excited me like nothing else. I wanted to stay there forever.

"Suck it. Please."

I pursed my lips and drew her clit into my mouth. I could feel it pulsing there, alive, warm, responding. Her hand on the back of my head held me close, but I wasn't going anywhere. She tilted her hips, and I slipped two fingers inside her. Shirley had let me explore her body this way, as well, but when I did it for Suna, she quivered with pleasure in a way Shirley never had. It felt good to be so in control, so in demand. I stroked her inner tissues, seeking out the deep centers of pleasure Shirley had shown me.

The techniques Shirley had taught me—keeping her on the edge of orgasm but not quite achieving it—served me just as well with my lips and tongue as it did with my fingers. From her sounds and movements, I could tell she was close, ready for a powerful orgasm.

I stood and quickly pulled the waistband of my shorts down under my cock. It bounced slightly, finally free, aimed at Suna's moist, waiting pussy.

There it was.

I was about to take that final step—do the one thing that Valka and I had been prevented from doing—and I was filled with a sudden sense of loss.

If I did this, that would be the end. No undoing it.

"Go ahead," said Suna, whispering desperately.

But I couldn't. I still had hope.

I knelt again, and placed my lips around Suna's clit once more. I sucked, pulsing in time with the heartbeat I could feel through my cheeks, while I stroked every other part of her sex I could reach. She climaxed in seconds, grunting and gasping, and then relaxed, laying back against the hard table with a sigh.

When she regained her breath, she rolled up onto her elbows and shook her head. "Why didn't you enter me? There is no danger to either of us."

I stood up. "I know. But it would have meant something to me. It would have meant giving up something I'm not ready to give up yet."

I couldn't say it to Suna, but I knew in my heart that Shirley's disapproval wasn't the reason I held back. I stopped because it would have been an admission that I'd never be able to do it, for the first time, with Valka.

I still had hope.

"Do you want me to help you with that?" She nodded in the direction of my unflagging erection and pushed a pair of breasts together invitingly.

Suna's invitation did make some sense. I had started this session with her intending to have an orgasm, and just because I turned down one invitation didn't mean I had to turn them all down.

Besides, I could tell from the smile on her face that she would enjoy it almost as much as I would.

She slid down off the table and took a moment to transfer some of the copious fluid from her pussy to the space between her lower set of breasts. I stripped off my uniform and took her place on the table with my legs hanging off one side.

She wrapped her breasts around my cock. It felt marvelous. Shirley had put her hands on my cock a dozen or so times, but it felt nowhere near as good as this. My breath caught. She slowly rubbed her body against me, and I tried to play with her upper breasts, but my hands wouldn't do what I wanted. I flopped onto my back and just let her go. She certainly seemed to know what to do.

Too soon, all too soon, I came. She smiled, stroking me all through my climax, spreading my semen all over her chest.

I lay there, panting, sweating, spots swimming before my eyes.

"Well, we are quite a mess aren't we?"

Suna stood and surveyed her handiwork. Her breasts gleamed in the dim light. My groin and thighs, as well as my chin, felt cool from the drying sexual fluids smeared over them.

"Next time, I'll bring some water."

"We could just go down to the water and rinse off."

"Won't someone see us?"

"They might. But there aren't any rules about taking a walk around the oxygen deck on your own time, are there?"

She had a point. We wrapped ourselves in our minimal attire and climbed down to the ground.

The warm, shallow water felt wonderful. Suna and I splashed about, rinsing off the evidence of our encounter in the hideout.

"So why is this called a *river*? I've never heard that word before."

"I'm not sure why. That's just what it's called."

For some reason, I found myself reaching out for her hand. I pulled her close and kissed her.

She gave me a gentle squeeze. "What are you thinking?"

I paused a moment for that to rattle around in my head. Why was I doing this? Wasn't I devoted to Valka?

"My mentor taught me that I could care for more than one person at a time, and if she was asking me to develop a relationship with her, then I should be able to have one with you, too."

"Relationship? That sounds serious."

"A little. Why?"

"Challers, you have to know," she said, shrugging one shoulder, "I'm not in this for a 'relationship.' I just want some fun once in a while, you know?" She spotted the furrow in my brow and squeezed my hand again, drawing me to a stop. "You're a Scout. Sometime soon, very soon, you're going to be going off on your cruise, and you'll be away for a long time. I just don't want you to think we're ever going to have anything permanent."

I could see her point. "I understand," I said. "Just for fun."

The next afternoon, while Shirley and I were on our way to the mess hall, we met Masters and Valka coming out.

Her smile melted away as our eyes met. "Challers." Her voice wasn't cold, exactly, but it chilled me to hear it.

My stomach clenched. I wanted to be anywhere else but there. I couldn't think of what to say, so I just blurted out, "How've you been?"

"Well enough. You?" Her eyes seemed empty, somehow. Something was missing there.

I shrugged. "The same."

We passed each other, the moment over, and I went into the mess hall. I caught a tear with the back of my hand and smeared it away. I wanted to turn around and call her back, but the words wouldn't come. There was nothing to say.

I moped my way through dinner. Shirley sat across from me, silent.

"I miss her," I finally said. It's all I could think to say. I couldn't talk about the guilt I felt over having given in to Suna the night before. I should have felt guilty about breaking two of Shirley's cardinal rules. Instead, what I felt guilty about was giving something to Suna that, in my heart, I knew I should be reserving for Valka and Shirley. It was all very confusing, and I couldn't talk about the things I had done. I couldn't even start.

"I noticed." Her eyes held sympathy.

"What did I do wrong with her?"

"You didn't do anything wrong. Your relationship just wasn't right for the Scouts. It didn't fit in anywhere, so it just broke. It happens."

"Is there any way to fix it?"

"Give it some time. You're both going to be in the academy for a while. There will be other opportunities."

I took a deep breath and tried to work up enough willpower to finish my meal.

A few minutes later, Trace walked in, trailing behind a tall, blond, muscular Scout with a swaggering walk. I could see why she didn't like him as soon as I saw him. I tried to make eye contact, but she wasn't looking up from the floor. Instead of the blustery woman I knew from the hideout, I saw a sullen child, her spirit beaten and subdued. The sight made my stomach twitch.

Shirley caught the direction of my gaze as I watched them getting their food. When they got to the end of the buffet, she waved to the big man. He smiled and walked to our table.

"Umber, may I introduce my new cadet, Challers Dizen."

Clearly, they knew each other, but that came as no surprise. There weren't that many people to know.

He nodded to me, and then to Trace. "Shirley, this is Trace Hom."

They sat next to us and started eating.

I tried to make conversation, but Trace completely closed down any attempt at conversation, eating with mechanical deliberation. She answered questions in monosyllables and shrugs, and never looked up from her food.

I gave Umber a questioning look. "Is something wrong?"

"A little nerves before jump day," he said.

"That close?" asked Shirley.

"Just four days." He patted Trace's back. "She's doing great."

Shirley rose from her seat. "In that case, we should leave you folks alone."

I followed suit. "Nice meeting you," I said. "Maybe we'll run into each other again."

On the way out of the mess hall, Shirley explained, "The last twenty days or so of academy training, cadets aren't allowed to have any orgasms at all. It can set anyone a little on edge."

"Really, why is that? The discipline, I mean, not the on-edge-ness."

"The longer you go without, the more orgone, and the farther the ship goes. The first jump is always to a distant, uncharted system. It's something of a final exam, to see how much you've learned at the academy. The further you go, the better."

"That sounds worth it." I wasn't going to say anything, but I was looking forward to a rest. Shirley had her hand in my pants every chance she got.

"Oh, it is! To go where no one else has been, to find new planets, that's the best part of being a Scout. The intelligence work, the diplomacy, the mail delivery, that's fine, but really, I mostly like being out among the stars."

"Intelligence work?"

"Scouts spend a good deal of time hunting down Pirate activity to call in the Fleet. Mostly, it means visiting a lot of empty star systems and making sure they're still empty."

I considered this while we walked. Growing up on Stakroya, the Pirates were always a nebulous threat, always out there in the darkness, ready to pounce. We got regular news reports about

Pirate raids that would leave a station gutted and the entire population thrown out of the airlocks. It hadn't happened to us, but we knew it could. They were the reason we needed the Fleet.

"Sounds like you don't actually find them very often."

"We don't. There aren't that many Pirates, but when you find them it's big."

"They don't have Scouts of their own?"

"We've never seen any. Finding Pirates is an all-or-nothing affair. A thousand star systems, all empty, for every one that has a rendezvous point or a mining ship. Even then, if the Fleet isn't on the bounce, the Pirates can slip away."

We arrived at our quarters and I set out my tablet to prepare for our nightly mathematics tutoring session. I had mastered the coordinate transformations and had started working on some of the rather complex theories for time-synchronization. Faster-than-light travel did some strange things to clocks, and I needed to understand some of the things Scouts put in their computers to handle it.

As the lines of the night's hologram simulation painted the air around us, I cocked my head. "Why don't we have our classes this way?"

"This is supplemental to the classroom work."

"Sure, compared to anyone else, but I'm not anyone else. Why can't we just do what we do here for the classwork?"

"It's for commonality of experience. When Scouts who haven't studied together talk about something, they need to use the same language. They need to have taken the same course."

"Physicality doesn't work that way, though. I'm learning more about your body and my body. I don't have a common experience with any other cadets."

"This is what works, Challers. You and I are learning how to bring each other to the heights of ecstasy. With dedicated practice, we'll be able to do that on a regular basis. It's too much to learn everything for everyone. It's impossible. After having gone through this process with me, though, your next partner will be easier to discover. Now, let's start."

All through my studies, the thought nagged at me, in the back of my mind, that I was being isolated. I wanted to talk to other cadets, and not just Trace. Valka wasn't happy. I wasn't happy. Trace wasn't happy. Were there any who were happy? The whole situation was starting to smell bad and I had only been at the academy a few days.

Still, I managed to get through the material with some confidence that I'd be able to handle the next day's class.

Chapter Fourteen

I waited outside the main portal, where I could just barely hear the music and voices from the promenade. Around me, the oxygen deck was quiet and dark. Shirley had fallen asleep early and the dark shift had only just started. Lucky break for me.

When a figure hurried out of the doorway, I came out of the shadows and joined her on the path.

Trace jumped at the sudden movement. "Challers! Vack-head! Don't do that to me."

"I wanted to talk to you about a few things before we met the others."

"Okay, so talk." She walked slowly, scanning the plants along the edge of the path.

"You've been here a lot longer than me. Tell me, are any of the cadets actually happy to be here? I'm not. Valka's not. You certainly aren't. What's going on? Is the academy just one big sexual prison?"

She grunted. "There are a few who like it a lot, like Jonno Smarka. To him, this place is a paradise. Most seem to tolerate it well enough."

"I know why Valka and I are upset. What about you?"

"It isn't enough that the Scouts lied to us to get us here. Then they force us to either stay and be their sex robots, or throw us to the Fleet or the Merchants?"

"I have a feeling that it's more than that for you."

Trace stopped, closed her eyes, and took a deep breath. "I used to be a man." She glanced at my face and turned away. "Pretty disgusting, hunh?"

"Well, it's kind of odd, but after seeing what Suna did to herself, I wouldn't say that. Why would I think it was disgusting?"

"Oh, vacuum take it! I'm leaving anyway; it's not like it matters what you think. Come on, let's get off the path." She picked out one of the plants from the border along the road and yanked it out of the ground. I followed her between the green vine-covered frames of the vineyard.

"When I got to the academy, I didn't really respond to my keeper. Didn't find her arousing in the slightest. So they switched her for someone with a different temperament, a different body type. Still nothing. Finally, they took me in for some tests—had me watch a bunch of sex holos while they measured my responses. They found out my secret. I like men."

Trace saw the puzzled look on my face and shook her head.

"Yeah, I know. Not supposed to be that way. I'm some kind of—I don't know—freak. But they knew *just* what to do with me." The sarcasm in her voice was sharp.

"And that wasn't what you wanted."

She sneered. "Of course not. I'm not interested in this kind of body on a sex partner; why would I want one of my own?"

"And they did it to you anyway?"

"They said that when my hormones changed everything would be fine—wait and see. Vack-heads. Besides, they didn't give me much choice. What was I going to do, go back home? Everyone would know what I was. Forget the Fleet or the Marines. I'd be dead."

"They'd kill you for that?"

"Orenva station has a strict code. My first—" She swallowed hard, closing her eyes. "My first lover was executed for 'corrupt morals.' If I went back . . ."

She shook her head.

"I take it having a female body hasn't helped any."

We stopped at the robot's leg. "Thanks to their 'adjustments,' my body's of use to them now. I can have an orgasm from just about anything, even if I don't want to. It's completely vacked. They've taken everything, Challers. Everything. I don't even have my body anymore. It belongs to them now; it answers their directions, not mine."

I saw her pain like she had never let me see it before. How could they not know they were torturing her? How could they see this and still do this to her?

I did the only thing I could think of, and put my arms around her.

She stiffened. "No," she choked, "I don't want . . . I don't want to . . ."

Sobs escaped, one by one, then a steady stream. Her body relaxed, letting me hold her, comfort her the only way I knew how. We stood there, under the dark frame of the robot, crying softly together, mourning the person she had been, that she could never be again.

When she quieted, I whispered, "So what are you going to do?"

"I don't know. I guess I'm just going to go on my training cruise tomorrow."

"Don't do anything extreme," I said.

She pulled away and looked up at me. "What do you mean?"

I hesitated. Should I even mention it? Too late to hold back.

"Back on Stakroya Station, during a hull survey, a classmate unclipped his tether, turned off the magnetics on his boots, and floated off. Before anyone could rescue him, he took off his helmet. The vacuum took him."

"No," she said, shaking her head. "No, I won't."

"We're friends, okay? And friends don't do things like that to each other." I wished I could believe her. "Promise me."

She put her head against my chest again. "I promise."

"Is there anyone else like you? I mean, men they've turned into women because of this."

"I guess. They seemed familiar with the problem."

"Maybe someday they'll let you pilot a ship with another man."

She pulled back and looked me in the eye. "What?"

"Maybe someday they'll let you just, you know, be who you are."

She snorted. "Never going to happen."

Suna's voice ended the moment. "Just couldn't control yourselves until you got inside, eh?"

Trace gave her a glare that would've split hull plates, then turned and twisted the robot's toe to open the hatch.

As she climbed up, I put my hand on Suna's shoulder. "I was just soothing the nerves of a friend. She's not having a good day."

"I was just teasing," she said, but there was regret in her eyes and in her voice. She was dressed the same as the last time I saw her, with colorful scarves tied crosswise over her four breasts and wearing a knee-length skirt. The look passed quickly and she leaned close to whisper, "I hope we can have fun together again sometime soon."

The thought did give my cock a little throb, but I shook my head. "Tonight I'm here for Trace. I think that would be inappropriate."

She pouted. "Doesn't have to be tonight," she grumbled, and climbed up the robot's leg.

When I reached the hatch, Trace was packing the pipe full of leaves. As soon as it was ready, she drew a deep breath through it and held the smoke in her lungs. She clearly meant to get the most out of it.

I noticed a new set of makeshift shelves near the hatch with some clean towels, a cylinder of water, some tubes of various cleaning solutions, and some basic cleaning implements.

Trace jabbed the mouthpiece of the pipe at the collection. "Whose idea was that?"

"Mine," said Suna. "We do need to clean up around here from time to time. We don't have any janitorial robots, you know."

I had to admit she was right. The place was a mess. I wondered how we had managed to keep our nighttime meetings here secret without bringing back telltale smudges on our clothes and bodies.

Trace shrugged. "Fine with me. It's your place now." She took another lungful of smoke and handed me the pipe.

Suna glanced at the holographic displays above the computer. "Oh, Zun's here." She touched the tablet and the hatch clanked open.

Zun turned out to be a Chevalier newgen, like the ones I had met down at the river. He wasn't naked, but I could see similarities in the way his face and body were put together. It bothered me a little, but I swallowed the little knot of uncertainty, and when Suna introduced him to me, and I bowed respectfully.

We took our places around the table. As before, Suna passed on her turn with the pipe, but Zun took a long pull from it before handing it to me.

"I'm going to miss this," said Trace, softly, as the pipe came around to her again. "The smoke. You folks." She took another deep draft of smoke.

"We're going to miss you, too," said Zun.

The standard response seemed trite, and I could see in his eyes that it felt that way to him, too. I know I felt helpless in the face of Trace's dilemma, and I had only known her a few days. Zun and Suna had known her for longer, it seemed, and they were no better equipped to deal with her pain than I was.

I took the pipe, filled my lungs, and let the effects dull the edge of my emotions.

"Let's play a game," said Zun. "Take our mind off things."

"You always want to play games." Trace took the pipe, but didn't draw so deep this time.

"Better than just sitting around," he said. From a carry-pouch, he took out a little holo device and set it in the middle of the table. To me, he asked, "Ever played Rubysocks?"

"No." The device looked like a portable desk emitter, but I had never seen that model before.

He waved his hand over it and it started up, displaying a bright red sphere in the center of the table. "Each of us tells a story. The one whose story makes the biggest impression on the others around the table wins the game. The story can be sexy or scary or funny, but it has to create a reaction. The device will measure the reactions from everyone around the table and declare the winner."

"I'm not much of a storyteller," I said.

"Oh, that's not true." Suna waved her hand dismissively. "Everyone has stories. It's part of the human condition."

"Does it have to be true?"

"No," said Zun. "Though sometimes that's the best. So who's first?"

"I'll go," said Suna and she waved her hand over the unit. The red sphere flashed and the name "Suna Vol" rotated briefly in the center, along with a chronometer set to ten minutes.

"It knows your name," I said.

"It reads your ID implant."

"So it's a Scout device?"

"No, but the ID implant isn't hard to read, if you know what you're doing."

"I'm just worried this will get back to them."

Trace shook her head. "You can trust Zun. He's been here longer than any of us."

"All right."

"Begin," said Suna, rubbing her hands together. The clock ticked down the seconds.

CHAPTER FIFTEEN

Suna stood up, beginning her story with a grand gesture.

"So there was this woman, captain of a Merchant ship that ran the routes between the Central Cluster and the Sandral Rim. It wasn't a big ship by Merchant standards, maybe five hundred hearts aboard, but it was hers and she was proud of it. Being small, it was also quick, by Merchant standards, easily making a thousand to one on the limit. It made port every few days, making short local hops to speculate on goods the bigger ships left behind as too small to bother with. Or they contracted out for short high-money missions from one star to the next.

"It was on one of these short contracts that her cargo-mistress came to tell her that something was moving inside one of the crates. Of course, stowaways are rare on a Merchant ship, but they happen from time to time. The captain opened the crate and they found a Marine, delirious with thirst. They managed to get him wheeled into the sick bay, and once they got some water into him, he recovered pretty fast. The Marine wasn't about to talk, though, so they locked him in the brig to sort out when they got to their destination.

"They thought they were safe with him there, but one night, while the captain was asleep, the Marine broke out of the brig, knocked out his guards, and made his way to the captain's stateroom. He slowly eased the door open, and a shaft of light from the hallway fell across the captain's face. She was beautiful, at least to his eyes. He knew right then that he had to have her.

"Marines, you know, don't get much contact with women, and a buck private like this one never does. So, even though the captain of this Merchant ship was just as over-endowed as the rest of her crew, he got a serious itch on for her. He crept in, on feet built and trained for silence, and stood next to the bed.

"Now, this Marine wasn't stupid. He knew that the bed had orgone collectors in it, and that if he messed around with it, there would be an alert or alarm or something. So, first thing he did was close the door and fix it so it wasn't going to open right away. Then he crawled into bed next to her and yanked away the covers, exposing her body to his eager eyes.

"Each breast was the size of a bucket with nipples as big as dinner plates. Her belly was even bigger. Her sex was invisible, lost under her spreading flesh. Even so, her skin was smooth and fair, and her long hair fell in golden cascades across her shoulders. Uncovered, she was only more beautiful to him.

"She woke up and asked him why he was there, but he didn't say anything, he just put one huge hand behind her head and pulled her in and kissed her. Nobody had ever treated her like that before and she loved it. She kissed him back, wrapping her arms around his huge, muscular chest.

"'Take me,' she gasped, but he never needed her permission.

"He stroked and squeezed her soft, tender body, exploring the soft folds until he found her warm, moist center. She moaned in ecstasy as his thick, calloused finger invaded, seeking out her feminine secrets. Probing and pushing, he plumbed the depths of her sex. An instinct took hold of him, something raw and primal, something all the alterations of the tank could never touch. He crept on top of her, putting his muscular thighs between hers, but she shook her head.

"She rolled over onto her huge belly, offering the twin globes of her posterior. 'Like this,' she gasped, hungrily. 'Much better like this.'

"The Marine took aim at her target and started thrusting for all he was worth.

"'Go ahead,' she cried, 'what are you waiting for? Put it in me!'

"'What are you talking about?' he said. 'It's in!'

"In disgust, she tried to pull away, but he was too strong. He grunted and groaned and strained and finally shouted a roar of triumph and collapsed on top of her, totally spent.

"Of course, this was the moment when the ship's security officer finally broke down the door. If the Marine had not been in a state of sexual exhaustion, they never would have subdued him, but they managed to tie him up and put him back in the cell before he came out of it.

The unit on the table let out a quiet tone as her timer reached zero.

"Vack!" She slumped down into her seat.

A score flashed on the sphere floating above the table. I had nothing to compare it to, but from her expression, I could tell it wasn't very good.

"That's how it goes," said Zun. "You have to keep your eye on that timer. Now, if I may . . ."

He waved his hand over the device, and the timer flashed his name and reset the clock.

"Begin." The timer ticked down the seconds, but Zun just leaned back in his chair and stretched. "Kal, my grandparent, tells this story . . ."

Zun screwed up his face in an imitation of an elderly person. "In my youth, I was something of a wanderer, traveling the trade routes in search of fortune and adventure. I had a bit of cash to my name, so I hired out space on Merchant ships and speculated on high-value cargoes, buying and selling at each station on the route. Of course, everywhere I went, there were interesting people to meet, and Corgela Station was no different.

"This particular station specialized in cybernetic enhancements—you know, robotic body parts of various sorts. I was in the middle of negotiations with a charming young creature by the name of Rol, when a sudden sneeze caused this person's ocular implant to sail across the table.

"I managed to catch it and when I handed it back, the poor thing was embarrassed beyond words. Needless to say, I got quite a favorable price for the power conditioners I was selling, but even better than that, I found that I had a bedmate that night.

"Rol turned out to be quite the sexual athlete. We were awake half the sleep cycle, trying out new facets and approaches." Zun sighed and shook his head wistfully. "Yes, that was quite a night. I'll maintain some decorum and not go into detail."

He cocked an eyebrow at Suna, who stuck her tongue out at him.

"So when it was time for me to get my cargo loaded and be off again, I asked Rol whether every client got this kind of treatment."

"'No,' she said, 'you just caught my eye.'"

The rest of us moaned in pain while Zun chuckled and took some smoke from the pipe. He still had more than half his time left.

"End," he said, and the timer flashed. The score posted was much higher than Suna's.

"Not bad," said Suna. "You even got bonus points for ending early."

Zun nodded once. "I know how to play this game."

"All right, my turn," said Trace. "Let's get this over with."

She waved her hand over the device, rose to her feet, and took a deep breath. "Begin."

"I had an older brother, and when I was young, I looked up to him, wanted to be like him. He was smart, worked hard, and always respected our parents. He showed me what it was to be a good son. Our station went overpop shortly after his eighteenth birthday, and it wasn't a month before the Fleet took him. Before he went, he asked me to remember him.

"And so I remember him. He was training for maintenance on the exterior crew. Had an expert rating at sixteen—would have had a master's rating at eighteen if it weren't for the supervisory requirements. He could handle a hullwelder like a surgeon's tools. He made me a sculpture of a woman from a scrap piece of hullplate, just using his hullwelder and grippers.

"My parents weren't happy about that sculpture. They said it was indecent. If you had a dirty mind, you might imagine she was pleasuring herself. I thought she was just standing that way. Knowing my brother, it probably *was* that kind of sculpture, but he argued for me and they let me keep it in my quarters. After he got taken away by the Fleet, I was glad they let me keep it.

"When my friends came around, they always wanted to see it. I'd take it out of the locker where my mom made me keep it most of the time, and put it on the table while we talked and played our games. They liked to look at her, at first, and talk about what women were like and all that, but after a while, she just became a part of the rituals of the day. Go into my room, take out the sculpture, and then do whatever it was we were going to do.

"I don't know about anyone else, but to me, she seemed like a witness, someone who saw everything that went on, heard all of our conversations, and never had any judgments or condemnations. After a while, I started talking to her at night, telling her about all my troubles. The feelings . . .

"Well. Anyway. When the Scouts came to pick me up, I wanted to bring her with me. There was just enough mass allotment, but instead, Mom took it from me and hid it. Maybe even destroyed it, or gave it to the void.

"I'd like to think she put the statue out an airlock. That she's out there, somewhere. Waiting for me.

Trace sat down. "End."

The score was even higher. I certainly couldn't argue with that. The story had struck me to the core. Trace had lost everything she had ever valued, whether it was given away, lost, stolen, or traded. All she had left was this vague, silly notion that her brother's sculpture was out there, in the void, watching over her. I hoped, for her sake, that it would be enough.

Zun nodded his head in Trace's direction. "That one will be difficult to surpass, Challers."

"I'm wondering if I should even try."

"Oh, please do," said Suna. "You couldn't do any worse than me."

"All right." I stood, and triggered the machine. I bowed my head, closed my eyes, and placed my palms together in front of my chest. "Begin."

I heard the device beep and knew it would be counting down. A bonus for ending early, eh? I could deal with that. Emotional reaction? No. The machine was probably reading *physical* reactions.

I opened my eyes and spoke softly. "A long time ago, a young boy sat on his mother's lap. He had his hands cupped, like this." I turned my hands to enclose a small space. "Holding something."

Zun and Suna leaned forward, looking at my hands. Trace cocked an eyebrow. Tough audience.

"'What have you got there?' she asked.

"'It's something wonderful.'" My whisper suddenly became a roar. "'See!'" I flung my arms wide, as if throwing something in their faces.

My audience leapt back. Zun nearly overturned his chair.

"End," I said.

Trace chuckled. "Nicely played."

I shrugged, and checked the score. "Well, not nicely enough. Even with the time bonus, you still won the competition."

Trace shook her head. "Not like it means anything."

"What do you mean?"

Zun put his chair back into position and sat down to catch his breath. "Winner of the game gets to ask one favor of the loser."

Suna gave me a little shrug. "Better luck next time."

To Trace, she asked, "So what would you like for your favor?"

"Remember me."

CHAPTER SIXTEEN

I would have liked to see Trace off, but she disappeared completely, as if she had never been there. I had only known her a few days, but when she was gone, I felt a hole in my life where she had been.

Like the bigger hole where Valka had been.

I threw myself into my studies. My research project on the Ovors got high marks, both from the automated instructor and from Shirley. There were even a few facts in there that she hadn't known—like how the Ovors had preferred the transcendent orgone drive early on, and had designed their stations to separate into individual pieces in order to travel to new systems.

When Astronavigation class finished the math section and started with the scientific and technical material, I actually found that I missed the math—for about five minutes. The reality of faster-than-light travel had always had a strong hold on my imagination, and being able to actually start learning it was an incredible treat.

Gradually, my evening Physicality sessions with Shirley became more and more intimate, though she never went so far as to actually let me penetrate her. When I asked her about it, she maintained that that particular act was reserved for our first session on the ship. Setting it aside would make the experience all the more powerful.

I saw Valka from time to time, usually passing in the hallways, and while she was polite, there was a coldness there that didn't seem to thaw with time. Every time it happened, I felt my stomach drop another notch closer to my toes. At least she looked healthy; she had gained more than a few milliLowells and the skinny, angular Valka I had known on the station was long gone.

The hideout was empty much of the time. I checked up on it once every few days, but rarely stayed any longer than was required to keep up the supply of dried leaves. I could see evidence that Suna had been there, cleaning the place up, but I rarely saw her. Either she had gotten what she wanted, or she realized she wasn't going to get it from me. That was fine.

About forty days in, Shirley told me that her old boyfriend, Robert, the one she had been recruited with, would be arriving in a few days. She planned to take a few days off from mentoring me to be with him. Robert's pilot, Grecca, would replace her while she was away. We would spend a day together, the three of us, to see how we got along.

Grecca met us at the morning Physicality class. She turned out to be a tall, willowy woman with pale skin and long, blonde hair pulled back into a braid running down her back. Her tight Scout uniform revealed a slender figure with only the vaguest feminine curves.

After a brief warm-up of partner movement exercises, Shirley gestured in the direction of a circular padded mat in the middle of the room. "Why don't you show her what you know, Challers."

I nodded and stepped out onto the mat. Mentally, I reviewed the movements I had learned, and then shook the circulation into my arms and legs.

Grecca smiled and stretched. "Is he that good?"

Shirley nodded in my direction. "Learn for yourself."

With a raised eyebrow, Grecca turned and strode out onto the mat. She definitely seemed at home there, moving with even more confidence than Shirley. She rubbed her hands together and then settled into a loose, fluid stance. Her movements were slow, balanced, and measured. Each step had the precision of a drop of water falling into the exact center of a bowl, ripples going out and coming back to the same point.

Her reach, I guessed, would be a bit longer than mine, so I waited for her to make the first move, standing in a ready position. She lashed out suddenly, grabbing for my wrist. I stepped back and to the side, but in the lunge, she had put one foot behind mine and I found myself falling. I twisted and rolled away, narrowly avoiding another grab for my ankle, but I was on the mat and she was still on her feet; a bad position for me to be in. I tried to reverse direction and roll up to my feet, but she was on top of me, and we crashed back down to the mat with her long legs wrapped around my midsection from behind.

On our sides, we grappled for a few seconds—she trying to get control of my arms by forcing them behind my back and me struggling for leverage to get her ankles unlocked. She was quicker, but I was stronger and she had a hard time working my arms backward, even with her good position. I managed to force myself to my hands and knees, lifting her from the mat. Shifting strategies, she tried to lean backwards to pull me back on top of her, but I ducked my head and rolled forward, sending her sprawling onto the map, and letting me slip my abdomen out of her scissorlock.

When I got back to my feet, my shorts had slipped down around my knees, pulled down by the grip of her thighs as I escaped. I could hear Shirley laughing behind me, but Grecca only smiled playfully as she sprang quickly to her feet. She didn't give me a moment to pull them back up. She leapt at me, knowing that I wouldn't be able to move quickly. I ducked, trying to roll down under her and kick off my shorts, but she adjusted quickly and landed on top of me before I could roll away. She quickly got my arms behind me, pinned between her arm and her body, and then rolled onto her side to get her legs wrapped around my abdomen again.

I struggled, but couldn't get free. "Augh! Submit!" I shouted, giving the signal that I admitted losing the bout.

Even though I went nearly naked most of the time at the academy, my face burned with embarrassment at my exposure.

Grecca chuckled. "Is that all I get? Shirley, you have been treating him too leniently."

Shirley stood nearby, shaking her head. "Perhaps I have."

"When Robert taught me to grapple, there was a penalty to pay when I lost. Are you ready to pay the penalty, Challers?"

"What penalty?"

"This."

Her free hand danced on my ribs—a light, rhythmic touch. Tickling. I didn't think I was ticklish, at least not much, but Grecca was an expert. Within seconds, she had figured out exactly what touch was required, and where, to send me into paroxysms of laughter. Only after I was panting helplessly did she release me, leaving me breathless on the mat.

I climbed to my feet, finally, and pulled my wayward shorts back into place.

"Care for another try?" she said.

"Depends. Do I get to do the same to you if I win?"

"Of course."

"Then let's go."

We took our places on the mat and started again. Grecca was fast and sneaky, but I knew I was a good deal stronger and she needed a lot of leverage to beat me. If I let her grab me on my terms, I could turn that to my advantage.

I lunged, knowing that she'd easily dodge me and grab my arm for a classic hip throw. As I was passing over her back, I grabbed her around the midsection with my free arm and held on, pulling her down as I fell. Her weight fell heavily on my chest, but she was more stunned than I was, and I managed to pull her arms in and pin them both with one arm across her chest. She arched her back and pushed with her legs to try to escape, but that stopped when I wrapped my legs around her, forcing my ankles between her knees, and took control of her legs as well. She was at my mercy.

"Well done!" cheered Shirley. "See, I told you he was good."

Grecca bucked and thrashed in my grip, but she didn't have the strength to break free. I tried to tickle her, but with her arms bound in front of her chest, I only had access to a small area of her underarms. Forcing her narrow wrists together, I took them in one hand and raised them over and behind her head, and then I had her. I took her elbows in one arm, forcing them against my shoulder, being careful not to put too much pressure on her neck. She was completely immobilized. I let go of her wrists and explored her armpits with my fingertips, ready to begin searching for the right spot to tickle her.

She sputtered a bit as I ran my fingers along the fabric of her uniform on her armpit, but it didn't have the impact I hoped it would. I caught Shirley signalling to me. She was lifting a curled hand, as if tugging on something. I got it.

I pulled up her shirt on that side to touch her bare skin. That was what it took. In seconds, I had her screaming with tickle-induced laughter. I gave her brief respites for breathing, just as she had done with me, in between thrashing, shrieking bouts under my fingers.

Oh, did that feel good! Having my tormentor at my mercy filled me with a sweet sense of power.

"Oh, please," she gasped. "Stop, stop! Submit!"

I was probably enjoying it a bit too much. I let her go and stood up, helping her to her feet. The hem of her tight white shirt had ridden up over one small, pink-tipped breast and I felt my cock twitch in response. She had been so undone that she hadn't noticed—or didn't care.

Grecca caught her breath and straightened her shirt. I caught the faintest hint of sexual tension in the air.

She had a huge smile on her face. "I forgot how much fun that was."

"Robert doesn't like it?"

"Not really room on the ship for it. Too many hard things to run up against."

Shirley walked out onto the mat. "So you like this game, do you?" Shirley smiled. "Ready for another round?"

"I think so."

"I'll warn you, I'm not nearly as ticklish as Grecca."

"You're also stronger. I can't just power through with you the way I did with her. But we'll see how it goes."

I'd like to say that I held my own in that bout, but it was no contest, as it had always been with Shirley. She was a master of this kind of combat, and had taught me every trick I knew. There was a quick flurry of moves and countermoves, and I was face down on the mat. She scooped her legs under mine and pinned my legs between her thighs and ankles, then maneuvered my arms into the small of my back one by one. I could buck a little and kick my feet, but her balance was excellent and I had no chance to dislodge her.

"Oh, you're in trouble now." Grecca strode into view and knelt down just out of reach. "Give it to him, Shirley. I want to see him squirm."

As a fighter, Shirley was my better, but she wasn't the veteran tickler Grecca was. She managed to get a few twitches and squawks out of me, but she sure didn't have me howling in hysterics.

After a few minutes, she grunted and sat back. "I'm not getting through," she said. "How did you do it?"

Grecca chuckled. "It's a light touch. You're working too hard."

I took the conversation as an unguarded moment and rolled suddenly to the side, knocking Shirley into Grecca. It was a little bit of a dirty trick, but if there's anything Shirley taught me it was to use every possible advantage. While they thrashed around trying to disentangle themselves, I leapt onto them. The air whuffed out of their lungs and I easily took control of Shirley's arms, locking them behind her back. Grecca somehow managed to wriggle out from underneath, but without use of her arms Shirley wasn't going anywhere.

"Well ,well," I said, "I think this is a rare victory."

"No fair." Grecca coughed, catching her breath. "I wasn't even part of the fight."

"You were giving aid and comfort to the enemy, so that makes you an entirely fair target."

"All right," said Shirley, "you've got me. Do your worst."

"My worst, eh?" I made sure I had Shirley's arms firmly in place, with one hand holding them against her back, and shifted slightly so I could use the other hand anywhere I wanted on her body.

"I can take it."

"All right. Don't say I didn't warn you."

I braced myself, then flipped her on her back, as suddenly as I could. I swept her arms under her back with my knees, pinning them underneath her. She tried to get her feet under her to push me up and off, but I grabbed one knee and hooked it with my elbow, curling it up and doubling her over. With the same hand, I grabbed her ankle, immobilizing her leg. Her foot, extended out in front of me, was the perfect target.

Slowly, I drew my hand closer to her foot. Her eyes grew wide. I saw her lips form the word *no*, but she didn't *quite* say it.

I showed no mercy. As soon as my fingers drew the slightest touch across the sole of her foot, she burst into laughter, and it only intensified as I continued. She thrashed and flailed, but she was wearing herself out faster than she was wearing me out.

"Stop!" she shrieked, finally losing her dignity and composure after several minutes. "Please!"

"You want me to stop?"

"Yes!"

I let go of her foot and immediately grabbed her breast, groping it the way I knew she liked, with her nipple squeezed between my fingers.

Her eyes sprang open and she gasped in surprise. "What are you doing?"

"Doing my worst." Her gasps turned to moans as I pulled her shirt up and worked my hand underneath. "You want me to stop?"

"Challers, you . . ."

"Yeah. You're used to being the one in charge. Well you gave me permission to do whatever I like, and this is what I like."

It was, I realized, the truth. I *did* like this game, I liked it a lot, and I was going to play it for all it was worth.

I didn't know if she'd ever let me play it again.

I squeezed her breast, pinching her fat nipple between my fingers, kneading and stretching the flesh. "What do you say, Grecca? Should I stop?"

"Vack, no." Grecca knelt again, a few feet away, watching us with one hand up her shirt and another down in her pants. "Make her come."

"Gotta do what the superior officer says, Shirley. Unless you want to countermand the order?"

Shirley was shaking her head tentatively, but she didn't say a word.

I twisted, getting my hand behind me and worming it up the leg of her shorts. One creeping push at a time, it approached her pussy. The angle was awkward, but she had stopped thrashing around, so I was able to get my hand right up to the edge of her cunt.

She was sodden—soaking wet.

I pushed on, working my way deeper, gradually slipping my fingers between her juicy lips.

"I think you like this, too. You're not used to this. Most of the time, you're the one in charge, the one deciding what will happen where and when."

I pulled her shorts down under her ass. I couldn't see very well, but I knew that her pussy would be much more exposed.

Her eyes were closed, her lips slightly parted, and I could feel her sweat soaking through my shorts. I reached behind me and put my hand on her pussy, finding her familiar sensitive places just by touch.

"Am I right? Are you as aroused by this as I am?"

She nodded, too far gone in her ecstasy to speak.

I didn't need to see what I was doing to do a good job. I knew Shirley's sex almost as well as my own. I rubbed and tweaked, and occasionally thrust a finger or two inside, watching her face for the clues as to which should happen when. After only a couple of minutes, I left her gasping and mewing on the floor.

Grecca helped me to my feet. "That was an impressive performance."

"Why thank you," I said.

Shirley made quiet little sounds, but they weren't really words.

Everything, once again, had changed.

CHAPTER SEVENTEEN

"Looks like he's all yours," said Shirley, as she stood up from the table, leaving her lunch half-eaten. "I'll see you in a few days." She gave Grecca a friendly hug.

"Have fun." Grecca winked.

Turning to me, Shirley took my hand and kissed the palm, the same gesture she had made when she first met me, and then left without a word.

"What is that?" I asked Grecca. "Kissing my hand that way? At first I thought it was a Scout thing, but she seems to be the only one who does it."

"I don't know. Shirley's done that as long as I've known her."

"How long is that?"

"I met her during my time at the academy. She came to visit Robert much the same way he's coming to visit her now." She pulled out her tablet. "So, a free hour until Astronavigation class. What would you like to do?"

"I usually spend it working on my independent research project, but that seems a little impolite."

"Why don't you show me what you've been doing? I saw the work that Shirley sent to Robert; it's really impressive."

"Okay! That sounds great." I pushed my lunch tray aside and took out my tablet. "My first project was on the Ovors. Now I'm working on the Sinden."

She set her tray on top of mine and sat forward, her expression full of eager anticipation.

"I don't really have anything compiled yet. I'm still just gathering sources."

"That's fine. Show me what you've got."

I opened the Sinden directory. "Here's a recording of a visit to a Sinden station."

I pulled up a holographic record, and ran it forward to the point where the recorder was about to open a hatch from the landing bay into the station proper. The portal was all sweeping, graceful curves of white and green. There was nothing utilitarian about it, nothing damaged or dirty.

Then the hatch parted revealing a wide, bowl-shaped room. The whole station seemed to be one huge oxygen deck; there were lawns of grass and stands of trees dotted with small buildings of the same elegant architecture. Splashes of color, probably flowers, could be seen here and there. Above, a domed roof soared, all transparent, allowing a yellow star to bathe the interior in warm light.

Most stunning, however, was a group of a dozen or so people standing a short distance downhill. They were tall, willowy people with pale complexions and elongated features. Their faces were elegantly defined and, even though each of them had long, flowing hair, the tips of their pointed ears were visible. They wore knee-length tunics of a satiny material in greens and blues accented with silver. While there was a certain androgyny to their features, it was easy to see that this race did have two genders. The one at the head of the group spoke, but I had the volume turned down.

"Those are odd looking people," said Grecca. "Beautiful, but odd. What's the story behind that?"

"I don't know, but I'm sure I'll find out. Some newgens have a practical body form, like Ovors, but sometimes I think it's just fashion. It's one of the more interesting things about this kind of research."

In the hologram, the Sindens parted, forming lines on either side of a path leading down to the nearest of the white buildings. Drawing closer, we could see that the building was a tall cylinder, its middle pinched in just a bit, and at the top, an array of graceful spires probed upward and outward. Writing of some kind was inscribed on the outer walls in horizontal stripes.

I closed that recording and brought up a galaxy diagram with a few blue highlights.

"The Sindens have only a few stations, way out on the downstream end of the Coreward Reach. They don't seem to be worried about expansion as much as preservation. According to some of my sources, they have records going back almost to the beginning of the Scattering, but for some reason, the Scouts have never gotten hold of them."

"Fascinating."

We paged through more of my sources, some of which consisted of passing references in logs, and external scans of their stations. What made them most fascinating to me was how little there was about them in the data banks.

"Have you seen many newgens, out there?" I glanced in the direction of the mess hall doors, as if they led directly out to the galaxy as a whole.

"Not really. We don't see too many other people out there. Robert and I have been pulling a lot of patrol duty, and that's pretty lonely. Well, except for each other. It gets like that sometimes. That's why you really have to be willing to get close to your partner."

"You're close to Robert?"

"Yes. Even though it starts off kind of contrived and artificial, you have to keep in mind that the medical section runs pheromone compatibility scans on recruits to make sure there'll be some chemistry between new partners. That gives something of a physical basis for the relationship. Beyond that, though, it's work."

"Yeah, tell me about it."

"Things not going well with you and Shirley?"

"You saw us on the wrestling mat. We're okay together."

"You're holding back, Challers. What's the problem?"

"Nothing. Really." I turned off the tablet and slid it back into its carry-pouch. "Come on, we need to get to Astronavigation."

In class, Grecca didn't sit up and behind me, but alongside me. It seemed like she was taking the course alongside me, so much so that I wanted to help her understand as much as I did. She knew the material, but her enthusiasm was entirely for me, rather than for the science itself. The same pattern held true in Technology and Medical. Rather than being another teacher, she was another student.

This subtle shift in her attitude, compared to Shirley's, put a whole different spin on the classes. Instead of a subtle feeling of being ganged up on—in spite of the fact that one of the teachers was a hologram—I felt like it was Grecca and me together, taking on the instructor. We covered for each other, coached each other, and generally made each class feel like a triumph.

Then, after Medical, came evening Physicality. I walked into the class and immediately threw off my uniform and jumped onto the bed. "So what's the lesson?"

"Hold on a moment," said Grecca. "Let's just take a moment to get centered."

She slipped out of her shirt and shorts, stepped into the middle of the bed, and sat down.

"All right, sure." I sat down facing her and took a few cleansing breaths.

There was a certain tension in my body, mainly from not having Shirley there for my first sexual session with Grecca. I was afraid that I wouldn't be good enough for her and, adding that to the basic fear of the unknown, I was nervous.

"Now then," she said, putting the soles of her feet together, knees apart, "I want you to sit like this."

I imitated her pose. From the exercises I had been doing, I was flexible enough that my knees nearly touched the bed. "Like this?"

"Yes, good."

She got up and sat in the space between my knees, facing me, and wrapped her legs around my body. Her hands fell naturally on my shoulders. No one had ever sat so close to me. She spoke softly, intimately.

"Medical makes sure that Scouts who are partnered together have compatible pheromone profiles. That provides a foundation for a physical relationship. Women, and to some extent men, need the right kind of mismatch in order to form a bond. But that's just the beginning."

Our noses were nearly touching. I could feel her breath on my lips as she spoke.

"There is a kind of comfort in being together that comes from that bond, that builds on it. It lives in the eyes, the breath, the hands. It's part of the body, rather than the mind or the heart, and it's essential. Feel my breath on your face, as I feel your breath on mine. Let our breathing come together, you breathing in as I breathe out. Look into my eyes, as deeply as you can, and hold on for as long as possible."

We sat that way for long minutes. I could feel the effect she was describing, right there as we were sitting.

"This is crazy," I whispered. "I can just feel it."

She hushed me gently. "Stop thinking about what's happening, and just let it happen."

This was like the meditation techniques we had learned before, but with a difference; instead of pulling inside myself, focusing on my own body and mind, I was focusing on her breathing, her eyes, the feel of her skin on mine. Time stood still. Words that had been running through my brain scattered away and disappeared. Even my awareness of myself seemed to fade into a single, transcendant *us*.

It felt marvelous.

I was tipping over, then, but it wasn't an unbalanced fall— more like a light drawing-down, as if gravity had been dialed down. We were floating towards the bed, stretching out face to face, embracing with hands and lips instead of legs and breath. Totally comfortable, totally at peace, there wasn't desire or impulse—I could only follow the slow rhythm of our heartbeats and our breathing. I was what I was, Grecca was what she was, and we were doing what we were doing. The moment had no history and no future, no cause and no effect, no meaning but itself.

And then, after no time had passed, we felt ourselves drift apart again.

I blinked and shook my head. "That was amazing. I should have been scared, but I liked it a lot." The warmth I felt had faded a little, but I could feel a lingering affection that wasn't there when we had started. "Did you make me fall in love with you?"

She giggled. "No, it's not mind control. It's just a little trick to engage some of the human instincts for bonding on a subconscious level. Robert taught it to me."

"It works," I said.

"So no sex today?"

"This isn't intimate enough?" She giggled at the confused look on my face and then soothed me with a tender caress on my cheek. "We can if you want. There's time before dinner."

Dinner. I knew I had forgotten something. My stomach growled.

She laughed. "Or maybe not. Come on, I don't trust that mouth near my tender parts until you're not hungry anymore."

"I don't bite!"

"Not yet, maybe, but we'll see when my visit's over." With a wink, she stood up and pulled her uniform back on.

When I was dressed again, she put her arm around me and we walked to the mess hall like boyfriend and girlfriend.

I never wanted it to end.

Chapter Eighteen

I walked with Grecca to the docking bays. The last few minutes of our time together was passing. As the hatch leading to her ship came into view, I stopped and took her hand.

"I want you to stay," I said, softly.

"I know, Challers, I know."

"You're a much better teacher for me than Shirley. I've learned more from you the last three days about sex and technology and, well, just being a good Scout. I think we'd be good together. Good for each other, and good for the Scouts."

"Challers, I can't." She put her hands on my shoulders and twined her fingers behind my neck. Her blue eyes sparkled, and there may have been tears waiting there. I could hear the emotion in her voice.

"Why not?"

"I haven't finished my own training cruise yet. I'm not a full-fledged Scout."

"So come back when you're done."

"By then, you'll have graduated and you'll be on your own training cruise. Look me up when you're done with that. I'd love to be your partner when you're a full Scout. We *would* be a good team."

That would be fine, except I still held out hope that I would be able to partner with Valka when our training cruises were done. I shook my head. Why did nothing ever go my way?

Another hand landed on my shoulder. "So this is the cadet, eh?"

He was a good head taller than me, with a short, dark beard speckled with grey hair.

Grecca pulled away and nodded in his direction. "Challers, I'd like you to meet Captain Robert Halko."

He took my hand and squeezed. Hard.

You want to play that game? I thought. *Fine. I can play, too.*

I squeezed back. I wasn't going to crush him, but I wasn't going to let him crush me either. It lasted maybe a half a second, but much was communicated in that grip.

"Pleased to meet you, sir," I said, exchanging a nod of respect with him. I felt like I had passed some kind of test.

"I've heard a lot about you, cadet." His voice was a deep bass. It reminded me, in some measure, of Masters. In fact, there were many things about him that reminded me of Masters. His build, his bearing—even the shape of his face.

"Good things, I hope."

"Very good things. From what she tells me, I can safely leave her with you." He turned in the direction of the hatch. "Is everything prepped, Grecca?"

"I haven't been in the ship yet." There was a tentativeness there that bothered me. Was she afraid of him?

I tried to catch her eye, but she turned away and hustled up the hatch. Yeah, she was afraid of him.

Robert and Shirley shared a goodbye kiss that was too intimate for my taste, so I walked a short way down the passage back into the academy.

They finished, and Shirley walked past me, head down. I fell into step beside her. She looked up, smiled a thin smile, and pulled me to her as we walked. I knew how she felt. It seemed like everyone I became even slightly attached to was pulled away from me just as I was really getting to know them.

"So how was Grecca?" said Shirley.

"Good," I said, not knowing what else to say.

"Kept up with your studies?'

"You know me. Scholarly and studious."

"Mmm."

"Have a good time with Robert?" I regretted the question as soon as I asked it.

She sighed. "Yeah. Too short, though. I guess it's time for, what, lunch?"

"You don't know?"

"Robert was on a totally different sleep-wake schedule; I have no idea what time it is."

I noticed, then, that some of her droopiness wasn't just sadness or loss, but just plain old fatigue. "How much sleep have you had lately?"

"Oh, I'm okay."

"Forgive me, Shirley, but that's vack-yack. You're floating dead. Come on. To bed with you."

She yawned. "But you have lessons . . ."

"I'm good. I'll show you what I've been doing, once you've had some sleep."

Too exhausted to protest any further, she let me guide her back to our room and get her settled onto the bed.

She woke up after a couple hours to find me sitting at the desk, reading from my tablet.

"Mmm, you weren't kidding about studying." She rolled out of bed and moved up behind me, her warm, soft breasts barely touching the back of my head. "More newgens, eh?"

"I've been researching more of the history of the Astrolo and Souree."

I didn't know why I was so fascinated with newgens. Perhaps it had something to do with the way the Chevalier newgens had surprised and troubled me the first time I saw them. In any case, I wanted to learn as much as I could about everything related to them.

"Never heard of them. Tell me."

"They're extinct now, or at least until someone decides to jump in the tank and become one. I'm not sure why anyone would want to, though."

I pulled up an image of an Astrolo, a young woman sitting on a hoverchair wearing a helmet and a uniform fitted to her limbless body. Robots flanking her held food and drink, ready to provide to her.

"What was the purpose of that?"

"I'm not sure. None of the sources agree on anything. Some say it was a religious group, others that it was some kind of status symbol, and still others that they were emulating a cultural hero. In any case, the last of them destroyed their archives and used the gentank to become Sourees a long time ago."

"That's another one I don't know."

I switched the screen to display another holographic image. This one looked fairly human except for the scaly skin and the feathered crest on top of her head.

"The Souree were a reptilian version of humanity. They were egg-layers like the Ovors. They were all killed when Raghar Station was destroyed by the Fleet."

"You have been busy." She patted me on the head and turned towards the fresher. "So what time is it, really?"

"In a few minutes, it'll be time for afternoon Physicality."

"Ooh, excellent. I want you to show me what you learned from Grecca. According to Robert, she's a supernova. "

"I can do that." I turned off the tablet and put it into its carry-pouch. "I don't know about supernova, though. I thought she was sweet."

Shirley came out of the fresher wearing a clean uniform. "Sweet? You couldn't have thought that when she had you pinned to the ground, tickling you until you were red in the face."

"Mmm. Maybe not then."

We left the familiar bed of our quarters for the equally familiar bed of our classroom.

"So," she said, hands on her hips. "Show me what you've learned."

I sat in the center of the bed, knees bent, feet together. "Sit here," I said, patting the diamond-shaped space between my legs. "Facing me."

Shirley sat and I positioned her legs on either side of me. Our faces were so close I could feel the heat of her body on my nose and her breath on my lips.

"Look into my eyes," I said. "Put your arms around me, but don't hold tight. Relax."

"I know this position," she said, reaching down toward my crotch.

"No," I said, "just sit. Relax. Look into my eyes."

Shirley giggled. She was seeing the same thing I was—a squashed one-eyed head.

"It looks a little silly at first, but just let that go. Relax. Breathe."

The moment Grecca showed me this technique was the moment the true depth of my feelings for her opened up. It wasn't true love, perhaps, but it was a kind of instinctive, basic intimacy. This was, I could see, the foundation of the surprisingly deep relationship we had built over those three short days.

Now that it was gone, I missed it, terribly. Everyone that mattered to me had been taken away. There was only one person who was a constant in my life, and I hoped that if I could build that kind of relationship with Grecca so easily, then with the right techniques, I might be able to do the same with Shirley.

I synchronized my breathing with Shirley, breathing in only when I felt her exhalation on my lips. I could feel myself falling into her eyes, losing myself there. The "she" and the "I" were becoming "we." I could feel it.

And then, suddenly, she pulled back, breaking the link almost before it could get started. She held my shoulders and smiled. "That was an absolutely fascinating experience! We're definitely going to have to do that again sometime soon."

"Wait, no. We only just started."

"Challers, if this is all you did for Physicality class for the last few days then we have material to make up."

I gritted my teeth, struggling to keep my rising pique in check. She moved to stand, but I put my hands on her thighs and held her down.

"Challers . . ."

"Listen. Shirley. This is important. You said that you can't have sex with someone without developing feelings for him. I know now what you were talking about, but there's more to it than that. You can allow a relationship to happen as a byproduct of all this, or you can deliberately set out to form a relationship, to create something real, something meaningful."

Shirley's brow knitted for a moment, and then her eyebrows twitched upwards. She was holding onto something, holding something back, holding it in. She put her hands on mine, ready to peel them from her thighs to escape.

"Shirley. Do this with me. Please. I want us to be more than business partners."

She blinked and swallowed, poised between jumping away and giving in.

In a whisper, she said, "You don't know what you're asking."

"So tell me."

Her gaze flicked back and forth between my eyes, as if she were searching for something behind them.

"Shirley. Tell me."

"No." She stood, pulling away from my grasp, almost shaking with emotion. "No, I can't."

What was it? Fear? What could she be afraid of? What was it that put her in such terror?

I put out my hand to comfort her, but she spun away from it, took a step, and then stopped. She put her hands at her sides, unclenched her fists, and took a deep breath. The armor that had seemed ready to crack solidified again, and when she turned back, the vulnerability was gone.

No, not gone. Hidden. She had buried it again, buried it where she thought I would never see it again.

"Why are you doing this to me?" I asked. "To us?"

She looked away. "Challers, I have a confession. You will be my fourth ship-partner since I joined the Scouts. That was almost ten years ago. Every one of them, when we were having sex, I would . . ."

She took a deep breath. "I would imagine that he was Robert. It was the only way I could do it."

"But everything you said about . . ."

"Yes, Challers, yes, I'm a hypocrite and liar. I never really believed any of it."

I put my arms around her, pulled her close. "I'm sorry. I shouldn't have dragged this out of you."

I had no idea her façade was so thin. Before, she seemed made of iron, and now she was crumbling right there in my arms. I didn't know what to do, so I just stayed there, holding her. It seemed so funny, me comforting her, after all the times she had done the same thing for me.

After we stood there in each other's arms for a few minutes, I asked, "So what do we do now?"

"We? *We* don't do anything." She pulled away again and took her tablet out of its carry-pouch. "I send in my resignation. The Service will find you a mentor who can actually do the job."

"What? No, not again. Listen, everyone I know is disappearing. Everyone I care about. Valka. Grecca." I almost blurted out "Trace" but stopped myself in time. "Now you."

She set the tablet on a stand near the door and activated it. "Challers, I've done you a terrible disservice. Unforgivable. You don't care about me; you're just well-conditioned."

I put my hand over hers, preventing her from entering commands on the tablet. "I forgive you."

Her eyes finally met mine. Something there told me I had gotten through to her, but it was like looking through a wall of ice.

She turned off her tablet and smiled. I could see the ice melting, just a bit, though there was still a good deal left to go.

CHAPTER NINETEEN

I hoped that the revelation the night before would change things. I had hoped that we could sit the way Grecca and I had, nose to nose, eyes to eyes, minute upon minute, building a sense of intimacy that could be the beginning of something more. I realized that Grecca had shown me the technique not because she wanted to form that kind of relationship with me, but because she knew how valuable it would be to have an emotionally close bond with Shirley.

What she didn't realize was how difficult it would be. If anything, Shirley became even colder, even more distant. She spoke hardly at all, except as needed, and would not look me in the eye.

In the morning, I awoke to the sound of Shirley sitting at the desk, talking quietly into her tablet. I propped myself up on my elbows and listened.

". . . I'd like to say you'd like him, if you got to know him in person, but I don't know. Maybe you wouldn't. He's still got some emotional rough edges to smooth off, and I know you don't like that. But even though he's sleeping behind me, right now, I still miss you, my love. I can't wait to see you again. Send a message as soon as you get this."

She touched the screen, the tablet beeped, and the pale glow from its screen flickered.

"A message for Robert?" I asked.

Her breath caught and she turned quickly. "You heard that?"

"Just the last part. Rough edges?"

"Maybe it took a rough edge to cut me deep enough that I'd feel it."

"I never wanted to cause you pain." I rolled up to sit facing her. "So what do we do now?"

"We go on with your classes."

"Like nothing happened?"

She put her hand on my knee. "We both know something happened. But you're so young in some ways, Challers."

"I'm not too young to understand. Tell me what you're thinking. Tell me why you're holding back."

She turned away.

When we arrived at morning Physicality class, Shirley went to a secure storage locker for a pair of bulky white pistols.

"Based on your stellar performance in wrestling, we're going to jump ahead to the next section. Marksmanship." She held one out to me, butt end first.

I took it by the handle and frowned at it, disappointed that we would not be wrestling again. This was, I was sure, another way to push me away. "I thought the Marines took care of the fighting."

"There isn't always a Marine handy and they aren't always cooperative."

"I remember the Marines on Stakroya." It occurred to me that the next time I met a Marine, things would be quite different. "Were you armed when you met them there? I don't remember seeing you carrying one of these."

"I didn't have time to retrieve it, but it doesn't matter. If it had gotten to a fight, the situation would have been pretty badly handled anyway—which brings up a good point. The reason you're learning how to use this weapon is not because the Service ever expects you to use it. But people will treat you differently if they know you're armed, and if they sense that you're confident with its use. It's a tool for taking control of a difficult situation. Hopefully, you'll never have to use it."

"Have you ever had to use yours?"

"I've never fired in anger. I expect no less of you." Next, she produced a light helmet for each of us. "This is to protect your vision and hearing, and to allow us to communicate. Ideally, you should wear one whenever you expect you might need to use your sidearm. That doesn't always happen."

The helmets had visors and ear protectors built in, and a headset radio to allow us to talk to each other. We put them on and checked to make sure they were working.

"Computer, display standard targets, please."

The lights dimmed and a set of silhouettes appeared on the wall opposite us.

"Your weapon is a mass driver powered by crisis orgone. We'll cover the details of its operation and maintenance in Technology class. For now, it's enough to know that we're remaining calm during this exercise in order to keep from punching holes in the walls."

She turned, took up a firing stance, and pulled the trigger. Three sharp cracks echoed against the walls in rapid succession and three spots lit up on the silhouette. Numbers appeared above it—ninety-eight in yellow and eighty-four in red.

"The yellow number indicates the chance that the target has been stopped. The red number, the chance of death. Depending on the circumstance, you might want that last number to be low, or high. Computer, display training targets."

Shapes lit up on the silhouettes: red areas on places like the head, neck, and torso; yellow on the knees, lower abdomen, and shoulders.

"You will remember from our anatomy studies about the location of sensitive and vital areas of the body. These are your primary targets. Don't worry about shooting to disable yet; the surest way to keep someone from killing you is to kill him first."

I looked down at the weapon in my hand.

An instrument of death. I felt unsteady.

"Challers?"

"I'm sorry. Just . . ."

I took a deep breath and imitated Shirley's stance.

"By your right thumb, there's a switch. Hit it once to take off the safety. That will put it in burst mode. Touch it again for single shot."

I did as she said and a tiny indicator lit up with three blue lights, and then just one.

"Good. Now give it a try. Squeeze the trigger slowly. If you jerk it back, you'll spoil your aim."

I lined up the sights on the silhouette and fired. The shot struck a bit below the neck. The numbers above the silhouette both said seventy-five percent.

Dizziness surged in my head. My stomach heaved and I had to swallow hard to keep the contents inside. I dropped the gun and put my hands over my face. The idea that I could have the power to take someone's life seemed alien, sick, *wrong*.

Shirley put her arm around me. "I'm sorry. This is my fault. I pushed a little too quickly. Let's take it a little slower. Computer, circle targets please."

The silhouettes disappeared, replaced by a simple red spot.

She picked up the pistol and put it back in my hand. "Give it another try, Challers."

I shook my head, too confused and scared to even speak.

"Challers." She turned me around and looked into my eyes. "If you let this get a hold on you, you're going to have a much harder time breaking it. Now hold up that weapon and shoot the circle. Just a test of coordination. Nothing more than that, not even symbolically. Now deep breaths. Remember your training. Remember your meditation."

She turned me around, took my wrist, and pointed it at the dot. "Shoot, Challers."

I felt queasy and my head hurt. Anywhere but there, I wanted to be anywhere but there with a death-spitting weapon at the end of my arm and no good purpose for it. I could imagine its orgone collector lurking inside it, eating my fear and pain.

Shirley persisted. "Come on. Deep breaths. Calm your mind. Squeeze the trigger."

I squeezed. The weapon bucked in my hand and a blue spot appeared on the wall, about a meter away from the circle.

"Good! Now this time, open your eyes, and aim."

I opened my eyes, again, just then realizing that I had closed them. My hands trembled too much to hold the pistol straight. "I can't do it."

"Nonsense," said Shirley. "You just did. Now try it again."

Deep breaths. Calm mind. Squeeze.

Dead center.

"Excellent!" She took her hand from my arm and stepped back. "Now again, on your own."

Another deep breath. *Crack! Crack!*

Deep breath. *Crack! Crack!*

Swallow. *Crack! Crack!*

One by one, lights appeared in the red circle, showing where I had hit.

"Nice grouping, Challers. You really are good at this, when you let yourself."

"Shirley, believe me. I don't think I could ever use one of these things on a human being."

"Whether that's true or not, you won't know unless the time comes to test it. And if it does, you'll be in much better shape to handle the situation if you have the skills to use this weapon effectively. Keep shooting. Empty it."

I held it on target and fired, thirty times or so, until the lights on the back turned red and it wouldn't fire again.

"Good." Shirley handed me a small block of metal and used her own weapon to demonstrate. "Here's how you reload. The port here opens when you've fired the last flechette. Slide the ammo in, close the port. That simple." She took up a new firing stance, this time down on one knee. "This stance gives you more stability, but it's not as quick if you have to dodge out of the way or engage hand to hand. Use this for ranges of twenty meters or so. Computer, reduce target circles by ten percent."

I looked at the "ammunition" in my hand. It was a flat block of metal, no bigger than the palm of my hand. I copied what she had done and the weapon accepted it.

In the new stance, after Shirley positioned me correctly, I squeezed off another thirty shots. It was getting easier. I was getting used to the feel of the weapon, but the shock of my first reaction remained, waiting for me. I could feel my nerves unraveling and I wanted to be done with this, to put these terrible machines away.

We practiced one more firing stance, on our bellies, and when that was done, I stood up and walked to the cabinet to put the pistol back where it had come from.

"Challers?"

"I'm done for today. I can come back tomorrow, but I'm getting jumpy. I feel sick. I need to move, to work some of this off."

"That's fair. Let's do some stretches, warm up, and then we'll check out your wrestling moves. Let's see if Grecca taught you anything while I was away."

I smiled, glad that she was agreeing, but still dreading the next time I would have to pick up a gun. "Same penalty for losing? You know I fight harder when something is at stake."

"Mmm, you do. All right. Same penalty."

CHAPTER TWENTY

The anticipation built while we did some calisthenics. I still didn't feel entirely well, and I needed the activity to burn it off. Once we got our blood moving, Shirley stepped to the edge of the wrestling circle.

"Ready?"

Shirley waited until the moment I spoke to rush across the circle, forcing me to either dodge her or immediately accept her grapple. Ten days before, this tactic was enough to throw me off balance and give her the upper hand. I had picked up a trick from Grecca, however, and I was ready. I spun and grabbed her arm, pulling it across my back. Her momentum carried her around in a tight arc. She tried to shift and catch me, but she was going too fast and landed on the mat with her arm twisted in my grip.

She blinked, stunned momentarily by the impact, then smiled up at me. "Nice throw, but you haven't got me yet." She lifted one leg up onto my shoulder and shoved with a grunt, yanking her arm out of my grasp.

I leapt on top of her before she could roll back to her feet, but she caught my ankle between her legs and scissored me onto my back with a powerful wrench of her legs. It was my turn to see stars. She wrapped herself around my body, pinning one arm under her chest and gripping my thighs between her legs. With only one hand free my options were limited, and I could feel her maneuvering to put me in the double arm-lock that would put me at her mercy.

I growled and strained, resisting the slow progress of her hold. In spite of my twenty kilos of mass advantage, our strength was equal and she had the advantage.

Power wasn't going to do it for me, so I reached down to where her knee crossed in front of my thigh and gripped the area just above her knee between my thumb and fingers. I squeezed, hard, and felt spasms loosen her grip. I kicked my legs and got them free of her encircling thighs. I let my captive arm go limp and rolled up onto my knees, pulling Shirley up with me. She was strong, but not terribly heavy. Before I could reverse the hold on her, she let go and sprang away.

"Did Grecca teach you that knee trick?"

"Yep."

"That girl really loves to—*wowf!*"

Without warning, I'd lunged and grabbed for her wrist. She pulled away, but I had placed my foot behind her ankle where I knew she would move and she stumbled. I hooked another foot while she tried to recover and we both went down, legs tangled. I was ready, though, and as she tried to recover, I grabbed her arm and pulled her in, maneuvering her into the same behind-the-neck arm lock that was her favorite hold. Kneeling astride her hips, with one arm pinning her raised arms to my shoulder, I had her helpless.

"And she knows a few moves you don't know."

Shirley grunted, trying to pull free, but she was caught. Unfortunately, bent over her the way I was, I couldn't reach her very ticklish feet. I pulled her shirt up over her tits and tickled her ribs and the parts of her belly I could reach, but I couldn't get much more than a twitch here and there.

"Hmm, I seem to be in a bit of a predicament."

"Forgive me if I withhold my sympathy," Shirley growled between struggles.

"I think I'm just going to have to hunt around for someplace else."

I explored the parts of her body within reach, letting my touch go soft or heavy as the mood struck me, carefully monitoring her reactions for any sign of ticklishness. The only tension at all seemed to come when I moved over her breasts, and I knew it wasn't laughter she was holding in.

It wasn't working. She just wasn't ticklish anywhere but her feet. If I was going to get hold of them, I would have to let her out of the shoulder lock, and she was struggling too hard to make that easy. I paused to consider my options.

Something came to mind, but it would definitely be taking this exercise to a new level.

"How dirty are we fighting?" I asked.

"Try not to do anything that'll put me in a gentank," she said. "But aside from that . . ."

"Good." I reached around in front of her and tweaked one of her nipples as hard as I could.

She shrieked in pain, and when I let go of her arms, her hands immediately moved to cradle her breast. In the moment her hands were occupied, I spun around and sat on her thighs, gripping her hips between my knees. I took her slender ankles in one hand and pressed them to the mat. With my weight on her legs, she couldn't move much except to thrash her arms; she had no leverage to throw me off or twist out of my hold.

"You're going to pay for that next time, Challers."

"Next time isn't this time."

I went to work on her feet, and her threats disappeared in a wave of laughter. The little cruelty of the pinched nipple felt good and I tickled her mercilessly. The last time I had done this, I gave her breaks to catch her breath, but something made me make the most of this opportunity. Even when she started gasping, "No," "Stop," "Please," in between desperate gulps of air, I kept it up.

And then I smelled something.

I released her and stood up.

She curled up, gasping for breath. Her shorts were soaking wet and there was a puddle on the mat beneath her.

"Shirley, I'm sorry. Oh, vack . . ."

Still panting, Shirley got to her feet. The front of her shorts was soaked too. "End of lesson."

If her expression left any doubt about her annoyance, her clipped speech removed it.

I had never made Shirley angry with me before. I didn't know how she would react, what she would do.

"I'm sorry," I repeated. My stomach started up with its twists and grinds.

"Enough," she said, and turned towards the showers.

I had gone too far, way too far.

"I never wanted this to happen."

"Of course not," she said, stripping off her fouled clothes and dumping them into the recycler.

I stood, nervously watching, until she waved her hand at the nozzles. "Go on, you probably need it too."

I undressed and got under the spray. I faced the wall, ashamed.

Shirley took a deep breath. "If we're going to play like this, we need to establish a rule. If either of us is in pain, or otherwise in real distress, then we have to stop right there. We need a signal we can give when it really, really has to stop immediately and completely. Struggling is half the fun, but an accident like this is not, and a real injury would be even worse."

"Um, yeah. I see what you mean."

"Each of us needs one. Don't choose a signal like 'no' or 'stop' or 'vack' or anything like that. You make it a word you wouldn't ordinarily say."

I considered. I would want my word to be something easy to say, but distinctive.

"For me, it'll be 'tablet,'" she said.

"Any reason it can't be the same for me?"

"Oh, show some creativity."

I had a sudden impulse to say Valka's name, but it seemed silly and I held back. "How about 'oxygen?'"

"Good."

We finished our showers, dried off, put on fresh clothes, and headed out to the mess hall a little early for breakfast.

And then, as we came around a corner, I was face to face with Valka.

"Challers!" she said. A tentative half-smile came to her lips. "You're looking good."

"You too," I said, but it was a lie. Even though she had continued to fill out, the haunted look I had seen in our last encounter was worse. It hurt to see her like this.

Masters came up behind her. "We have a class to get to, Valka."

"I'll catch up, if it's all right?"

"Don't be too long." He gave us both a stern look before continuing down the hall.

Shirley patted me on the shoulder. "I'll get a tray for you. See you inside."

"Thanks."

Valka stood nervously, her arms wrapped around her middle. "I wonder if it would be all right with you if I sent you a message, once in a while?"

I had my doubts. We couldn't really be together anymore, so why prolong the pain? Not only that, I couldn't understand why she would want to make this connection with me again. She was the one who had ended our relationship. Weren't the reasons for that unchanged?

But in spite of my doubts, I said, "Sure." I leaned down to give her a nice, polite kiss on the cheek.

She stiffened as I got close, but afterwards, she smiled. "Thank you."

I had the first message on my tablet the next morning. I didn't want to watch it while Shirley was around, though, so I left it unread for the day. The distraction of knowing it was there balanced with the satisfaction of knowing how much she had wanted to send it to me. During my free hour after lunch, I went out for a walk on the oxygen deck and brought my tablet with me. I wandered down to a quiet spot by the river and set it down to play her message.

From what I could see, she had recorded it sitting at her desk. Only her upper body and head was visible.

"Thank you for letting me send this to you, Challers. I want you to know that I miss you. I'm sorry for dumping you the way I did; I really could have handled it better. I know it'll be hard to forgive me for the way I treated you, but I still want to be your friend." Her eyes were dark and hard to read.

"I thought you might want to know what's going on with me, so, if you're still listening, I'd like to just go over things. I'm sure we're studying most of the same things, so I won't bore you with all that. It bothers me that I don't get to see or talk with any of the other cadets here. I know I wasn't much of a social creature back on the station, but I get lonely a lot. I guess that's why I end up thinking of you so much."

She sighed and shook her head. "I promised myself I wouldn't get like this." She looked up and tried to smile, but didn't quite make it. "I've been learning about some of the jobs the Scouts do. You'd think delivering the mail would be a boring job, but when you get down into the information infrastructure of it, all the networks and coding and all that, it's fascinating stuff. I guess you wouldn't be interested; you never were back on the station, but you know me, I'm not happy unless I'm messing around in the guts of a computer. I'm learning a lot."

"Could you send a message back to me, about your research project? I really am curious to know."

Then, finally, I could see the hope in her eyes, the hope that I would respond, and I felt that spark I had been keeping alive inside my own heart flare up in response.

The recording cut out. She hadn't told me what was bothering her, but she had reopened the way between us, and that, at least, was good.

Chapter Twenty-One

"Having a good day?" Shirley gave me an amused expression as I walked into Technology class.

"I got a message from Valka." I replayed it for her.

"That's great!" She gave me a little hug and pulled away to look at me, eye to eye. Her lips were pursed around a little smile and I could see satisfaction in her eyes.

"What?"

"Look at yourself. When you first came here, Masters and I were intruders on your relationship with Valka. Now you're inviting me to celebrate with you when that relationship is reawakened."

"Yeah, I guess I have changed a lot since then." I thought of Trace and Suna, and smiled to myself.

"I knew you could do it." She leaned in and kissed me on the lips. It wasn't a particularly passionate kiss, but it was more than a peck.

"You kissed me," I said.

"Why yes. How observant."

"You've never kissed me like that before."

"I haven't?"

"You've never kissed me at all. Not on the lips."

She bit her lip. "I guess I haven't."

I saw a glimmer in her eye, something going on behind them, and I had a suspicion what it was. Before I could pursue it, though, she took her place at the desk behind me.

"Time for class," she said and summoned the holographic lecturer, and that was that.

After we returned to our room from dinner, I got my tablet out.

"I'm going to send a message back to Valka, and I want it to be just from me. Could you give me ten minutes?"

"Certainly, Challers."

When the door closed behind her, I pulled up the recording program and my finger hovered over the touchpoint that would start it up. I wanted to make sure I knew what I was going to say. I waited a few seconds longer, then jabbed the screen.

"Hi, Valka. Yes, I listened to your message. Thank you so much for sending it. Of course I forgive you. Will you forgive me for driving you away? I'm sorry I hurt you, even if I still don't understand how.

"I know what you mean about being isolated. I've hardly spoken to anyone but Shirley since you and I split up. It seems really strange, compared to the crowds on Stakroya, but even with all the people around, were there really that many people we could talk to? I know you didn't talk to your parents much, and I didn't have many friends outside my family. I think a lot of them knew we wouldn't be staying on the station for long and didn't want to get close.

"Your research project sounds fascinating. Will you send it to me? I'd love to see it. My research project about the Ovors got very high marks. Shirley is letting me continue my studies into some of the other newgens in that part of the galaxy. Pretty funny, after I reacted so strangely to meeting the Chevalier newgens down by the river, huh? But it's fascinating. It makes sense, though. So much about how we put our societies together comes from basic physical needs: food, water, shelter, sex, companionship, all the rest. When you change how those needs work, you change the way society works. I wonder what it's like to live on some of those newgen stations?

"I suppose that's all for now. I can't wait for another message from you."

I cut the recording, attached my Ovor research project to it, and sent it into the academy's messaging system. It struck me that it was the first time I had used it. Before then, I didn't have anyone to send one to.

While I waited for Shirley to return, I sat back in my chair and thought. Did I really want to get back into a relationship with

Valka? She had hurt me when she pushed me away and it still hurt to think about, even after the time that had passed.

Then again, the hesitation I felt that night with Suna told me that, deep down, I really did hope I would get together with Valka again, that somehow she would be my first. I didn't know how that could happen, though. After our training was over, Valka would go on a ship with Masters, I would go on a ship with Shirley, and our first times would be there, in those ships, propelling us out to some distant star to start our training cruises. There didn't seem to be any other way, or at least, any other way that didn't lead to the Fleet or the Merchants.

And if I couldn't be with the woman I loved, then I was going to love the woman I was going to be with. To do that, I needed her to love me.

The door opened and Shirley poked her head in. "All done?"

"Yeah." I shut off my tablet and put it away. "I've been doing pretty well in my classes so far, right?"

"Oh, yes, quite well. Why do you ask?"

"Would it be allowed for us to go out to the promenade, and maybe visit some of the clubs? I've been past there several times and I never see any cadets in there."

"It happens sometimes. You just don't see them in uniform."

"In that case, I think I deserve a reward for how well I'm doing." I cocked my head to one side and smiled, trying to look challenging rather than petulant.

She considered for a moment, then shrugged. "All right, sounds like fun. Let's go."

It turned out that there was a clothing synthesizer near the exit for just that purpose. With a few minutes work, we had a sharp outfit of trim black pants and a loose gray vest for me, and a knee-length white dress for her. Even though we weren't in uniform, we were still wearing the colors that marked our respective ranks.

When we got to the promenade, I led Shirley to a dark club with lots of flashing lights and loud music. I had passed it many times before and of all the clubs on the promenade, this was the one I wanted to go to.

At the door, I growled to myself. "Vack, Shirley, do I have credit here?"

Shirley nodded. "You do, but save it. I'll pay." She waved her hand over the bouncer's handheld implant reader and we went in. "You get a payment to your account every thirty days. You can check it on the tablet; I'll show you when we get back."

I nodded and led Shirley out to the dance floor in the middle of the club. All in all, it wasn't very big, but even so, it wasn't crowded. I knew from my nighttime excursions that people didn't start coming out until later. There were just a few other couples, and they were all focused on each other. Most of them seemed to be Scouts, dressed in white, though there were a few colorfully dressed civilians, as well.

Mentally, I thanked Valka for insisting that I learn to dance— or at least, that I let go of the feeling that I looked like I had a nervous condition and just *do* it. Shirley wasn't familiar with my style of dancing, but she adapted quickly, incorporating some of the moves from partner movement.

I kept my eyes on her face, on her eyes when she'd show them to me. When she looked up, she always saw me looking directly into her eyes. It couldn't have been too hard to figure out what I was doing, but she didn't say anything. It felt, more than anything, like a struggle. Wordlessly, I was trying to get her to open up to me, to let herself feel something for me. The music made conversation impossible, and after agreeing to come out, she could hardly stop after only a few minutes. She was trapped, in a way. It seemed odd to be trying to win her over like this, but everything seemed odd.

When the music turned to a somewhat slower song and I moved a little closer, she smiled and took a step back.

"I'm a little tired!" she shouted over the music. "Let's get a drink!" She mimed a glass and pointed to the bar at the back of the club.

The music there was a bit less intrusive and we could hold something of a conversation. Shirley called up the menu on the counter controls and punched in an order. The mechanisms in the back of the bar delivered two glasses, one of which she handed to me.

"Alcohol's allowed?"

"In moderation. Getting drunk isn't." She raised her glass and touched it to mine, then took a sip. Seeing a quizzical look on my face, she said, "Old tradition. Probably dates back to the First System."

"What does it mean?"

"I don't know. It's just what you do."

I tasted the drink. I didn't know what it was supposed to taste like. I liked it, sort of, but it wasn't what I was there for. I looked around the club.

"A lot of Scouts come here, looks like."

"Yeah, it's good to get out and away from the ship in between missions, to get to know people. When a cruise is over, you'll have a chance to pick a new partner from the available candidates, and it's good to know who they are."

"Do you always get your pick?"

She shrugged. "Not at first. The more prestige you have with Command, the more likely you are to get your pick. But if someone with more asks for you, then that's who you get."

"I see. How do you get prestige?"

"Discovering new resources, volunteering for dangerous missions, recruiting. Anything above and beyond the usual duties."

"That's why you recruited Valka and me."

She blushed. "Partly. That's why we went out looking for someone to recruit. The medical analysis said we'd be compatible and, I have to say, it was right."

"Medical analysis?"

"Female attraction is a funny thing. It has a lot to do with things like how you smell. The computers can tell, based on our genetic makeup, how likely we'd be able to make a connection."

"I see."

"If it makes you feel any better, Valka has the same compatibility with you that I do."

I nodded, looked around the club again, and then back at her. I drank some of the wine, watching her over the top of the glass.

"You're doing it again, aren't you?"

"Doing what?"

"Looking into my eyes. How did you put it? Creating something 'real.' Whatever that means."

"Yes. I am. Do you want me to stop?"

"Challers." She gave me a dubious look. "Think about what you're doing. Are you saying that staring into each other's eyes is actually going to create something beyond what we already have? We live together, we study together, we have sex on a regular basis. I like you. I have the crazy idea that you like me too. What more do you want? What more do you expect to accomplish?"

"Are you saying it's meaningless? Silly?"

"I wouldn't put it that way, but yes. I think it is a little silly. There's a lot more to a relationship than gazing into each other's eyes."

"Is there any harm in it?"

"No, of course not. Except maybe as a waste of time."

"We're here, having fun. Wasting time." I leaned closer and set my glass down, still half full. "So no harm at all. It's safe, right?"

She took a big swig of wine and shook her head. "You're a romantic, you know that?"

"What's that?"

"Someone who believes in the power of love to overcome every obstacle—that all you need is to love someone deeply enough, completely enough, and everything will turn out all right in the end."

"In that case, maybe I am. And why not?"

"It's going to hurt when you realize the world doesn't work that way. Falling in love, *really* falling in love, leads to a great deal of pain."

"And yet you still love Robert, even though every time you have to say goodbye, you hurt all over again."

She looked down. "That's different."

I finished my drink and took her hand. "Come on. Finish your drink and let's dance."

When she looked up, she wore a crooked smile and shook her head. "All right, Challers. All right."

We danced close, closer even than when we practiced our partner movement exercises. I held her close and, before long, she was holding me, as well. We had our thighs between each other's legs, grinding against each other. She might have been trying to get me turned on enough that I had to leave, or it might have just been the way she wanted to dance. It didn't matter, though, because she was finally letting me in, letting me through the doors of her eyes.

We stayed there, our dance slow and sensuous in spite of the changing music, for what seemed like hours. Our gazes stayed in that mutual reflection the whole time, and by the time we were too tired to stand any longer, I could tell that something had changed. It wasn't anything overt, or even anything I could point to in any logical way, but I could feel in my heart that I had finally gotten through. We didn't try to talk. The thudding music made it impossible. I didn't care. Words would have been a distraction.

The dance floor slowly became more and more crowded, until there simply wasn't enough room for us anymore and I pulled Shirley away. We went back out to the promenade and found a bench that wasn't too besieged by the swelling traffic.

I took her hand in mine. "There. That wasn't so bad, was it?"

"It was marvelous, Challers. Thank you."

"Do you feel any different?"

"It's a very intimate thing, looking into the eyes like that. It touches something very primal."

"You didn't answer the question."

"You're asking so much. I don't know if I can give it to you."

"You can. You are. You just have to let it happen. All those things you told me, about opening my heart, about loving more than one person? It's not a lie, Shirley. You may not have been saying it sincerely, but I listened to what you said and I agree with it. Don't you think we'll be better off if we're honest with each other, if we let ourselves feel the things that go with what we're doing?"

She closed her eyes. Her voice grew tight and strained. "I'm scared, Challers. Vack! I'm not supposed to get like this with a cadet. I'm supposed to be the authority!" She choked back a sob and looked away, trying to hide her tears from me.

"I won't lose my respect for you if you cry, Shirley. You brought me through the math section of Astronavigation when I thought it was going to wash me out. I owe everything here to you."

She curled sideways, into my arms. I could hear, in her breathing, that she was using the meditation techniques she had taught me to keep control.

I pulled her to her feet. "Come on," I said. "Let's go out to the oxygen deck. I know this quiet place down by the water."

CHAPTER TWENTY-TWO

We sat by the water, my arm around her, for an hour or so before I thought of something worth saying.

"Valka and I used to sit in the communications center for hours at a time, looking out at the stars. It had a big window for some reason, and if the station was oriented right and we turned off all the lights, it seemed like the whole galaxy was laid out for us. We didn't talk, at least not the whole time, and we didn't spend the whole time kissing, either. We just sat together, enjoying just being together."

"We've never done that," she said.

"Until now. Shirley, I know I can love you. In perfect honesty, I still worry whether that's going to make me love Valka less, but if anything is going to make our time together worthwhile, it's going to be allowing ourselves to fall in love. And that means doing silly things like taking long walks by the river and gazing into each other's eyes. There's one thing I can't do, though, and that's love someone who doesn't love me back. That would hurt even more."

"Do you really think you can *make* love happen, just like that?"

"I think you know it's possible. Whether it actually works for *us* is a question I can't answer without your help."

She kissed me. It wasn't just a touch of the lips, either. She rolled her head up, nuzzled under my chin, and then pushed me onto my back and kissed me like I had never been kissed before. Her kiss was insistent, almost desperate. I submitted to it, rolling with it, then returned the passion and desperation. It didn't have the same quality that kissing Valka had, there wasn't the overwhelming sense of *rightness*, but it felt good that I had gotten through to her.

After what seemed like only seconds, she pulled her shirt up over her head, quickly followed by the rest of her clothes.

"What's this, time for class all of a sudden?"

"No class, Challers. No questions. No answers." She straddled me and pulled my shirt over my head. Her nipples dragged over my skin as she ran a trail of kisses down my chest and abdomen.

"Shirley?"

"Don't talk." Her legs made a small splash entering the water. She pulled down my shorts and engulfed my flaccid cock in her mouth. It seemed almost like hunger that drove her, using her lips and tongue to work it towards erection. The sudden passion confused me, but I had no intention of complaining. I lay back on the ground and enjoyed her attentions. Somewhere in the corner of my mind, I noticed that I was sliding down the slope into the water.

She pulled me in completely and wrapped her legs around me. "I can't wait to have sex with you on the ship, in zero gravity. It's incredibly liberating."

She paddled with her hands and pulled me out into the deeper water.

I splashed, panicking a little at the way the water seemed to want to pull me under.

"Like this," she said. "Watch my hands."

I imitated her movements and found that I could keep my head above the water level by pumping at it the right way.

I was panting, half from fright and half from erotic tension. My cock bumped against her ass as we floated in the water and I knew that it would only be a slight motion to slip it inside her.

I wanted it. I wanted it so bad I could taste it. But even as we drifted there in the water, I didn't want it enough to actually do it. The fact that Shirley wasn't pushing herself down onto me told me she was holding back too.

I felt a shudder pass through her body. "I think we need to get out of the water. It's colder than I thought."

I had to agree. I could feel the cold seeping into my flesh.

"Uh, how?" I tried to alter my paddling to produce some sideways motion.

"Try and go that direction."

"I *am* trying!"

We drifted further and further downstream. The current in the center of the river was faster than it was near the edge. The glowing rectangle of the entrance to the promenade had disappeared behind something. I couldn't tell how far we had gone. The only light came from starlight filtering down through the transparent ceiling and the distant lights of the far side of the ring, not nearly enough to see by. I felt like I was floating in nothingness, floating in the void. My heart pounded in my ears and my breathing came faster. I fought down the urge to thrash against the water.

The only thing that kept my wits about me was the firm grip of Shirley's legs around my waist. "Stay calm, Challers, let me use my legs. I think I can get us out of the water."

"Don't let go of me!"

Panic flashed through my brain. I thrashed in the water and my head went under the surface for a moment. The river couldn't have been very deep, but for that moment, it felt infinite. I got my head back to the surface and gasped for breath.

"Don't worry! I'm not leaving you." Her ankles unlocked from around my waist and we drifted apart a little. I splashed and sputtered, trying to keep my head out of the water. She turned her back to me. "Grab my shoulders, but don't push down. Just put your hands there."

Her skin was slick and I could feel goosebumps under my fingers. It took every scrap of will I had to keep from climbing on top of her to get that much further out of the water. She swept her arms and legs in wide arcs and, gradually, we moved through the water. I couldn't see well enough to even tell where the bank was, so thick was the darkness.

Then, suddenly, I felt Shirley's body lurch under me. It felt like something had grabbed her. She slid down, then forward, briefly going under the water, but then straightened up. She had found something to stand on, some solid ground under her feet.

We pulled ourselves out and lay there, shivering. I was coughing, panting, gasping.

I looked around, but all was blackness. Once I had caught my breath, I felt around. My groping hands found fibrous, dense vegetation in every direction. We lay on a thick, spongy mat that felt like miniature grass.

"I can't find a way out," I said, nearly frantic.

Shirley's hand found my hips. "Cuddle close," she said. "We'll wait here until the end of the dark shift, then we'll find a way when the lights come on."

I settled down and found my place behind her, curled up around her back spoon-fashion. My arm, draped over her side, found a natural place on her breast. Gradually, our body heat returned and the shivers faded away. The air wasn't really very cold, and once the water on my skin had evaporated, I felt almost normal again.

I felt my erection return and, with it, the passion that had been driving me ever since we left the promenade. I turned Shirley on her back and ran my hand over her body, feeling her skin from neck to crotch, figuring out where she was in the pitch dark.

Shirley put her hand on my chest. It might have been a gesture of caution, but I was too turned on to stop. I wanted her, badly. I stroked her breast and felt the nipple harden against the palm of my hand.

"After all that, you're still aroused?"

"I can't help it." My erection bumped against her leg. I leaned down and nuzzled her chest. When I located her nipple, I took it between my lips and sucked.

She let out a soft sigh and ran her fingers through my hair. "This is nice."

I slid my hand down and found her pussy. My fingers slid between her warm, wet lips. Her nipple popped out of my mouth. "No fancy bed. No lessons. No rules. Just you and me and the darkness."

I felt her body tense a little. "Challers, just because . . ."

"No, Shirley." I probed her more deeply, touching her most sensitive places in the most effective ways I had learned.

She let out a long breath and arched her back. "Challers, what are you—what are you doing?"

"Shh." I stopped any further protest with my mouth on hers, while I shifted my body between her legs. Guided only by touch, the head of my cock found her slick vulva and bumped against her lips.

She made a weak sound of protest into my mouth and I pulled back, giving her the chance to refuse me. I wasn't going to rape her, but I wasn't going to take anything less than a *no* to stop me.

Having worked so hard to engage her, to break down the shields around her heart, I found my own barriers failing, as well. I had pledged to myself that if there was any way to do it, Valka would be my first, but that promise was lost in the chaos of my thoughts and emotions. Right then, I wanted Shirley, and I wanted her badly enough to let all my other promises fall aside.

"I want this," I said. "Not for the Scouts, not for training, but for us. For you. For me."

I kissed her again and she returned it with passion. Her hands moved over my neck and through my hair. Nothing about her said she wanted me to hold back.

I thrust in.

Her breath came sharply in, as did mine. All the times she had pleasured me with her hands, with her mouth, even between her thighs or between her breasts—nothing was as sublime as the feeling of her soft warmth wrapped around my cock. I moved slowly, savoring every moment.

"Challers," said Shirley, "you have to . . . oh . . . you have to stop."

"It's too late now."

"No . . . Challers." She whispered between sighs. "Listen . . . oh . . . you have to stop."

I paused my slow thrusting with my cock buried to the hilt. I could feel her pussy squeezing me with pulsing spasms around my shaft. She wasn't making any move to stop me. In fact, her hips were tilting up to admit me.

"We're already doing it. Just let it happen. Let go."

Then I felt her hand on my chest. "Challers." She was mustering her will, calming her voice. "Stop. You have to stop."

I rolled onto my side next to her. To keep going like that would have been rape. "I don't understand. What good is it to stop now? We might as well finish."

"No, Challers. There's something transcendent about the first time, something special that can never be recaptured. We can't squander it. We will have that time, I promise you. It just can't be now. I'm sorry."

I heard genuine regret in her voice, but whether it was regret at letting things go too far or that we had to stop, I couldn't tell. Probably both. My hands drifted over her body. I could tell, just from touch, that she was still very aroused. Her nipples were taut and her body was almost hot to the touch.

Her hand found my erection and caressed it. "I'm sorry to jerk you around like that. Can I make it up to you?"

"Does that mean what I think it means?"

"Yes. How would you like it?"

"Your breasts," I said, my voice stolen by a fresh wave of heat.

She pushed me onto my back and I felt her warm, soft breasts enfold my cock. I was too aroused to care what she used, as long as she did something to ease my ache. After only a minute or two, I gasped and jerked, and splashed her chest with cum.

When I was done, she pulled away.

"Wait, where are you going?"

"Just getting some water to rinse this off." I heard a few splashes of water, and then she snuggled up next to me, still a bit wet.

"You don't need to, ah, have an orgasm yourself?"

"No, I'm fine. I'm happy right here." She squeezed me, and as sleep crept up, it occurred to me that I was, too.

CHAPTER TWENTY-THREE

I awoke to find light filling our mossy bower, the rays filtering down between the leaves of the shrubs that surrounded us. The foliage was still too dense to just push through, but it was a simple matter to crawl out into the shallows of the river and stand up.

I bent down and tugged Shirley's ankle. "Come on, wake up. Dark shift is over."

She emerged, bleary-eyed and hair tangled, with leaves and bits of moss stuck to her here and there. We looked around. Now that the lights were on, we could see that we were only a few feet away from a road.

Shirley looked around and pointed off in the distance. "I'm pretty sure that's where the entrance to the academy is."

"We should get walking, I guess." My stomach growled.

Shirley chuckled. "Or maybe find something to eat."

I looked in the direction of the closest wall of the ring. "What else might be nearby?"

"Most of the folks who live here at headquarters work in support jobs. There are factories manufacturing spare parts, food processing facilities, that kind of thing. We should get back to the academy, though. If we find a console somewhere, I'll call to have someone come out and pick us up."

We started walking back in the direction of the academy. The ring shape of the oxygen deck allowed us to see the route to take, so there was no chance of getting lost. Several large robots came by as we walked, but when we tried to wave them down, they just kept on going.

We held hands.

Walking with Shirley was totally different from walking with Valka. She didn't have just one way of staying close. We walked hand in hand, or elbow to elbow, or sometimes with an arm around her shoulders. It felt wonderful, free, like she and I were the only people in the universe.

A voice suddenly called out from behind us. "Ey, out da way!"

Something large and orange flashed past us, careening wildly down the narrow path. It skidded to a stop, throwing up a cloud of dust and nearly tipping off of its three wheels. It settled back down and a bald head poked up over the top of the machine.

"Hey, you folks in trouble?"

"Yah," said Shirley. "We need a ride. Can you call the academy for us?"

"Nope. Radio's broke. Climb in the back; I'll give ya a ride. Where ya goin'?"

"The academy."

We clambered into the little cargo area behind his one-seat control couch. It was half full of greasy boxes of tools and barrels of lubricant. As dirty as I was, I didn't want to sit on any of it. Instead, I stood up and gripped the framework overhead that held a ladder and some poles. Shirley took a place next to me.

He screwed up his face and clucked his tongue. "It's a little outside my duty zone, but I suppose I can give you a ride. Name's Joco Gata. You?"

We lurched into motion and sped off between the fields and orchards.

"I'm Captain Shirley Smith, and this is Cadet Challers Dizen."

"Ohah, you're Scouts?" The man handled his little vehicle like a maniac. We held on tight as he bounced along the track and made idle conversation. "So why you folks naked?"

Whenever he looked over his shoulder to get a look at Shirley's boobs, he swerved precariously to the right.

"We went for a swim and got carried downstream. By the time we got back onshore, it was too dark to see, so we just waited for the lights to come back on."

"Heh. Must have been some swim." He gave me a wink and went back to leering at Shirley.

The fact that he was right made his leer even more embarrassing. For the first time in a long time, I felt ashamed, not just for myself, but for Shirley, as well.

"Ya know, I used to be a Scout, years ago."

"What happened?"

"Turns out I wasn't really good Scout material. But I'm good with robots, so they let me stay on as a tech."

"Do you miss going out in space?"

"Sometimes, but I'm happy here. I got a comfortable place, got lots of robots to mess with, and I get to meet interesting people." He winked at me and gave Shirley another lurching leer.

My stomach growled.

"Ya hungry? My lunch is in the red box back there; you can have it if you want."

I ignored another gurgle from my midsection. To eat, I would have to let go, and no food was worth the risk that would entail. "No, I'm fine."

The road dipped down near the river, where our clothes were still scattered on the grass.

Shirley pointed over his shoulder. "You can let us off right over there."

The little truck skidded to a stop, nearly throwing us back in the water. I leapt out, more than a little glad to have my feet back on the nice, stable deck. Shirley waved to Joco as he spun his little machine around and sped down the road.

We pulled our clothes back on.

I shook my head, watching him disappear in the distance. "What a creep."

"Oh, I don't know," said Shirley. "I think he had his own kind of charm. He certainly seems to be enjoying life."

"Enjoying looking at you."

"Really, Challers. It's one thing to get jealous of someone who might, in some perspective, be a threat to you. But him?"

"I'm sorry. So easy to let those feelings take over, you know?"

She gave me a hug. "I know all about letting feelings take over, Challers."

Valka's image stared at me across the little desk. It seemed that she was even more drained than before, tension twisting her features.

"Challers, I'm worried about Masters. He's turning inward. Not really talking to me, not really opening up. Could you ask

Shirley if something happened while they were together, or maybe if he said anything to her about something before they were together? I've tried everything I know to reach him."

Her gaze dropped to her hands, clutched together in front of her. "I know you don't like Masters much, or at least, my relationship with him, but I'm kind of stuck with him and, well . . . I hope you understand. I need to get through to him."

The message cut out and I slumped back in my chair. My first thought was, "How dare she? Wanting me to help her get closer to Masters?"

Then Shirley walked into our quarters and put her arms around my neck and kissed my cheek. "Another message from Valka?"

At that moment, I knew I had to help her. How could I deny Valka the kind of relationship with Masters that I had with Shirley? I squeezed her head to my cheek and then rose to my feet.

"She wants my help," I said.

"What kind of help?"

"I'm not sure. I need to figure out how to give her what she needs."

"Well, if there's anything I can do to help, let me know."

"Actually, there is. Can you tell me what it was like on your cruise with Masters?"

"What do you mean? It was a cruise. We were just delivering mail most of the time, making the circuit from station to station. Not really much of a big deal." She turned away, and I could feel a tension come over her.

"There's more you're not telling me."

"I'd . . . I don't think it's proper to compare one partner to another. I'm sure Valka will do fine with him."

I stood behind her and put my arms around her, hands resting lightly on her belly. "I don't think you're sure at all."

"You're right. Masters is . . . wounded. Somehow. It happened during his stay at the academy, but I swear, I don't know what it is. I tried to get through to him, but after a while, it just turned out to be easier to let him be. Whatever was bothering him seemed better left buried."

"Valka seems to have picked up on that. She's trying to get past his defenses and having a rough time of it. You never looked into the matter?"

"What could I do? We were out on our cruise." She sighed and her shoulders slumped.

"There's more you're not telling me."

She gently pulled my arms away from her and stepped into the fresher. "I really shouldn't. It's not my place to talk about him. It's between Valka and Masters, really, to work this out." She picked up a washcloth, wet it under the tap, and ran it over her face.

"This is for Masters and Valka. If he's as wounded as you say, he's not capable of making this work between the two of them. She needs our help."

She let out a deep breath and closed her eyes. "The woman he arrived with . . . Cassandra. She was reassigned by headquarters halfway through the academy."

"Reassigned? To where?"

"I don't know. He never found out. It's a secret. Completely need-to-know."

I stepped closer and put my arm around her. "It hurt you, to see him in such pain, closing himself off like that."

A tear ran down her cheek. "Yes. It was like . . . it was like living with a walking corpse. He walked and talked and made all the right movements, but there was never a connection there. I think he decided that if he couldn't have Cassandra, he wouldn't have anyone."

I kissed her. "I've kind of felt that way myself, here and there. It must have been terrible."

"I'm sorry, Challers, but I just don't have the information. I can't help Valka. I couldn't even help myself. If there had been anything I could do . . ."

I squeezed her. "Come on. Let's go to bed. I don't think Valka knows about Cassandra. That'll be a place for her to start."

She turned and hugged me back. "I'm so glad you didn't go that way, Challers. If you had, I don't know what I would have done. I was so afraid, so afraid that when you and Valka broke up, it would happen all over again."

"You held back because you thought I was going to go the same way, turn cold and dark, and you didn't want to get pulled into the same black hole with me."

She nodded. "I'm sorry. It was the exact wrong thing to do."

"We got it worked out. They can too. I'll tell her about Cassandra. Maybe she can use that to get more information."

"Please tell her not to do any searches in the system for her. It really is need-to-know. If she does look, it could easily get traced back to us."

I made a noncommittal sound.

"I'm serious, Challers. Cassandra is a taboo subject. Just looking for her name almost got me kicked to the bottom of the prestige ladder. Make sure she understands. Command doesn't make a big deal about many things as long as we complete our missions. Some things, though, get their attention. Cassandra's one of them."

"Okay, I'll warn her."

I returned to my tablet and started my own recording. "Hi, Valka. Shirley doesn't know much about what happened with Masters. He was already pretty closed off by the time she met him. I'd like to talk about it, though, face to face. I'd like to meet you down by the water, where we met those newgens the first day of class. Maybe tonight, after the dark shift begins on the oxygen deck? Let me know when you can come." I ended the recording, sent it off, and sat back in my chair.

"Do you want me to come with you?" Shirley came out and ran her fingers through my hair.

"No, it's best if you don't, I think. She came to me for answers, and I'm going to give them to her myself."

Chapter Twenty-Four

Lights from the far side of the river reflected on the surface of the water, merging and splitting and sweeping out short, quick elliptical arcs.

Valka sat down next to me, close enough to hold hands if she wanted to, but she wrapped her arms around her knees instead. "So."

"Thanks for coming," I said, looking over to her face.

She stared into the water. "You have something for me?"

"Not a lot. Masters hadn't told Shirley much more than he told you."

"That's not hard. He hasn't told me anything." Valka's tone held frustration and sadness.

"Her name's Cassandra. She was pulled out of the academy about a quarter of the way through, and disappeared. Anyone who looked into it got slapped down, hard. It hurt him pretty bad."

Valka sighed. "I figured it was something like that. He looks at me sometimes and I can just tell that he's wishing I was someone else."

"Yeah. Well, anyway, Shirley says not to look into it. It's too dangerous, for all of us." I looked back out over the water, at the lights winking out one by one in the far side of the ring. "At least people like Shirley and Robert have some hope that someday they'll have a cruise together."

"Robert?"

"He's the guy Shirley was recruited with. Her true love."

"And they've never had a cruise together. How old is she? How many years has she been a Scout?"

"She said she's been a Scout for ten years. That makes her what, almost thirty?"

"Vack. I wish I had a safe tablet."

"What do you mean?"

"Anything you look up on your tablet is keyed to your ID. I've seen the data taps. You can't do anything without the Scouts knowing. Too much sniffing around sets off alarms. I know. I tried."

"You did? What happened?"

"I got a stern talk from Director Kal. She said that, prodigy or no, if I went poking around secrets beyond my station, I'd get sent to the Merchants."

"Vack."

"Yeah."

My jaw fell open, and I looked over my shoulder at the robot standing in the vineyards behind us, my heart beating fast. "Wait. Wait . . . come with me." I stood up, grabbing Valka's hand. "Come on. I need to show you something." I pulled Valka towards the vineyard, nearly breaking into a run.

"Have you gone crazy?"

"No. You have to see this." I stepped over the border of narcotic plants. There was no time to pick one and no need. In minutes, we were in the hideout. Luckily, it was just the two of us, alone. I pulled a chair from the table in the center of the room and set it in front of the tablet. "There."

Valka looked around. "What is this place?"

"A refuge. I come here sometimes to get away from the academy. No rules, no supervision."

"You set this all up?"

"No, it's been set up like this for a long time, long before we got here. A cadet named Trace brought me here and showed me everything. Look. This tablet. It's logged in. Not you, not me. Autonomous."

"No. Tablet's don't work that way. Someone has to be nearby, someone with an implant, or it just shuts down." She leaned down and examined the case in minute detail. "Oh, vack." She pointed to a lump stuck on the side of the unit.

I looked. There, suspended in semi-transparent epoxy, was a tiny silver square. "Someone dug out his implant to keep this tablet running."

It was an operation that couldn't have been done painlessly and, what's more, the Scout who did it would be discovered in no time. There simply was no way to get around, no way to get anything done at the academy, without it. Someone sacrificed everything to keep that tablet running.

"Yeah." Valka examined the holograms suspended over the table. "You need these?"

"They keep watch for us, let us know if anyone's coming."

"Fine." She waved her hand through the interface and the images floated up out of her way. "Watch them. I need to see what this thing is connected to."

She pulled up new screens and interfaces, typing commands on virtual keyboards faster than they could be spoken. I watched for a while, recognizing some things from when we were data management students on Stakroya, but many of them were new to me.

"You've been studying."

She smiled up at me briefly before going back to work. "You can't give me toys like these and expect me not to play with them. Now quiet. I'm working."

I pulled up a second chair and sat down behind her to watch the monitors. Normally, no one was going to show up on them, except possibly Suna or Zun, but given what she was doing, the chances of that were somewhat higher.

Not too much higher, I hoped.

For an hour, the only sound was the little beeps and clicks the tablet made to acknowledge commands. I kept watch as well as I could, but my gaze kept drifting to the back of Valka's head and body. Even from the back, even after everything that happened, she was still beautiful to me.

Finally, I caught myself nodding in my chair and stood up. "Valka. It's getting late. You need to get some sleep. Masters is going to get worried about you."

"I doubt it."

"Suspicious, then. You need to go back to the academy."

She sighed. "You're right. This is going to have to wait."

She shut down the screens she had been using and returned the external monitors to their old positions.

"Did you learn anything."

"Lots, but nothing really useful—yet."

I opened the hatch and started down the robot's leg. "Like what?"

"The cable that runs down the robot's leg doesn't just go to the toe sensor you use to open the hatch. It's connected to a major information hub, probably running down into the soil to the next level below this one. It's pretty sophisticated. It functions by rerouting data requests that were sent from elsewhere, so it doesn't get profiled by the system. Its activities get lost in the noise."

"Wow. Impressive. So what did you learn with all this?"

"I spent most of my time just getting familiar with this system. Next time, I can start trying to track down where Cassandra went."

"You really want to get them together."

"Masters can never be whole until they are. I can't just let him suffer like this."

Hmm. Suffer. That wasn't a word I had thought to associate with Masters, but if Valka said he was suffering, then he was suffering. An ugly little part of me was glad—the jealous part that I thought I had killed. I shoved that thought out of my head. What if Valka had been taken from me the same way? What if the possibility of piloting a Scout craft with Valka wasn't even a nebulous possibility for the future? How would I react to that? Besides, if I could give Masters the love of his life, maybe he'd leave me mine.

"Right. Well. First step to getting them back together is finding her. Are you coming back tomorrow night?"

Valka nodded as we stepped back out onto the road. "Yah. I don't know how long this will take; I don't want to pass up any opportunities."

My heart leapt. Maybe we weren't going on a date, but the fact that she was coming back, that I would see her again, left me giddy.

When I got back to our quarters, Shirley was waiting for me. "How did it go? Is she going to investigate?"

I groaned. I didn't want to lie.

Shirley shook her head. "You made it clear how bad it could be if she pokes around in this?"

"Yes, she knows."

"Then you've done what you could. If she's smart, she'll let this go. Find some other way to get through to him. I should probably have a talk with him, myself."

I nodded.

Over the next few days, I slipped out to meet Valka at the hideout every night. It felt a lot like when we were studying the Scouts' data for the secret that would get us selected. Hours spent poring over immense mountains of data, looking for correlations to a secret that wasn't quite contained within it, because there were holes.

Someone had expunged massive amounts of data to conceal what had happened to Cassandra. Her name didn't appear anywhere. As far as any of the records were concerned, Masters had arrived alone, which we knew wasn't possible. Everyone arrived as a part of a couple.

Very quickly, it occurred to us that Cassandra's disappearance would likely cause an imbalance—a male Scout with no partner. We looked for him, looked for disruptions in the pairings that such an assignment would cause. We found more than one, but most were easily eliminated. Trace's switch from male to female, of course, caused a surplus on the female side, but it appeared to be balanced by another switch in the opposite direction, though we couldn't find exactly where.

"Here he is," said Valka and pulled up a record on her screen. "Joco Gata."

"That name sounds familiar." I snapped my fingers. "I met him. He's a robot tech; he works nearby."

"That makes sense," said Valka. "This is his tablet."

"What?"

"It's his ID implant glued to the side. I assume it's his."

"Why did he get thrown out of the Scouts?"

She did a few more queries. "Looks like he got too curious. Had several disciplinary actions because of information breaches. It says he was a mentor at the academy, but doesn't say who his student was—to me, that's a sure sign that she was his student. He was probably looking into her disappearance."

"That sounds right; look at this setup. Seems like exactly the thing someone would set up for surreptitious access to the network. One thing doesn't fit, though. Why does his ID implant have access to all this information? Wouldn't it have been locked down when he was kicked out?"

"It doesn't. That's just signed into the tablet; that identification isn't going out beyond here. There's a slave process running on the hub that hijacks data queries from elsewhere on the system and substitutes its own. When the response comes through, it plucks the response out of the stream and reports the message lost back to the system."

"Wouldn't that eventually cause the hub to get reported as faulty?"

"Not if we don't use it too much."

"That explains why you're storing most of the information locally. So it looks like Joco is the one who set this system up. He may even have set up the whole hideout. I wonder if Suna or Zun know about him?"

"Who?"

"Suna and Zun are newgens who come around here from time to time. I haven't seen either of them for a while, though."

"I hope they won't mind us using the computer."

"Doesn't matter if they do. This is too important. Just be careful, okay? Looks like Joco's under the equivalent of house arrest over this."

"I will."

I stood up. "All right. I think I need to talk to Joco and find out if he knows anything about what happened to Cassandra. Maybe talk to Suna and Zun, too."

In order to catch the newgens attention, I set up a new holographic monitor on the tablet and opened a simple text document with big glowing letters.

WE NEED TO TALK. MEET HERE ONE HOUR AFTER DARK SHIFT STARTS.

Leaving that open while we were out would catch their attention next time they came to the hideout.

Joco wouldn't be so easy to get to, though. I only knew where he was during the light shift, and even then, only a vague notion. I needed a reason to go down to the river again to look around for him. Maybe I could claim I dropped something? No, that wouldn't work; we were naked going down the river. There didn't seem to be any good excuse to go looking for him.

Sending him a message for a rendezvous was out of the question. Even though we could send it pretty much anonymously, we couldn't be sure it wouldn't be intercepted. The Scouts didn't have their eye on me, as far as I knew, but they were definitely watching him.

The next morning, a thought occurred to me. Suna was a newgen. So was Zun. From the few conversations I had with them, I knew they had communities of similar newgens not far from the academy. Where were they actually located?

While Shirley was having her morning shower, I took out my tablet and did some research. There were several groups of newgens, numbering from a few dozen to a hundred or so, scattered around the headquarters. A group of Chevalier newgens lived quite close, just a couple of kilometers along the ring. Some more inquiries found that their living and working areas were just beyond where we had met Joco. If we went there, we'd travel right through his area.

Shirley came out of the fresher and looked over my shoulder. "What have you got there?"

"The historical information is so impersonal. I want to interview some newgens in person. There's a group nearby. I thought I could go interview some of them."

"Sure, why not? You're doing well in most of your studies. We can bring our tablets and do some review along the way."

We dressed and packed up our things, but instead of making our way to the promenade, Shirley took me down a corridor I had never used before. The sign over the door read *Transit Hub*.

I groaned inwardly. Of course the station would have some way of moving people and goods quickly; it was too big to depend on just walking. I had expected something like Joco's little truck, but instead, we found ourselves climbing into what amounted to a large elevator car mounted in a tunnel that ran around the ring of the station rather than up and down. Shirley waved her implant over the car's reader, spoke our destination, and we started moving. We were going to go right past him.

CHAPTER TWENTY-FIVE

As we sat in the accelerating car, Shirley turned to me. "What's wrong?"

I tried to wave it off. "Nothing."

"You're worried about Valka, aren't you?"

Air started rushing past the car and a strong vibration ran through the frame. What could I say? I couldn't lie to her, but at the same time, could I trust her with the information? There was little else I could do but take the risk.

"We're looking into it."

"Challers!" She put her hand on my knee. "You can't."

"We can." I lowered my voice to a whisper. I hoped that if there were listening devices in the car, the noise of the rails and the wind would make it hard to hear what I was saying. "We found a place where we can get secure access to the network and it won't get traced back to us. I found out who Cassandra's instructor was at the academy."

"Who?" she whispered back.

"Joco."

She nodded, recognizing the name. "So that's why you wanted to come out this way today."

"Yeah, except this route's going to go past him. I expected to go out on the oxygen deck."

"That would be a long walk, wouldn't it?"

I rubbed the bridge of my nose. "I guess I didn't really think this through."

"If you had told me what you were trying to do, I could have helped."

"You're not going to try to stop me?"

"I guess I owe it to Masters since I never tried to help him while we were partners." The car slowed down, approaching our destination. She helped me to my feet. "We'll figure something out. Besides, talking to the newgens will be good for your research. Just be careful."

We disembarked and walked into a large circular plaza, several levels high, with balconies on either side. It was empty, except for a desk in the center of the floor where a single newgen sat working at a console. He didn't look up as our footsteps echoed through the vacant hall.

"Excuse me," I said. "I wonder if we could talk to someone?"

He looked up from his console and looked me over, lingering a bit on my cadet uniform, and then over at Shirley. "About?"

"I'm doing research on newgens—history, culture, that sort of thing."

"I see." He arched a thin eyebrow and went back to his console. "I shall contact Kal Oreis, our arts director. It will not be a problem to make time for you. Please proceed to the second balcony on your right. Director Oreis will meet you there."

"Thank you."

We made our way up the wide ramp leading to the balconies. "I have the impression I am being indulged."

"You're a Scout," said Shirley. "We're the whole reason all of them are here."

At the top of the ramp, we were met by a tall Chevalier newgen in a short white tunic with a red stripe down one side. Her long black hair made me think of her more as female than male, even though I knew the concept was meaningless for them.

"Welcome to our little community," she said. "I am Kal Oreis. You're interested in learning more about newgens."

"Yes. I'm Cadet Challers Dizen, and this is my mentor, Captain Shirley Smith."

"Pleased to meet you both. How can I help you?"

"Ahm . . ."

I kicked myself for being so unprepared. If I had been thinking, instead of feeling sorry for myself, I could have thought up some questions on the way. Now I looked like an idiot standing there in front of someone who was clearly an important person in the community.

Shirley saved me. "Perhaps we could start with a tour? I'm sure Challers will remember the questions he prepared once we get started."

Kal smiled. "Of course. If you'll follow me?"

The newgens lived in apartments that ringed the central plaza on the upper levels, and worked in offices below them, monitoring automated factories in other parts of the station, analyzing and balancing resource needs, and operating mining drones in the asteroid belt. Exactly the same kind of thing you'd see on any other station.

"What do you do for fun?" I asked.

"Oh, the same thing anyone else does. Games, sports, long walks out on the oxygen deck. Gossip. Come on, I'll show you."

We found the recreation area in a set of terraces overlooking the oxygen deck. Water cascading down from fountains near the top filled tubs and pools as it flowed down to a stream that ran across the oxygen deck to the river. Some pools steamed with warmth, some had a thin covering of ice. Most were empty, but there were newgens in groups of twos and threes and fours lounging here and there.

Director Kal turned to me and smiled. "Care to join me for a swim?"

Suddenly, I found it hard to breathe. "Oh, I don't think that's necessary."

From the look in her eyes, I could tell she had more in mind than just a dip in the water.

"Mister Dizen. You're here to learn about our people. As you've seen, we're really no different than you, all very mundane, except for one thing. Sex. If you've come here to learn about us, then there's really only one way to do that."

I felt Shirley's hand on my shoulder. "Actually, Challers, an encounter like this was already planned. It could have come a little later, but given your interest in newgens, I thought today would be perfect for it." She moved next to Kal and took my hand. "Director of art includes the sexual arts, Challers. It's part of the job."

My heart thudded. "You could have warned me."

"Would you have paid any attention during the tour if we had?" Kal kicked off her slippers and descended a set of stairs sculpted into the side of a pool. With her back to me, she pulled her tunic up over her head and laid it on the side. Her slim back was muscular, but not enough to dispel her femininity.

"I guess not."

Shirley took my hand and led me to the edge of the water. "Come on. You can do this."

"Are you coming with me?"

"Oh, of course. I wouldn't miss this for anything."

We stripped off our uniforms and joined Kal in the waist-deep water. I was glad for the luxurious warmth of the water, because otherwise, I would have been trembling. All of the anxiety I had felt talking to the newgens by the river had returned. Back then, I was worried that they would want to have sex with me, but with Kal, it was coming true.

Shirley stood behind me, urging me forward by simply not giving me anywhere else to go.

She whispered, "Touch, Challers. There's nothing to be afraid of. Touch."

I put one hand on Kal's ribs, and she turned her head and smiled over her shoulder at me. She took my hand and moved it around to her chest to cup one small, firm breast. I felt her nipple rub against my fingertips.

Slowly, she turned to face me and lifted her face towards mine. Our lips met and she put her hands on my sides, not quite an embrace, but close. She smelled like butter. Shirley pressed close behind me, squeezing me between their bodies. I felt something brush my thigh.

"Was that . . ."

"Yes, Challers," said Kal, "that was my cock."

"Do you want me to touch it?"

"I would like that very much, but if it makes you uncomfortable, then don't."

I felt my breath catch in my throat. I was as nervous as the first time I was naked with Shirley, or the first time I stole a kiss in the communications room with Valka. All the control and reserve I learned in my sessions with Shirley evaporated.

Shirley reached around me and stroked my cock while Kal's hands caressed my chest and shoulders. My own hands felt most comfortable on Kal's breasts, so I kept them there. I closed my eyes and let my head roll back, enjoying the sensation of four hands roaming over my body.

I could feel Shirley moving around to my side, and then there was a splash and we separated. I opened my eyes. Shirley had lifted Kal out of the water and set her on the side of the pool, so she could bend down and take Kal's rigid cock into her mouth. After a few slow plunges, she took the organ in her hand and turned her head towards me.

"Give me your hand," she said and reached out to me.

In a daze, I gave her my hand, and she pulled it in and put it on Kal's body, just below her cock. Folds of skin connected the underside of her penis with the lips of her pussy. In truth, it was all one organ—no clear boundary where cock ended and pussy began. The entire area was hairless, either from a depilatory or by design. I stroked it as Shirley went back to sucking the male end, and Kal lay back on the hard stone patio that surrounded the pool. Kal took my hand and guided it to her breast, inviting me to play with it the way I had before.

"You like this?" asked Kal, between sighs of pleasure.

I swallowed. I had to admit, the novelty of Kal's body excited me. There was something unnameably frightening about it, but the fear was more like the lurch of going out of an airlock for a hull inspection—not something to be avoided, but an excitement to savor.

"Yes," I said. I was aroused watching Kal become aroused, but also by watching her cock disappear into Shirley's mouth.

"Then after," she said, "it'll be your turn."

My turn for what? The possibilities drove my anxieties to new heights, yet I couldn't deny the erotic power of the images in my imagination. Then Kal arched her back and growled, gripping my hand tight to her chest. Shirley rose from between her legs, licked her lips, and swallowed.

"Marvelous." Kal sighed and opened her eyes. She propped herself up on her elbows and raised an eyebrow at me. "Ready?"

"No," I said, boosting myself up onto the edge of the pool, "but I'm not going to let that stop me."

Shirley and Kal traded places. Kal bent down between my legs and Shirley rose up to kiss me. I tasted Kal's cum on her tongue. It tasted faintly of apples, reminding me that Kal wasn't quite human—at least, not the way I thought of humans. Shirley's breast grazed my chest as she leaned over me, touching just with the tip of her nipple.

At the same time, Kal's lips and tongue played up and down the almost painfully hard shaft of my cock. She was teasing, it seemed, taking her time. With my mouth and hands engaged with Shirley, I could do nothing to encourage Kal. She licked and kissed every part slowly before even making the slightest motion to take it into her mouth, and then it was only the head, and just for a brief moment.

I groaned with frustration into Shirley's mouth. She pulled away and gave me a questioning look.

I looked down and said, "Kal, please . . ."

Kal replaced her mouth with her hand and smiled up at me. "Yes?"

"I can't take any more of this."

"You don't like it? It certainly seems like you do." Her smile turned mischievous.

"No, I mean, please . . ." I needed her mouth back on me; her hand wasn't enough, not nearly enough. "Suck me."

"Gladly." Even inside her mouth, though, she managed to make it last. She moved only enough to maintain my erection at full intensity. I tried to protest, but Shirley put one fat nipple into my mouth and the conversation was over.

I closed my eyes and concentrated, falling back on the meditation techniques Shirley had taught me to reach orgasm faster. Focusing my attention on my cock, I pulled the sensations around me and dove into them, accepting them along with all the erotic imagery that was playing in my imagination. Then, unbidden, Valka's image came to mind. Instead of disapproving, however, I imagined her there, her mouth around my cock, or her breast in my mouth.

I opened my eyes and thrust the images away. Shirley had warned me against that, and I wanted to be there for both of them, a full participant in what we were doing. I took Shirley's breasts in my hands and guided her away from my face.

"I want to watch Kal," I whispered. She nodded and helped me up to a sitting position.

Kal used a technique I had felt Shirley use on me several times before. With my cock nestled in the back of her soft throat, she moved her tongue up and down the underside of my shaft while her hands caressed the base. It felt wonderful, of course. Kal knew as much about oral sex as Shirley did—perhaps more, as she was touching an organ that she herself possessed, more or less.

My orgasm finally arrived, teased to a dizzying height, and I felt my body pulse again and again, filling her mouth with my cum. She tried to swallow each jet as it came, but there was too much, and when the cum started dripping out of her mouth, she pulled back. The last few spurts hit her cheek, chin, and neck. With a groan, I collapsed back into Shirley's arms.

CHAPTER TWENTY-SIX

Shirley and I strolled along the path next to the river. I was quiet, focusing on my thoughts about the experience with Kal.

"You're awfully quiet," said Shirley. "Something bothering you?"

"Does every Scout have sex with a Chevalier newgen?"

Shirley chuckled. "No, you seem to be developing a specialty in newgens, and since the Scouts have need of someone who can operate in those circles, I've been developing your talents that way."

"I see."

She gave me a questioning look. "Is that a problem?"

"Well, I would have liked to have talked about it."

"It wouldn't have been the same experience for you if I had. Was it that bad?"

"It wasn't bad exactly, but I am a little worried."

"About what?"

I took a moment to figure out what to say. "You remember Trace, that cadet who was about to leave for her training cruise? I talked to her before she left. She used to be a man. They put her through the gentank to turn her into a woman because she prefers sex with men."

"Prefers?"

"I guess not exactly. She wasn't capable of having sex with women at all. I suppose that's more than just a preference."

"That makes sense."

"It does? *She* didn't seem to think so."

"Oh, no, I'm talking about her mentor, Umber. He was a woman last time I saw him. I bet he went into the gentank in order to take the job."

"Umber used to be a woman? But he was such a . . ."

"Swaggering fool? Yes, well, he always did like playing a role."

That gave me a bit to think about. Trace's situation seemed a little different in that light.

Shirley put her arm around me and squeezed. "Don't worry. Just because Kal had a penis doesn't mean you're like Trace. We're not going to make you into a woman. At least, not permanently." She saw the look of alarm on my face and chuckled. "Oh, it happens. As something of an educational experience for students who fall behind in certain areas. It can be useful to find out how it feels to be the opposite gender, for some people."

And that turned the whole situation back at me again. Would I want to do that, to feel how it was to be a woman? How about a newgen, like Kal or Suna, or one of the other types I had studied?

"Was there something wrong with Trace?"

"Someone like Trace isn't well suited to being a Scout. I'm surprised they went to such lengths to accommodate her, actually. Do you know any reason why they didn't just send her home?"

"She said that people like her got killed on her station."

"Good enough reason to keep from sending her home. You're worried about her, aren't you?"

"Wouldn't you be? She was miserable."

"I'm sure she'll be fine. As much as Umber can be, well, Umber, he's a dedicated Scout and I'm sure he wants the best for Trace."

"I hope so."

We walked in silence for a few minutes, bringing us down to the water, where we then turned towards the academy.

Shirley scanned the area and frowned. "You know, the odds of us meeting up with him are pretty slim. Chances are, he's out in the fields somewhere fixing a robot, not driving that little cart around."

I shrugged. "I gotta take the chance."

We stayed alert while we walked, keeping conversation to a minimum. I kept the pace slow to give us more time to spot him. We passed the little bower where Shirley and I spent the night, and then after a couple more kilometers, we spotted the dust cloud. That had to be him.

"Vack," I said. "Look how fast he's moving. We'll never catch up."

The dust cloud zipped along the edge of the oxygen deck where the long, high row of buildings that made up the rim rose up out of the terrain.

"That's if it's even him."

The dust cloud suddenly changed direction, moving toward us.

Shirley pointed to a side path running between rows of fruit trees. "Looks like he's going to come up that way."

After walking a short distance up the path, we finally got a good look at the creator of the dust cloud. The truck was the same type that Joco had been driving. Before we could go far up the path, however, Shirley pulled me off the path and under the trees.

"A skimmer," she hissed. "Headed straight for him."

I peered up through the leaves. I couldn't see anything, but I could hear a mechanical whine from off to our left. It got louder, shifting in front of us, then dying down.

Shirley tossed her head back in the direction of the river. "Come on, we should go. The only people who have those skimmers are station security."

"No. I need to know what's going on. This could be *my* fault."

My stomach clenched at the thought that our investigations had put him in danger. I ran towards the sound of the idling turbines, head down under the foliage, moving from tree to tree.

"Challers! Oh, vack . . ."

Shirley quietly moved along behind me.

I saw them before I could really hear them. The whine of the turbines, even at idle, was loud enough to prevent me from hearing their conversation without getting dangerously close. Joco stood a short distance from his truck. He seemed to be explaining something, his palms out in front of him in a gesture of innocence. The two Scouts standing in front of him weren't hearing it. Their words were angry, punctuated with pointed fingers.

One of them drew a pistol. Joco dropped to his knees. I could almost hear him pleading. He hid his face in his hands. The weapon was aimed at his head. My guts wrenched into a knot. There were more cries of innocence.

I wanted to run forward—not knowing what I could do to save him, but I couldn't let it happen without trying.

Not again. This time, I wanted to *do* something.

But Shirley had one hand firmly clamped around my wrist, and her other on the branch of a tree. She shook her head, her eyes wide with fear.

Bang.

Joco slumped to the ground. The two Scouts turned calmly, boarded their craft, and flew away.

I tried to run to him again, but Shirley still held me back. "No, no, wait until they're out of sight," she whispered.

The whine of the skimmer's turbines faded, and we crept out.

He was dead. There was no chance we could have saved him, even if there had been a gentank handy. The bullet had smashed his skull and his blood was seeping into the dust.

I turned and retched.

"We can't stay here," said Shirley. "They'll have called this in; someone will come to clean this up."

"What do you mean, 'called this in?' They just murdered him! We're the ones who need to report this!"

"Those were Scouts, Challers. From Security. That wasn't murder; that was an execution."

"For what? He didn't do anything; he never hurt anyone! He didn't deserve that!"

"I know, Challers, I know. But if we get caught here, we're not going to get better treatment."

She pulled me away, back under the cover of the trees. We hurried away, through the trees for as long as they lasted, and then back out onto the path before Shirley figured we were far enough away.

The Scouts had killed Joco to stop him from talking. One thought kept running through my mind. Could they have known I was trying to find him? My research on the tablet that morning hadn't been secret.

"Should we be going back to the academy?"

"You mean, will they be looking for us? I don't think so. If they had expected us, they wouldn't have just left after they shot him. They probably would have set up some kind of ambush. I don't know exactly why they killed him, or why they waited until now to do it, but I don't think it's anything you did. They may have detected your queries without knowing exactly where they were coming from and just decided not to take any more chances with him. Whatever it was, if they knew you were coming today, they wouldn't have just flown away like that."

"And what if they're waiting for us when we get back?"

"We don't have a lot of choice. This is their station. If they want us, they can find us. The alternative is to go down to the docking bays and steal a ship. We could probably manage it— they're not guarded—but after that, there'd be no turning back. They would be on the lookout for us wherever we went."

I sighed. "And I'd never see Valka again."

"That would be the least of your worries. We need to go back to the academy and act as if nothing happened."

"How can I work for an organization that does that to someone?"

She moved in front of me and looked me in the eye. "Challers, you haven't got any choice. If you don't, you'll wind up like him."

I crossed my arms. "They've got a secret they'll kill to protect. I'm going to find out what it is. This isn't just about Masters anymore."

"And Valka?"

"It's not Valka you're worried about, is it? It's Robert. If you go rushing off with me on this, it's him you would never see again."

"Challers . . ."

I narrowed my eyes and gave her the glare her cowardice had earned. "Don't worry. I won't involve you any more in any of this. Just keep yourself out of it, and I won't drag you in again."

I stepped around her and continued down the path.

We walked the rest of the way in silence.

By the time we got back to the promenade, the light shift was over.

"You go on back," I told Shirley. "I have some things to take care of."

"You're not going to do anything rash, are you?"

"Just go on to bed; I'll be along."

"Be careful, Challers. For both our sakes."

I climbed up into the hideout to find Valka already hard at work.

She glanced over, gave me a quick smile, and returned her attention to the screens. "Any luck with Joco?"

"None at all. He's dead. The Scouts killed him."

"What?"

I told her what had happened, leaving out the sexual encounter with Kal. The closer I got to the moment when Joco was killed, the angrier and more grief-stricken I became. I was nearly sobbing by the time I got to the end.

"The whole time it was happening, all I could see was Bendel—like it was happening all over again."

Valka sprung from her chair and wrapped her arms around me. She was the only person who could understand, the only person who could comfort me. I let the tears flow. I had thought my grieving for Bendel was over, but the wound ripped wide open again with Joco's murder.

When I was only an infant, my parents took in a young man who had lost his mother and father in an accident. He watched my sister and me, and cleaned up around our quarters, in exchange for sleeping space in the corner and a share of the food. It wasn't much, but it gave my mother more time to work and that was good for all of us. Bendel had a girlfriend, a pretty young woman named Teltie, who was at our quarters often enough that I thought of her like a big sister.

Bendel died because he had tried to keep the Merchants from taking Teltie away. He stood in their way, shouting threats, and finally picked up a chair and started beating them with it. They shoved him away and Teltie disappeared into the Merchant ship. A few days later, a Fleet frigate arrived. Three Marines walked straight from the airlock to our quarters, dragged Bendel out into the main passageway, and shot him while I watched.

The hatch clanked open.

"Oh! You're here." Zun climbed through the opening and pulled it shut.

I tried to regain my composure. "Sorry, I didn't see you coming."

"Is something wrong?" His glance darted back and forth between Valka and me.

A few deep breaths got me straightened out enough to talk. "Zun, this is Valka. We're . . . um . . . we were recruited together."

Zun smiled and nodded. "Pleased to meet you."

Valka nodded back. "Do you know anything about the man who set all this up?" She waved her hand through the holographic displays hovering over the tablet.

"No, no, it was all here when I found out about the place."

Valka raised an eyebrow and gave him the look I knew well, the look of being caught in a lie. "Are you sure?"

Zun looked at me again, then took a deep breath. "I can't tell you."

Frowning, Valka touched the side of the tablet. "This ID chip belongs to Joco Gata. Does that name sound familiar?"

This was getting nowhere

"Zun, he's dead," I said.

His hand went to his mouth. "No. No, I don't believe it."

"Some Scouts found him, shot him out in the fields. I saw it happen."

Zun went pale and staggered. I caught him and got him settled in a chair. "Oh, poor Joco!"

While Valka made sure Zun didn't pass out completely, I went over to the drying racks and packed a pipe. I hadn't taken any smoke in a while, but this seemed like an excellent time to get back in the habit. I returned to the center of the hideout and drew on the pipe to get it lit.

"Zun, I need to know if Joco ever said anything about someone named *Cassandra*. Anything at all."

He shook his head, stunned, staring. I offered him the pipe and he took a desultory puff.

Valka took his hand between hers. "Zun."

Zun spoke softly. "No. But Joco was always closer to Suna than to me. She might know something."

"Where do we find her?" I asked.

"Sector four. Ovor maternity school. She left a few days ago." Zun took a longer draw on the pipe and let it out slowly. "She won't be back for twenty days or so."

I nodded. "Thank you, Zun. I want you to go home. I wouldn't want you to get into any trouble with the Scouts over this. Don't come back until things blow over."

He nodded and rose to his feet. The smoke had calmed him down some and, with a little help, he managed to get to the ground safely, and then off towards his community. Valka and I stood under the robot and watched him disappear into the darkness.

"I'm going to have to go find Suna," I said.

"How are you going to get there? It's way out in sector four. You can't just go for a walk."

"I'll figure something out. I can't make another 'field trip,' and not just because it would be suspicious to take two of them close together like that. Maternity school is strictly for Ovors. They wouldn't let me in."

"You could wait for her to come back."

"And what if the Scouts know about her affiliation with Joco? At the very least, I have to warn her."

"I could send her a message through the system. It wouldn't be traceable back to us."

"Yes, but if it were intercepted, it would tell them that she's involved. The act of warning her might put her in danger."

"Sounds like there's only one way to do it. You're going to need to become an Ovor."

Chapter Twenty-Seven

I tried to remember, standing in front of the gentank, exactly why I was going on this crazy mission. I could just wait until Suna was done with maternity school, couldn't I?

No, she was in danger, and she had to know. If we were lucky, the Scouts had no interest in her. If not, they'd kill her to keep whatever she knew about Cassandra secret. Security had waited until Joco was alone to kill him, so I hoped we could get to her at the school before they did anything.

This was necessary.

Valka opened a panel in the side of the gentank and yanked out a connector.

"What are you doing?"

"This unit has a bad communications module. It's only on the network intermittently. If I disconnect it, it's not going to raise any alarms, because it's already on the list to be repaired. But since it's not in a place where it's needed right now, no one will be out to fix it anytime soon. It won't be able to report that we used it, or what we did. When we're done, we can wipe its memory and no one will ever know."

"We have all the supplies we need?"

"For the last time, yes, everything checks out. Now get in, I'll keep an eye out while you are inside and distract anyone that might come along. What are you afraid of? Everything's all set. Just get in."

Trying hard to keep from shaking, I pulled off my uniform, unclipped the air mask from the side of the cabinet, and strapped it over my head. I took a deep breath and settled my body in the pale blue gel. It was warmer than I expected, and thicker. I smelled something in the air, and had just enough time to decide that it was the anesthetic before I was unconscious.

I woke up slowly, the interference gradually clearing in my head. Gentle hands took my shoulders and pulled me up out of the gel and cleared it from my eyes.

Valka smiled. "How do you feel?"

"A little weak, and a little sore, but . . . oh . . ." My voice had changed. It still sounded like me, in a way I couldn't put my finger on, but it was higher. I looked down to see four full, round breasts. "I'm female."

"Of course you are, silly. They don't let men into maternity school, do they?"

Valka helped me out of the tank and over into a nearby shower to rinse off the gel.

Somehow I thought I would be made into a *male* Ovor. When Valka found the necessary template to load into the gentank, she hadn't been very specific about what, exactly, it would do. There was nothing to do about it now. There was no time to get a new template, no time to get back into the gentank. I would just have to deal with it and focus on the task before us.

Valka's hands felt wonderful on my body. It wasn't overtly sexual, but there was a sensuality to it that made me feel comfortable and warm. She worked her way down, encouraging the sticky stuff to let go under the warm water.

She stopped before my mind had cleared completely. She put me into the warm air vent to dry off and I felt the abrupt loss of her touch like oxygen stolen from my lungs. It took me a minute to catch my breath. When I was dry, she handed me shorts and a shirt of bright colored fabric that we had fabricated for our trip.

While I dressed, Valka stripped off her uniform. I was glad to feel a little tingle from watching her disrobe, because it meant I was still attracted to her in spite of the change. I put the mask over her face, helped her to climb in, and ran the commands to engage the template we had loaded. With the lid closed and the cycle locked in, I went out to the front room.

The maintenance robot we had brought with us lay partially disassembled in the middle of the floor. I knelt and started tinkering with it, using a set of tools left from when Valka had been there. This was how we spent the hour waiting for the gentank to do its work. If anyone came to investigate, I had an excuse for being there. On the headquarters station, just like at home, people doing repair work were invisible, especially if what they were working on was as humble as a maintenance robot. We had seen folks doing this kind of work many times and none of them wore Scout white or black. Still, I had never seen an Ovor working this kind of job, and I feared that if someone were to find me, the novelty of it would be enough to attract attention.

I could feel a kind of warm heaviness coming over me, but it wasn't drowsiness. It didn't distract me much and I was able to keep watch without much difficulty, so I passed it off as an Ovor thing and just kept poking around. Even with a prepared cover story, I worried that someone would come by and ask what was going on. If someone went in the back and saw the gentank running, everything would be ruined.

My fears turned out to be unfounded, and after a tense hour, the gentank beeped that its cycle was complete. I hurried over to it and helped Valka out. Like I had been, she was weak and sore, and needed help to get into the shower. As I rinsed the gel off, I could feel the warm feeling growing throughout my body. My breathing was getting quick and I felt like I wasn't getting enough air.

"I think the steam is getting to me. I'm going to go sit down; I don't feel well."

Valka stepped in front of me and gave me a lopsided grin. "You're not sick, Challers."

"No, I'm serious. I think something might have gone wrong with the gentank."

"Nothing went wrong." She put her hand on one of my breasts and leaned in close to kiss me. "You're not sick. You're aroused."

"This is how it feels?"

She nodded. "Yes. This is how it feels." She pulled my shirt up over my head and threw it out of the shower. "Your nipples are hard. Your face is flushed. I know the signs."

I didn't understand. I knew what arousal felt like, or at least I thought I did. Maybe it did feel different for a woman. I nodded weakly, too stunned by the possibilities to speak.

"I don't think we should waste this opportunity. Don't you agree?" She pulled off my shorts and gently pushed me against the wall. "We've got a few minutes. Let me show you what you can feel."

Her lips met mine, and then she slowly dragged her four breasts across my chest. Our nipples touched, sending little flashes of pleasure down my spine.

It was really going to happen. Finally, Valka and I were going to have sex. Just the idea filled me with joy.

Her fingertips touched the skin just below my navel and moved slowly down towards my pussy.

"Please don't tease me," I said between gasps.

"Oh, but that's the best part. Have to build up the anticipation." She traced a lazy circle over my abdomen and thighs.

I grabbed her hand and shoved it against my crotch. "Do it, Valka. Please."

She chuckled and stroked my pussy lips. A part of my mind was aware that they had become warm and swollen, but that part was now very small and quiet compared to the lather of anticipation in the rest of it.

Then she knelt at my feet, gently pushed my thighs apart, and licked. At first, it was a tentative touch—a stroke here, a poke there—but gradually, she gave it more and more energy.

My eyes practically fell out of my head. How could anything feel like that? How could anything feel so good? I gasped with the pure pleasure of it. My head thumped against the wall of the shower but I didn't care. My knees shook and wanted to buckle, but she held me there, as the broad softness of her tongue ran through my new sex, dragging over my clit with every stroke. There was no finesse, no exploration, just a relentless, insistent, driving stimulation.

Oh yes. This was arousal, like nothing I had ever felt before. Each touch of her tongue pushed me another inch higher on a wave that seemed to have no crest. Desperate to reach the top, I grabbed my breasts, squeezing them, pinching my sensitive nipples between my fingers. It wasn't like my cock had been shrunk down to the size of my pinky finger without losing a single nerve ending—though, in a way, that was probably true. It was a completely different experience. My consciousness seemed to expand rather than contract, taking in everything. The feel of steam in my lungs, the faint antiseptic scent of the gel, the slick feel of my skin under my hands, the hard floor under my feet, and the unbelievable touch of Valka's tongue on my clit—it all combined in a synaesthetic whirl of sensation, twisted together in a mind-bending cyclone of pleasure.

I whimpered something incomprehensible as the first shudders of true orgasm racked my body. My vision blurred. My knees buckled and, once again, Valka held me up, pinned to the wall, helpless under her tongue. As I paused and caught my breath, I thought that would be it, but Valka kept at it, and within moments, I felt my body launching into another cycle of arousal, even greater than the first. I cried out this time, her name I think, and I felt her slip her fingers inside me. In a more lucid moment, I would have been able to name the places she touched, but at that moment, I was too far gone for conscious thought. My whole body quivered as a third orgasm ran through me and I screamed in ecstasy. Every orgasm I had ever had as a man paled in comparison.

She relented then, finally, standing again under my shoulder, helping me to stay on my feet. I stared, mute, unable to put any of my experience into words. She put a gentle hand over my pussy, as if to protect it from further stimulation.

"When this is over," she said, "I think you will be the best lover the Scouts have ever known."

Then she flicked a finger across my nipple and shudders, weaker this time, echoed through my body again. I put my hands over them, but I had only two hands and four breasts. She flicked again and another spasm made me let out a little gasp.

Valka giggled and I had to laugh a little myself. Then she flicked a finger against my clit, and the laughter dissolved into another sigh of pleasure.

"Stop," I said. My voice was little more than a breath. "That's . . . oh . . . enough. You've made your point."

Then she kissed me. It wasn't like the quick little pecks we had shared now and then, but a deep, languorous kiss, making full use of tongue and lips and teeth.

When I regained something of my composure, we climbed into the warm air vent and dried each other off.

"I have something I need to tell you," I said, my higher voice still sounding unfamiliar to my ears.

She shushed me. "It'll keep. We have an hour ride in the transit car in front of us. There will be plenty of time to talk."

We tied our hair back in braids and dressed in the clothes we had prepared.

I knew, then, why it was that more Scouts didn't go through this kind of transformation. There was a disconnectedness, as if everything that was happening to me was artificial, a simulation. The change had a price, I could tell, a price borne by living through the slightly altered perceptions of a body not wholly my own. In time, I could get used to it, but going through this kind of change too often probably wouldn't be good for my mental state.

As we made our way carefully through the empty section of the academy, my thoughts drifted to Trace. She had gone through something similar to this and hated it. I could understand like I couldn't before. I loved the feel of a woman's body, so having one of my own to play with wasn't such a terrible thing. If I didn't feel that way, though, this body could easily be a prison.

Once Valka had diverted control of the transit car and we were on our way, she turned to me with a serious look in her eye. "All right," she said. "Something's on your mind."

I had to take a moment to collect myself, to remember what I had wanted to say after we had gotten out of the shower. Then another moment to think of exactly how to say it.

"I love you, Valka. Even with everything that's happened, I still love you."

She giggled and shook her head. "That's just the hormones. A really good orgasm can make you feel like that for a while. Don't pay it any attention."

"No, I felt like this before. I'm sure of it." I brought my gaze up to her eyes. "And I think you still love me, too."

"Tell me that when you're a man again, and we'll talk." She gave me a broader grin than I had ever seen.

"There's something else," I said.

She nodded.

"I love Shirley, too. When I thought I had lost you, when I gave up hope, I turned to her, and made something of a bond."

"I hoped you would."

I leaned over in the seat and hugged her. Maybe it was just the lingering chemical influence of the encounter, but in that moment, I could not imagine loving her any more than that. She was perfect.

Chapter Twenty-Eight

The trip to the Ovor maternity school took something like an hour, and Valka and I talked the whole way. I coached her a little on Ovor customs. I didn't know whether the Ovors here at headquarters would follow the same rules as their counterparts out on the stations, but it couldn't hurt to know.

But that was a cover. I was nervous. I couldn't get the sex we'd had in the shower out of my mind. When the conversation paused, I just came out and said it.

"Do you like me better like this? I mean, as a female."

She gave me a quirky little smile and looked out the front window of the transit car. "Better isn't exactly the right word. More like, I just couldn't stop myself. When I saw that you were all excited like that? I wanted to just make you come and come."

"Do you like women more than men?"

"No. I like men too. Men are . . ." She shrugged. "Different."

"Of course. What I mean is, would you rather have sex with a woman than a man? Because there was this cadet, Trace, who liked having sex with men. Only men. The Scouts turned him into a woman."

"That's rather drastic."

"She hates it. Hates her partner, hates her life. I worry about her sometimes."

"Well, you don't have to worry about me. I like having sex with men just fine."

"Fine?"

"All right, so Masters isn't exactly the best partner in the world. It's not like I can't orgasm with him. I'd just like it better with someone a bit less wrapped up inside himself."

"Like . . ."

She rolled her eyes. "Challers, we're *not* going to be having sex any time soon."

"We just had sex."

"I mean with you as a man."

"Why not? We're already breaking all kinds of rules here, enough to get us killed, what's one more?"

Her shoulders slumped and she closed her eyes. She sagged in her seat. A breath laden with emotional cargo passed her lips and she shook her head. "I can't."

I put my arm around her and pulled her close.

"You don't understand, Challers. You *can't* understand. You're so innocent, so sweet . . ."

She sniffed and sobbed. I had a hard time keeping myself from breaking down, too, and I didn't even know what she was crying about.

"Valka, what's wrong? You can tell me. You can *trust* me. Okay, so I'm a virgin. So what? So are you. What's the big deal?"

That just released a whole new burst of tears. "No, Challers. No."

"Don't do this to me. Don't tell me there's some reason that you don't want me, and then not tell me what it is. Is it something I did? Something I said? Something that makes me always a boyfriend, never a lover?"

"Oh, Challers, no. You've always been a good guy."

"Then what? I think I deserve that much, at least. To know why? Don't I?"

She took a long, calming breath. I recognized the meditation trick from Physicality class. She spoke quietly with her eyes on the floor. "For a long, long time, back on the Station, my father was . . ." She swallowed. "He would come in my room at night and . . ." Her voice trailed off and she choked a bit.

"What?" She was trying to get me to fill in the empty spots for her, but the blanks were just *blank*.

Her tears suddenly flashed into anger. "Do I have to diagram it out for you? Do I have to show you a damn holo? Vack, Challers, how dense can you be?" She was nearly shouting at me.

"Are you saying he beat you up?"

"No! Come on, Challers! Don't make me say it!'

"Say *what*? I don't know what you're talking about!" I slapped my hand on the seat between us.

She turned and shouted at me. "He'd fuck me, Challers! He'd vacking *fuck* me!"

The image of Valka's father, huge and stern, loomed in my imagination. How could someone so much in authority take such advantage? I couldn't imagine why anyone would want to do anything like that. It was completely alien. But he had never liked me and this told me why. The thought of him, on top of . . .

No. I wasn't going to imagine it. I pushed the thought aside and tried to calm my angry stomach. I breathed, remembering my meditation exercises, keeping oxygen in a brain that very much wanted to fade into hypoxia. Time went by, seconds that felt like hours, and I realized that Valka's expression was shading from anger to resignation.

"See? You're horrified. Vack! I shouldn't . . ." She sobbed thickly. "I shouldn't have said anything."

"What? No, no, Valka, I'm just stunned." I put my hand on her shoulder. I felt like an idiot. I couldn't think of what to say that would make things any better, so I just said what I felt. "I'm horrified by what happened. I'm not horrified by you. I love you. I could never be horrified with *you*. Come here." I turned her around, held her close, and let her cry.

After a long time, her tears dried up and her gasping sobs quieted to quivering but mostly even breaths.

"I'm still here," I said when I judged the time was right. "I'm stunned and I don't know what to say, but I'm still here, and I still love you."

"Thank you." She managed to uncurl herself enough to give me a peck on the cheek, and then she lay her head down on my lap.

I stroked her hair. "I wish I could sing or something. I'd love to sing you a lullaby, but I don't know any."

"That's okay. Just being with you is enough."

I looked up to see a light approaching on the side of the tunnel. "Unfortunately, you can't stay there much longer. We're here."

She blinked and looked around as if waking from a deep sleep. "We are?" Her voice seemed to convey dread at the end of our trip.

"You can wait here, if you like. With luck this won't take long."

"No," she said, getting to her feet. "I'm fine. I'm coming with you. You might need me." She sniffed and rubbed her eyes.

"All right."

There was a sign at the station indicating that the maternity school was just up the main corridor, at the end of which, we found a pair of huge wooden doors with an iron clapper attached to the front of one. That impressed me; making anything out of real wood was unusual, let alone anything that large.

"I don't see an intercom or anything," said Valka.

"I guess this is the way to summon someone." I lifted the clapper from the iron plate that was under it and let it fall back against the door. It made a satisfyingly loud noise in the quiet corridor.

"It's dark shift; do you think anyone will come?"

"They have to have someone to handle emergencies in the middle of the night. Someone will come."

It took another two knocks, but eventually the door opened. An Ovor girl, just on the edge of adolescence, pushed the door open and looked us over. She was wearing a white thigh-length robe with long flowing sleeves. I started to speak, but she put a finger to my lips and shook her head. Evidently, we were to keep silent. I nodded to Valka and followed her in.

The corridors were dark except for a pale orange glow coming from recessed indirect lights near the ceiling. The girl led us a short way down a side hall and indicated a doorway. Through it, we could see a small sleeping chamber.

"No, no, I . . ."

The girl stopped me with an upraised hand. Clearly, she was not going to hear anything I said. Before I could try to get through to her, Valka pulled me in and closed the door. Behind it, there was a pair of short robes similar in cut to the one the girl had been wearing, but blue in color.

"What are you doing? We need to get to Suna."

She glared at me and whispered, "And we're not going to do that by talking to that one. Look, there aren't any cameras and I don't think the door is locked. Once she's gone back to bed, we'll sneak out and have a look around. Maybe we can find Suna." She handed one of the robes to me, and then put on the other one.

"Of course. I'm sorry, I guess I was just too focused on getting to her as soon as possible."

"Just keep your head straight and your eyes open, Challers." Valka poked her head out and looked both ways. "Looks like it's empty. Come on."

As we crept through the empty halls, I shrugged my shoulders and pulled at the garment around me. It felt heavy and constricting even though it was only loosely tied.

"What's wrong with you?" Valka whispered.

"I guess I got used to wearing the cadet uniform."

"Well get used to *this* and keep alert. You're not doing me any good like this."

All the rooms along the corridor where we were staying were the same—small apartments with two beds. Some were occupied, but most were empty. Luckily, the doors were very quiet and we could peek inside without waking anyone.

About halfway down the hallway, I stopped. "We're not going to find her here."

"No?"

"No. All these Ovors? They're not carrying eggs. No belly. I'm not sure what they're here for, but it's not for help giving birth."

"Hmm, okay, so?"

"So Suna came here with a belly full of eggs. I'm thinking she'll be in a different wing."

We doubled back and went out to the entrance. Sure enough, across the main hall, there was another archway. We crossed over and started looking through those rooms.

As I had suspected, the Ovors on this side of the school had huge bellies, even larger than a pregnant puregen would look. Unfortunately, this made our search harder. I had to get a good look at each one's face to know it wasn't Suna. Still, I felt that we were on the right track and the corridor wasn't very long. We were going to find her.

That's when I blew it.

I opened the door and saw a male Ovor dressed in a green robe, sitting in bed, reading from a tablet. He looked up, saw me before I could duck back out of sight, and smiled. He gestured for me to come closer. I shook my head and pulled the door closed.

We ran back towards our room, pausing at the corner to look back. His door was opening. My heart thundering, I pointed back towards our room.

"He never saw you," I hissed. "Get back, I'll try to distract him."

Reluctantly, she complied. Once she was out of sight, I crept back out into the hallway.

He smiled again, a genuine smile full of warmth. He gestured for me to join him in his room.

I went in, he followed me, and he closed the door behind us.

"There," he said quietly. "We can talk now."

"Isn't that against the rules or something?"

"So is wandering the halls during dark shift." He stepped over to a low table and poured two small glasses of a thick white liquid, and offered one to me.

I took it, but didn't drink. "I couldn't sleep. I was just . . ."

"You were looking for someone, maybe?" He took a sip from his glass and licked the residue from his lips. "Maybe I can give you what you came looking for."

There was a twitch in the front of his robe and if it was what I thought it was, I wanted no part of it.

"I'm looking for a friend. I need to give her a message."

"Maybe I can help you. Then we both can accomplish our goals."

"And your goal is?"

"Expansion of the species, of course. That's what we all want, here, don't we?" He pulled off the belt of his robe and it fell open. Underneath, he was naked. His cock, only half-erect, seemed monstrous.

I gasped.

"There's nothing to be afraid of. In fact, if experience is any guide, I'm sure you'll quite like it."

"No." I went to the table and set the drink down. My hands were trembling. "No, I don't think I will. I'll go back to my room now, thank you."

His hand caught my arm, just above the elbow. His voice went cold. "We have a duty to perform. Leave now, and I'll report you to the headmistress."

"I said *no*." I grabbed his hand and twisted, forcing it up and behind his back in a classic armlock.

He squawked in surprise, but I knew he was going to shout for help any second. I needed to end this confrontation, fast and quiet. My other arm went around his throat and he began struggling in earnest.

We fell, bounced off the table, and landed on the floor in a heap. The impacts were far less forgiving than falls on the practice mat back at the academy. Still, I managed to keep my forearm across his throat, stifling any shouts he might make.

He was bigger than me, though, and stronger. He grabbed my arm with his free hand and pulled. Air flowed into his lungs again.

Instead of screaming, he purred, "Oh, so that's how you like it, eh? I can play that game."

With his arm still in my grasp, he pulled his legs under him and rose up onto his hands and knees. I tried to force his arm higher, but he had tensed the muscles in it and I wasn't strong enough to make the most of my advantage.

I tried to rear back, forcing his arm into an even more painful position, but he pushed off and flipped backwards, slamming me into the floor and blasting the air out of my lungs. He pulled his arm free and clambered to his feet while I lay gasping.

"Not bad," he said. "You're pretty scrappy."

He pulled his robe off his shoulders and threw it aside. His cock stood fully erect. The bastard was turned on by this. The thing loomed over me.

I tried to speak, but I couldn't get any air. I shook my head, nearly choking. He knelt down and pulled my robe open.

"Tsk, tsk, you're not supposed to be wearing anything under this. Another violation. Quite a naughty girl, aren't you?"

I coughed, finally able to draw half a breath. "No," I croaked. "Stop."

"Oh, we've gone way past that point," he said, leaning forwards to grab my neck with his hand. He leaned on me, hard, and I had to hold him back with both hands to keep him from crushing my neck. My shorts, tied at the waist, pulled away when he yanked on the knots.

Thrashing, I tried to get him off me, but he was too heavy, too strong. I felt his cock bump against my thigh.

"Hold still," he growled. "You're not going to do the Service any good this way."

The Service? Did he mean the *Scouts*? Of course he did.

There was no time to consider the implications. His cock bumped against my thigh again, and then he was in position. Through the red haze clouding my vision, I saw a smile of satisfaction come over his face

"Just relax," he said, "and think of the Scouts."

CHAPTER TWENTY-NINE

No. It couldn't end like this. I wasn't going to allow it. I grabbed his thumb, prying it loose from my neck, and yanked.

It broke with an audible snap. He growled and pulled back, cradling his injured hand. I reached up for the bottle on the table next to us and swung it with all my strength at his head.

He dodged. It landed on his shoulder with a crunch. He gave a strangled cry and collapsed to the floor. I scrambled to my feet, still dizzy from lack of air, and brought the bottle down again.

He lay still.

I've killed him. My first thought spun through my brain and I retched, thankful that there was nothing in my stomach to bring up. I bent down and put my fingers on his neck. There was a pulse, weak but steady.

The door opened. I spun around, ready to use my improvised weapon on whoever had come to investigate the scuffle.

Valka flinched. "No! Challers, it's me!"

I put the bottle down and pulled her into a hug. "He was about to rape me. I had to . . . I had to . . ."

She put my head down on her shoulder and patted my back. "It's all right now; he can't hurt you."

After a minute or two of soothing, I got my head back together and slipped out of her arms. "We have to do something about him, in case he wakes up."

"Don't worry," she said, taking the bottle. "I'll handle it. Go look for Suna. I'll catch up with you."

"You have something to tie him up with?"

"I'll find something. Go on."

I crept back out into the hallway, still trembling but glad to have something to do. I searched more carefully now, listening for movement and peeking before entering fully. As the number of available rooms dwindled, I worried that I was wrong, that Suna wasn't there, that this whole endeavor would turn into a fiasco.

And then I found her. She slept, facing the door, her face serene in the dim light spilling in from the hallway. Relief swept over me and I slipped inside.

I knelt down beside the bed and shook her shoulder. "Suna. Wake up."

She blinked awake and squinted at my face. "Hmm?"

"It's me, Challers?"

"You're not Challers," she mumbled, eyes fluttering closed.

"I used the gentank so I could come talk to you. Suna, you're in terrible danger."

"Mmm. Thanks for the warning."

I shook her again, whispering desperately, "Suna! They shot Joco."

Her eyes opened. "What?"

"They shot Joco Gata."

"Who did? Why?"

"The Scouts. I saw it happen. Suna, you're in danger. If they find out that Joco built the hideout, if they trace you to it, they'll come after you, too."

She pushed herself up to sit on the edge of the bed. "How did he die?"

"They shot him. They flew out to where he was working in a skimmer, got out, asked him some questions, and shot him. They think he was trying to look into Cassandra."

The color drained from her face.

"That name means something to you," I said, trying not to make it sound like an accusation. "You have to tell me what you know."

She glanced at the door, then back at me. "I promised Joco I'd never tell, but it looks like that doesn't matter now. Challers—he knew too much. If I tell you, you'll know too much, too."

"If they learn that I came out here to talk to you, I'm dead anyway. Tell me."

She closed her eyes and shook her head. "I can't. I can't be part of it again."

"I need to know what happened to her. I'm going to find her. Did Joco ever tell you?"

"You won't be able to get to her." She sighed and covered her face with her hands. "I can't believe he's dead."

"If you want to fight back against the people who killed him, you have to tell me what you know."

"All right, all right." She took a deep breath. "He was always something of a loose crate, always bucking the rules and making trouble. It eventually came down that he had to do something to raise his prestige, or get forced out. Well, he couldn't count on finding a new metallic belt, or charting any distant stars, so he went on a recruiting run and found Cassandra and Masters. She turned out to have a real talent with the gentank. When she submitted her first research project, on the possibility of editing templates to alter or improve the final product, command went berserk. They had never seen anyone with a mind for gentank science like hers. They took her away. When Joco started looking into it, they forcibly retired him."

"Did he find out where they took her?"

"Yes. There's a research station in Globular Cluster X-42. It's orbiting a type-A supergiant on the side closest to the galactic disk."

"Is there anything else you can tell me?"

"A ship goes out there once a month to bring supplies and personnel. It's the most secure place anywhere, even more so than here."

"What's it called?"

"Everest Station. Are you really going to try to go there?"

"Originally, I was just trying to reunite Masters with Cassandra, but it's more than that now. The Scouts are corrupt. I can't work for them anymore, and if I can crash their system a little by getting Cassandra out of their hands, then I'm going to do that. This is personal."

"Good luck, Challers. I don't know where you get the courage for this. Try not to get killed, okay?"

I chuckled. "I'll make it as hard as I can. Have you got somewhere safe you can go?"

"I can stay here. They've been asking for people to stay on full time, and I'm actually pretty happy doing this." She rubbed her stomach. "I don't think the Scouts will bother me. It's supposed to be a retreat from all that."

"Good." I gave her a hug and a peck on the lips. We had, after all, been lovers once and I felt better knowing that she'd be safe. "Do you know of any way we can slip out, right now?"

"Nothing is locked. Anyone who wants to leave can just leave. It's not that kind of place."

I started to tell her about the man in the other room and what he'd tried to do, but I decided she didn't need to know. If I could just walk out, I would just walk out

"Take care of yourself."

"Goodbye, Challers." She lay back on the bed and I pulled the sheet back up over her.

I filled Valka in on everything I had learned on the way back to the academy.

When I was done, she frowned.

"Doesn't something strike you as odd about what happened there, Challers, especially given how easy it was to leave?"

"No, not really."

"Your research paper said that Ovors can choose whether their eggs will become fertilized."

"Yes, that's true. There's a gland that secretes a spermicide in the vagina unless the Ovor specifically empties it before sex. That was in the report."

"And the guy who tried to rape you was clearly trying to fertilize you."

"I see what you mean." I pondered a moment. "Maybe he assumed that since I was there, I had already taken care of that?"

"Maybe. I've been trying to find out where that gland is, and I can't feel it. There doesn't seem to be a muscle or anything to empty the gland. Isn't it supposed to be under conscious control?"

"Yes, but maybe that's just because we got made this way in the gentank. We just don't have the right memories or something. That doesn't make any sense, though. The gentank is supposed to wire up the nerves to handle the new body shape—otherwise, you wouldn't be able to walk when you get out."

"Right. Something else has crossed my mind and if it's true, things are worse than we thought. First of all, that 'maternity school' hasn't been there long, or the Ovors would be overrunning the station. From what I could see, they should be producing eggs by the hundreds every month, and you don't see thousands of Ovors around the station. Just a few hundred."

"Okay, so it hasn't been around long."

"Second, Cassandra is this incredible genius with templates and the gentank, and she's been working at this Everest Station for what, six years now?"

"Right."

"What if the first modification she did was to take away that gland from the Ovor template."

"Why would they do that?"

"Look around. This station was clearly built for a much larger population. What happened to them? Where did they go? Not only that, look at the way the Scouts will take just about anyone who fits their psychological profiles. Look at how they tolerate all kinds of bizarre behavior in what's supposed to be a military service. They need people desperately and that's the one thing they can't just manufacture."

"Unless you've got a race of Ovors that have lots of eggs."

"Exactly."

"So if they created the maternity school when they got the altered Ovor template, and they're using it to repopulate the station. So what?"

"That comes around to my third consideration. What do the Scouts and all the other services need the stations for?"

"Oh, raw materials, manufacturing . . . no, wait, that's not true. They told us so many times I just accepted it, but there's all the manufacturing and resources they need right here."

"What they need them for is people. People raised in the right kind of poverty, raised in the right kind of repressed, twisted culture that when the Fleet or the Merchants or the Scouts come along, they don't make too much of a fuss about having their children carted away. Do you know what my mother said when Palla Rossing got taken by the Merchants? She said, 'At least she'll have enough to eat every day.'"

I thought back to the day I said goodbye to my own mother. She hadn't made even the slightest protest to me leaving the station. She saw it as a way to a better life.

"Oh, vack."

"Vack is right, Challers. If this experiment works, they won't need the stations anymore."

"They need the stations. They need them to be separate, so if there's a revolt, they're easily isolated, easily purged."

"Fine. They can bring in the gentanks and force everyone through them. Then it won't be ten or twenty overpop in a year, it'll be a hundred, two hundred. The ships could stop by every month and pick up another load. "

"Okay, it sounds to me like you've got something, but one thing still doesn't add up. Why are there so few Scouts? If they're getting a couple Scouts a year from every station, that'd be, what, a few hundred at a time. They could fill up the academy right now."

"They're competing with the Fleet and the Merchants, remember, and they need people too."

"But why? There must be something . . . of course. Pirates."

It was my turn to leave her puzzled. "Hmm?"

"Okay, we've got a lot of assumptions strung along with only a few facts, but so far, everything lines up . . . especially if the Pirates aren't just scattered raiders, but a full military force that's fighting against them. You've seen the histories; there have been wars across the galaxy that left it with a quarter or even half of its population dead. Doesn't it look like that's what's been happening here? They have to be desperate for manpower."

"And these hyper-fertile Ovors are the perfect answer to that problem. Challers, we have to go get Cassandra. It's not just for Masters, not just for revenge. We can't risk this going any further. She's the key to it all; without her, they can't make the changes to the templates."

"But they already have them."

"You know as well as I do that an initial design never goes completely perfect. They're going to need to adjust things for this project to work. Taking Cassandra away from them is going to be the best way to keep them from doing that."

"So what do we do?"

"When we get back, we need to convince Masters and Shirley to go along with us. Once we graduate, we'll have two ships; we can go looking for Everest Station."

"And then what? Four people aren't going to be able to just walk onto the station and take her."

"We can figure that out when the time comes. For now, our job is to lay low, stay out of trouble, and graduate."

"Right. I just hope I can keep up the charade that long."

"What charade? You've seen the cadets. How many of them look happy?"

I thought of Trace. It wouldn't take much acting after all.

"You're right."

I steeled myself. I could do it. My path was clear. While the future didn't look rosy, I could see the way that might lead to making things right.

We talked some more, making plans on how to stay in touch so the Scouts wouldn't be able to hear us, plans on how to approach getting Shirley and Masters to help us.

Then the car arrived at the academy transit hub and the doors opened.

Shirley stood on the dock, a pistol on her hip, flanked by two similarly armed Scouts—all three with grim expressions.

My mentor's voice creaked under the strain of speaking. "Cadet Challers Dizen, Cadet Valka Parl, you are under arrest."

CHAPTER THIRTY

"NO!" screamed Valka, rushing out of the car. "You can't help them! Shirley, don't you understand? They will never let you be with Robert! It's a lie. The prestige ladder, the lotteries—they're all lies. Shirley, I've seen it. You know it's true."

Shirley set her jaw and drew her pistol. "Are you going to come quietly? Or are you going to keep spouting the lies your Pirate friends told you to say?"

The betrayal ripped through my guts.

"How could you?" I screamed and she backhanded me with her pistol, knocking me against the side of the transit car. I tasted blood, but it was sweet compared to the bile of betrayal. Shirley had told me she would stay out of it, that she wouldn't go to Command. *She lied.*

Shirley and her escort put us in restraints, both wrists and ankles, and marched us back into the transit car.

"How could you do this to me?" I asked.

"Stay quiet," she said. "You're already in enough trouble. Don't try to drag me into it; you'll only make it worse for yourself."

Shirley wouldn't look at me. Valka stared down at her feet. The two guards just glared.

When we arrived at our destination, about a half hour later, they escorted us through an unmarked set or doors. Inside, a couple of muscular guards in white Scout uniforms stood with pistols at their hips in front of another pair of unmarked doors.

"Prisoners Challers Dizen and Valka Parl," said Shirley.

The guard nodded and stepped out of the way. The doors slid sideways as we passed through.

My heart felt like it was sliding into my belly. I was ready to cry, ready to scream, ready to jump on Shirley and beat her senseless, but I knew that would only get me shot.

We continued into a maze of convoluted passages. Shirley turned at one intersection and when Valka tried to follow us, the guards got in her way. "Your cell is this way, prisoner."

"No!" cried Valka. Tears fell from her face and I found myself stifling sobs, as well.

I turned to Shirley, who had stopped to look back at us. "At least let us say goodbye."

She gave a curt nod. "One minute. No more."

The cuffs on our wrists wouldn't let us hug each other, so we just laid our heads on each other's shoulders and cried. I wanted to say something hopeful, but the words wouldn't come. It would be a lie to admit that our outlook was anything but void-black, and there had been enough lies.

"I love you," I said, my voice cracking. It was the only thing that would still have meaning.

"I love you, too. No matter what happens to us, remember that."

"I will. I promise."

We had said the same thing to each other, back before we even started looking into becoming Scouts. That promise had been broken as soon as the slightest strain was put on it, but that promise was built on a lie. Now, with a new relationship built from the shards of the old, I knew it meant something. I would remember her as long as I lived.

We turned our heads and kissed, but it was hard to maintain through the tears.

"Time's up," said one of the guards and we were shoved apart.

As they carried Valka away, I could hear her shrieks of grief echoing from the walls.

We walked along for a bit and then a section of wall suddenly slid up, revealing a tiny cell. Shirley removed my restraints, stripped off my clothes, and gently pushed me inside. I didn't resist. She stood in the doorway, her face unreadable.

"Oxygen," I said and she looked away. I didn't really think using my safe word that way would get me out of this prison cell, but it did hurt more than I could stand to see my life crumbling around me.

As the door closed, she mouthed a word, almost imperceptibly. It could have been *sorry*, but I couldn't see how she could be sorry for any of this.

The room was two meters wide, two meters long, and two meters high. Too small to walk in and barely big enough to lay down. The floor, walls, and ceiling were made of the same soft-but-resilient material as a Scout bed and glowed faintly. A covered hole in the corner with a water sprayer above it was clearly for sanitary purposes.

I wailed until my voice was raw, all pretense of dignity gone now that I was alone. I beat my fists on the walls. In between, I sat and sulked, imagining a thousand ways to get my revenge on Shirley. When that was done, I lay down and tried to sleep.

As soon as I closed my eyes, the lights flashed and a loud crash rattled my teeth.

I started, my sleep spoiled, heart pounding. "What?"

"Cadet Challers Dizen, who are you working for?" The voice was synthetic. Impersonal. Pitiless.

I squinted against the bright light. "I was just trying to help Masters and Valka."

"Someone contacted you. Who was it?"

"I don't know what you're t . . ."

Another klaxon split the air. I clamped my hands over my ears. Then it was gone and the lights went out completely.

Did they want Trace? Was that it? Trace didn't have anything to do with this. They couldn't want her.

"Who is your contact with the Pirates?"

"I don't have con . . ."

My denial was obliterated by the noise.

"We know everything. Your entire life has been recorded. All that remains is whether you will redeem yourself and cooperate, or if you will refuse and prove yourself completely useless."

"Trace. Her name was Trace."

"Good. So Cadet Trace Hom was part of the conspiracy?"

"There was no conspira . . ."

Another blast of sound interrupted me. "Do not lie to us, Cadet Challers Dizen. You were in a conspiracy with Cadet Trace Hom."

"To maintain the hideout in the robot. That's all."

The blackness stretched in silence. I waited for a response. There was nothing. I groped, found the corner, and curled up in a ball.

Everything seemed to be going so well. The Scouts didn't seem to have taken any notice of our activities. Shirley's betrayal bit into my stomach. I vowed to make her pay for it if the opportunity ever came.

Might as well have vowed to visit the Norma Arm.

When I woke up, I smelled food. Groping in the darkness, I found warm bread, some tea bulbs, and cut raw vegetables. I ate them all as fast as they would go down.

Sleep came at irregular times, often interrupted by the disembodied, angry voice. Always, they wanted to know who I was working with, who I had spoken to, and what I had said.

Before long, with the constant assaults on my sleep, the irregular food, and the light and dark, everything outside the room started to seem unreal. I started having nightmares. The world took on a dreamlike quality and the dreams became more vivid. The difference between sleep and wakefulness blurred. I fought hard to hold on to what was real, but in the isolation of that little cell, the fight was a hard one.

In the meantime, I told them everything. I told them about Trace, and the hideout, and Suna, and Zun. I gladly told them all about Shirley and everything she had done to make my activities possible.

And when that wasn't enough, I made stuff up. It didn't seem to matter. Talking resulted in food and sleep. Refusal, or even hesitation, was punished. Before long, I had constructed an elaborate fantasy in my head full of lies and betrayal, doublecrosses and triplecrosses, with plenty of names to give up to my captors.

Time passed. I don't know how long. Ten days? Thirty? A thousand? I had no way to tell.

The door of my cell opened. The walls outside were green instead of white.

"Good news," said a man. "We're going to reward you for all you've done. You're getting your old body back."

"Thank you," I said. "My old body?"

He didn't explain further. He led me out and down a short corridor to a gentank where a couple of technicians were waiting.

I wasn't sure, right then, whether I was dreaming or not. They opened the gentank and helped me down into the blue gel. Something inside me tried to protest, tried to tell me not to do it, that they would be able to make me into whatever they wanted, whatever was useful to them.

That voice was small. The greater part of my mind wanted to just go along to make sure they didn't start with the klaxon, with the lights, and let me sleep. Inside the gentank, I knew I would sleep. I had the strangest sensation of deja vu, that this had happened to me before, but I couldn't tell whether it was in a dream or real life.

I could swear I knew that technician, that I'd seen him before, but all my thoughts were lies—things I had made up and things I had dreamed.

All except that little voice in the back of my head.

It got louder.

They still need you for something or they would have killed you like they killed Joco. They don't need your mind anymore; it's broken. So they need your body. They're trying out a template that Cassandra made, trying it out on someone they don't care about. They're lying to you.

My imagination fixed on the dozens of newgen templates they could use. Would they make me into a limbless Astrolo, put me completely at their mercy. They could combine Astrolo and Ovor, and just turn me into an endless egg factory. They could take what they had done to Trace to its logical conclusion and turn me into just another component of their drive system, orgasming on command, a living orgone factory.

Or they could be using this as a convenient way to finally dispose of me. The gentank would simply unmake me, take me apart into my constituent molecules and store them away to use on others.

I tried to fight the horrific possibilities flooding my mind, to somehow escape from what I knew would be a fate worse than death, but the conditioned, compliant, dreaming part of my mind had become too strong. That little voice still screamed in my head as the lid of the gentank came down. The chemical smell came and I slid into sweet unconsciousness.

CHAPTER THIRTY-ONE

Masters's face swam into view, a vision in the mist, blurry and indistinct, but I knew it was him. Only it wasn't Masters. It was Robert.

"Challers?"

"Unh." I recognized the voice. Blinking, I wiped the gel from my face.

"Challers, we need to hurry. Can you walk?"

I wasn't in the gentank anymore; I was propped up on the edge of it. I guessed that I had been yanked out still unconscious.

"I . . . I guess."

I looked down. I really was back in my old body. I swallowed and stretched. The fog that had clogged my mind cleared a little. This was *real*.

"Wait," I said. "Where's Valka? Where's Shirley? What's going on?"

"There's no time to explain, just come with me. We can get you cleaned up when we're aboard my ship." He shoved me, still covered in goop, into a Scout uniform and handed me a pistol. "Do you know how to use this?"

Another shock of reality. I remembered that day in the target range when I realized I could kill, in quick flashes of memory, each like a bucket of cold water in my face. I definitely wasn't dreaming. I thumbed the safety and selected three-round bursts.

"Yes." My stomach protested with a painful somersault, but I swallowed the bile back down.

"Good. If we're lucky, you won't have to use it. Ready?"

I was still sore and dizzy from the aftereffects of the gentank, but I nodded. "Let's go."

We hurried away from the lab, through the twisting corridors. I was lost, but Robert knew the way. He peeked around corners as we went, kept an eye behind us, alert every moment for an assault or ambush. I kept quiet.

"Where are all the guards?" I couldn't see how we would be allowed to just walk out.

"We know how to plan a mission, unlike some cadets I know."

"That wasn't our fault!"

"Wasn't it?" He turned to look me in the eye momentarily. "Do you think Command doesn't have people watching for just the kind of thing you were doing? When you killed that Ovor in the maternity school, they knew the next car leaving the station would have the perpetrator."

"Killed? We didn't kill anyone!"

"Didn't kill anyone? His head was smashed like a melon!"

Valka. That was Valka. She had stayed behind to "take care of" the Ovor man who had almost raped me. That was indeed the most expeditious way to take care of him.

I shuddered. "I didn't know anything about that."

"That may be, but it was what got this whole mess started. They scanned the car as you were travelling back, figured out who you were, and came and got Shirley. She could either arrest you, or she could get arrested herself. It's a fine position you put her in." He rounded a corner, raised his weapon, and fired two short bursts.

Two Scouts lay on the deck, neat holes in the centers of their chests. The wall behind them was splattered with gore. Robert was channeling some serious crisis orgone into that weapon. As we ran by, I swallowed hard to keep the contents of my stomach where they belonged.

"Stay sharp," he said. "The gunfire is going to attract attention."

"Then why did you shoot them? Couldn't we have talked our way past or something?"

He opened a side door to a ramp circling up the sides of a wide shaft. "Too risky. By now, they know you're not in your cell; they're going to have people converging on us."

"What about Valka?"

"They're listening, Challers. Just follow me and stop asking questions."

"I'm not going anywhere without Valka."

"Vacuum take it, Challers!" He slapped me across the face. "Shut up and run!"

I ran. Every stride could have been taking me farther from Valka. I stumbled, wanting to turn around right there and make sure we were getting her too, but for once in a very long time, the rational part of my brain took hold. If Robert could rescue me now, I could rescue Valka later. With my own freedom, we would still have hope. I pushed on, past the numbered maintenance hatches set every few meters along the ramp.

Shouts echoed from below. "Stop!"

Robert swung his pistol downwards and fired a burst. Ricochets sang through the shaft. I felt the ramp vibrate as more rounds struck the floor beneath us.

He pushed me towards the wall. "Run. If you see them, shoot!"

We hustled together, using the ramp floor as cover, trying to keep the angle between ourselves and our pursuers close enough that they couldn't see us. For a few seconds, we were safe, but another burst cut across our path. We dropped to the floor and I crept up to the edge of the ramp. One of them on the ramp below was going down. He was angling to get a good line of sight on us while his partner climbed the ramp. Another burst slammed into the ramp.

I looked back at Robert, who still lay where he had dropped. He groaned, clutching his arm. Blood dripped from under his hand. One of the rounds fired from below had caught him high on his right arm.

Vack. Now it was up to me. I peeked over the edge again. I could hear the running footsteps of the man's partner on the ramp below me. I didn't have more than seconds until he caught up. Another burst of gunfire rattled the ramp and I ducked back behind the edge.

The man shooting at me was right out in the open. There was no cover for him. All I had to do was peek over the edge and shoot.

And become one of *them*.

Become one of the people who would kill to advance his own agenda, one of the people who considered his own life more important than anyone else's. There wouldn't be time to shoot to maim. I took a deep breath, trying to quell my fear, quiet my heart. I wanted as little crisis orgone as possible going into that weapon. I didn't know how worked up I would have to be to put a hole in the side of the station, but I didn't want to find out.

I rolled to the side, raising my weapon over my head to poke it over the edge of the ramp. I fired a burst to get him to flinch, then aimed and fired again. He went down.

I leapt to my feet, catching Robert's elbow as I went. Had I killed my target? There would be time to worry about that later. For now, we needed to run. I fired a couple bursts down the ramp, just in case the second pursuer was close, and we took off.

Luckily, our destination was only seconds away. A door at the top of the ramp opened and we dived inside. It was an emergency airlock, a type I was familiar with. The heavy door closed and Robert slumped against the wall, grimacing with pain. The outer door had red lights around the edge, indicating that the exterior was a vacuum.

My rescuer's face was pale and sweaty. There was an awful lot of blood.

I looked around the tiny chamber for some way to keep the door from opening again, but there was nothing.

"Great," I said, "now we're trapped." I took the first aid kit out of its vacuum-proof container and applied an emergency bandage to Robert's arm. It bonded instantly, and I could see the relief of the built-in anesthetics wash over his face.

He smiled and shook his head. "No. We're almost free."

He stumbled to the outer door, hit the button, and it slid open. A short plastic transfer tube led to the belly hatch of a Scout ship. We crawled through and closed the hatch behind us. A hand reached down to help Robert up the hatch to the main deck. Once he was up, I got to see who it was.

Grecca.

She practically yanked my arm out of its socket pulling me up the hatch for a bear hug and a kiss on the cheek. "You made it!"

"We did, but Robert's injured. We need to get him into the tank."

"No," said Robert, "not yet. I'm alive, I'm not going to black out. You two are going to have to power the ship while I keep us from getting recaptured. As soon as they figure out where we went, they're going to launch the drones. We need the fastest orgasm you've ever had."

"Can do, captain," said Grecca.

"You going to make it to the bridge on your own?" I asked.

"I'll be fine. Go get started."

Robert made his way to the bridge, steadying himself with his good arm.

Grecca took my hand. "Come on. The quicker, the better." She led me back to the chamber. "The rendezvous point is fairly close, so we don't need a good orgasm. We just need a quick one." She knelt in front of me, pulling my pants down as she went.

"Rendezvous? With who?"

"Shirley, Masters, and Valka."

"Valka! You mean . . ."

"Yes, she's being rescued right now. Or at least, that's the plan. We won't know until we get to the rendezvous point. Concentrate, Challers, we don't have time for talk. Now lie down. We don't want to be standing if Robert has to make evasive maneuvers."

Valka. We were going to see Valka. My heart leapt, but at the same time, I knew how dangerous getting away would be. I lay down in the middle of the chamber.

Shirley's voice crackled from the intercom. "I'm strapped in. Starting up, hold on tight."

"Ah, here we go," said Grecca, removing the crumpled pants from my ankles. She moved closer and gave my as-yet-unawakened cock a lick. "Bleah!" She made a foul face and spat. "You taste terrible!"

"The gel from the gentank," I said and propped myself up on my elbows. "There wasn't time to clean up."

"Well, this isn't going to work like this." She got to her feet just as the ship lurched to one side, and she stumbled and flailed for balance.

I took her hand and pulled her back down to the floor. "There are other ways. Kneel down, we'll do it like new recruits."

I hadn't had an orgasm for a long, long time, and while my body was freshly remade from the gentank, my mind was more than ready. We quickly stripped off the rest of our clothes and knelt facing each other.

"First one to come wins," I said with a wink.

"No fair! Men always win those races."

"Tough. Just try, it'll help me." I wrapped my hand around my cock and concentrated on her body, watching as she stroked her breasts and pussy. My body reacted, filling my hand with hardening flesh.

"That's it," she said, "do it for me. Do it for Valka."

One hand drifted back and forth between her nipples, making them into tight little knots of pink flesh. The other drew two fingers between her pussy-lips, making small, liquid sounds as she stirred her juices.

The ship bucked again, nearly toppling us, and I tried not to imagine the threats that could be causing Robert to have to maneuver that way. I focused my thoughts, blending all the skills I had learned in Physicality to let my body take over.

Grecca stroked her slim, pale body and let her head sag backwards. I let my eyes drink in the sight of her, enjoying her erotic display. I didn't know whether she was really trying to orgasm, or if it was all for my benefit, and I didn't care. I just enjoyed it.

A momentary vibration sang through the ship. I passed it off as the first rumblings of orgasm manifesting in the orgone collectors of the ship and refocused my attention. My hand was slick with the first secretions mixed with the lingering gel from the gentank. With the growing tension in my body, it became impossible to keep my eyes open. All the anxieties of our escape, all the excitement and rage and pain and confusion mixed together right behind my navel and then shot down into my pelvis. I came with an intensity and desperation that I had never felt before, and as the drumming concussions of the ship's drive hammered in my ears, Grecca threw herself on top of me.

"We did it, Challers! We did it!"

CHAPTER THIRTY-TWO

We did it! We had successfully escaped from the Scout headquarters.

I climbed onto the bench ringing the chamber, heedless of the mess of gel and semen on my body, and opened a terminal from a side panel. We hadn't gone far—only a fraction of a parsec—but it was enough to put us out of danger for the time being. Not only that, according to the plotted course, we had gone straight to our rendezvous point in one jump.

I pressed the control for the bridge. "Robert? Looks like we made it."

No reply.

"Robert?"

Grecca made a panicked cry and ran up the narrow passage to the bridge. I followed close behind. Robert lay unconscious in the pilot's seat.

She made a quick check of his pulse and breathing. "We have to get him into the gentank."

"You go get it open," I said. "I'll get him out of the seat."

"Got it." Grecca ran back into the passageway to open the floor plates that covered the small gentank built into the Scout ship, while I opened the controls and slowly dialed down the gravity. When Robert became light enough to lift, I slowly eased him out of the control couch and into my arms.

There were bruises on his head, fresh ones, and more on the rest of his body. Had he fallen on the way to the control couch? It didn't matter; the gentank would make him right. I lowered him down into the gel and Grecca fixed the oxygen mask over his face before letting him fully submerge.

The little screen on the side of the tank read, "Diagnosing."

I stared at it, feeling my own heartbeats counting out the seconds. After what felt like days, I asked, "That should flip over to 'Treating' very quickly, shouldn't it?"

Grecca's brow furrowed. "Yes, it should. It's been like that too long."

She touched the control next to it to get a more detailed readout. "Multiple subcutaneous and internal contusions, cause unknown. Heart, lung, and liver function seriously compromised. Brain damage extensive."

I shook my head. "Brain damage. That's not good. How did he get brain damage? He got shot in the arm."

"I don't know. This doesn't make any sense." She stood up and looked towards the bridge. "I'm going to check the ship's logs, see if there's anything in there to explain this."

"Good idea. I need to clean up."

After a quick shower, I made a visit to the pantry to get some protein bars and electrolyte drinks. There wasn't much else there, but there was enough food to get us to wherever we were going.

Which would be where? I put the food on a tray and started back towards the bridge. The plan for "where to go from here" lay in the injured brain under the deck plates. The gentank wasn't good at repairing brains; that was its only real weakness. Suddenly, our escape seemed a lot less secure than it had been.

I set the tray down next to Grecca's control couch and sat in the copilot's seat. "Find anything?"

"I was just pulling up the sensor records."

A holographic display appeared between us. Dozens of contacts had shown up shortly after we took off from the side of the station.

"They look like fighters," said Grecca.

"They're fast." The little blips swarmed after us, quickly overtaking the ship.

"Yeah. See that warp signature? It's pulling a hell of a lot of orgone. Whoever's piloting those things, they're going to be one hurting . . . whoa!"

Ten of the drones suddenly disappeared from the screen. "What happened?"

Grecca shook her head. "I don't know. It's like a bunch of them self-destructed. There was a huge ripple in the space-time structure. Look." Grecca added new data to the screen. Bright lines streaked out from the disappearing drones towards the ship. "See those green spikes? Those are focused warp energy. A weapon."

"What would those things do to us, if they hit?"

"To the ship? Not much. It's hardened against that kind of thing, or we'd never be able to make a jump."

"But not us."

"No. Any of that energy that got through the hull would scramble our insides."

"Or Robert's."

Long seconds of silence stretched as we watched the pursuit. The ship dodged and weaved, evading the deadly lances of green that shot out from the diminishing swarm of pursuers.

Grecca waved her hand at the display. "I can't believe all those people committed suicide to try to stop us. If there's anything the Scouts can't afford, it's to throw away lives like that."

"No, wait. Look." I froze the display and zoomed in on one of the drones. "That thing's tiny. No way to put a pilot, life support, and a warp drive in there. They're not using grown people. They're using Ovor eggs."

She looked over at me, eyes wide with horror. "They can't!"

"It's the only explanation that makes any sense." The hologram sprayed flickering red and green light across her face.

Grecca took data from the sensor record. fed it back into the computer, and put the math up on a secondary screen. "It's impossible. Look, there isn't enough basal orgone in something that small."

"Then it's not basal orgone." I felt my stomach tighten and I nearly moaned out loud from the pain of it.

"What?"

"They're not just using Ovor eggs to power those drones, Grecca. They're torturing them. That's stress orgone."

Grecca gasped and put her hand to her mouth. "No one could be that evil. What could motivate someone to do that?"

"It's a war, Grecca."

"What do you mean? There's no war."

"The Pirates. How long has the Fleet been protecting the stations against them? As long as I've been alive. As long as my grandfather was alive. How many lifetimes before that? You were at the headquarters. How well is that going? There's hardly anyone there. They're barely holding things together."

"That's no excuse! I don't care how badly you're losing a war; you can't use babies like that."

"It's not a war like they had after the Scattering. It's not fleets and conquest; it's raids and counter raids. Atrocities and massacres. Remember those holos we saw of the bodies floating outside Ureela Station? It doesn't matter which side did it. That's the kind of war this is."

I was nearly shaking with rage and despair. Searching for something else to focus on, I pulled up a status report from the gentank. "Robert's stable, but he's not coming out of the tank for a little while."

Grecca pulled up the navigation system. "We're at the spot where we were supposed to rendezvous with the ship carrying Valka. Nothing on sensors, though."

I tasted bile. All I had gone through, all Grecca and Robert had gone through—it would all be meaningless if Valka hadn't made it.

"When were they supposed to show up?"

"Robert didn't tell me the plan." She turned back to the sensor recordings and ran it forward, zoomed out to maximum range. The arc of the station stood out, its immense form dwarfing the buzz of attacking drones. "There," she said, pointing. "Another ship leaving the headquarters."

"Who?" I peered at the little blip streaking away from the station.

"Shirley and Masters. It was their job to get Valka." The recording ended. "And that's when we jumped."

"Were they leaving from the right place? That was coming from a different part of the station than we did."

"Valka wasn't in the prison."

"Where was she?"

Grecca sighed. "Ovor maternity school."

I cringed. "Oh, vack."

On top of everything that had happened to her, with her father, and Masters, now this. As much time as had passed, she would probably be carrying eggs, eggs fertilized by one of their professional rapists. It sickened me to think that she had been subjected to that.

I looked up. Grecca's eyes were full of sad sympathy.

I swallowed my rage and took her hand in mine, drawing strength. "So was that their ship?"

"It looks like it. I can't tell if they made it, though. They hadn't jumped by the time we did."

I looked out the front window, as if my eyes could make some kind of contribution to the sensor array.

Grecca touched my shoulder. "All we can do right now is wait. For Shirley and Masters to show up, or for Robert to wake up." She took one of the protein cakes, took a bite, and waved it in my direction. "Eat."

I waved her off. "I'm too worried. My stomach gets funny when I'm like this."

She lay back in the control couch and stared out into the void. There was nothing more to say, so we said nothing. There was nothing more to do except sit and wait.

Sleep crept up on me while I stared out into the void and the blackness covered me like a shroud.

An alarm on the console woke me. While I blinked and swallowed, trying to fight my way to full consciousness, Grecca brought up a display.

"Sensor contact," she said. "Just one. It's Shirley."

I reached for the communicator controls. "Glad to see you made it."

Shirley's face appeared. "We had a little trouble, but we made it. No one's seriously hurt." Her brow furrowed. "Where's Robert?"

"He's alive," I said, "but you better come aboard."

We maneuvered for docking, the belly of our ship to the belly of hers.

Shirley was first through the hatch. "Where is he?"

"In the gentank."

Shirley pushed past me, hit the control to lift the deck plate covering the gentank, and activated the diagnostic screen.

"Severe brain insult to the right parietal lobe," she read from it. "Multiple cerebral hematomas, autolyzed. Damage to motor cortex." She let out a shuddering breath. "Paralysis."

I put my hand on her shoulder. "I'm sorry."

"Let's get him out," she said. "The gentank has done everything it can."

Grecca and Shirley pulled Robert's semi-conscious body out of the gel and maneuvered him into the fresher to wash off the gel.

"Go talk to Valka," said Shirley. "She needs you."

I found her in the main chamber of Shirley's ship, sitting crosslegged in the middle of the bed-floor. She had a white robe wrapped around her body, but even so, I could tell that she still wore an Ovor body, belly swollen with eggs, four breasts piled on top.

She looked up at me with eyes full of hope and shame. Her mouth opened to speak, but I bent down, took her hand, and pulled her into an embrace.

"I was so worried about you," I said.

"We had to stop," she said. "I wanted to get back to my old body before the rendezvous. Challers . . ." She choked back a sob. "I can't. If I did, I'd destroy the eggs I'm carrying."

"It's all right," I said softly, holding her head to my chest. "It's you I love. It doesn't matter what your body looks like. Once you've delivered your eggs, we'll get you back to your old body." I felt a surge of pride in her. She had put the lives she carried ahead of her own immediate interests, and mine.

We held each other, there, for a time, until the communications panel on the side of the chamber beeped. I walked to it and pushed the button. "Go ahead."

Shirley's voice came through the link. "I know you need time together, Challers, but you need to come back here. We have to sort out what happens next."

We gathered in the drive chamber of Robert's ship. The bed geometry had been altered to make a seat for him. His left hand was stuffed into his pocket at an odd angle. His left eyelid drooped and the corners of his mouth didn't match. Even so, his aura of authority was still there. Shirley, Masters, and Grecca had distributed themselves on the benches around the edge of the room.

"Challers, Valka," he said, speech slowed and slurred. "Sit down. You deserve an explanation."

We sat next to each other. I took her hand in mine and held it in my lap. She smiled at me, then looked to Robert to continue.

"You're probably wondering why I took the suicidal step of rescuing the two of you from the Scouts. After all, what possible benefit could I gain from it? It would have made more sense to just keep my head down and just . . ." He groaned and took a raspy breath. Shirley jumped to his side, but he waved her off with his right hand. "No, no. I'm fine."

He chuckled hoarsely. "Looks like I'm going to have to make this short. I am a Pirate agent. It was my job to infiltrate the Scouts and send back information about where the Scout cruises were going, so our fleets could stay one step ahead of them."

"So why end it to help us?" I asked.

"Cassandra's why," he said with a half-smile. "I knew she existed, I knew how valuable she was to the Scouts, but I didn't have a way to investigate without risking my cover. You handled that part for me."

I leapt to my feet and crossed the chamber. "You burner! You were playing me the whole time, weren't you? You had me on your string, watching me, through Shirley! I wasn't doing it for you, vacuum take you!"

He sat there and looked me in the eye, cool as space. "And where were you planning to go once you had rescued her? You need me, Challers, and I need you, and we don't have time to play games. You help me rescue Cassandra and I'll sponsor you for the Pirates. I'll vouch for your actions. We have to move fast, though. When the Scouts figure out what's happened, they're going to act to secure her."

I glanced at Valka. She nodded.

My guts were clenching and spasming, threatening to bring up what little I had in my stomach, but I knew there was only one way out of the situation I was in, and that was to change sides.

I gritted my teeth. "I'll do it."

CHAPTER THIRTY-THREE

Globular Cluster X-42 was, like any other, a tangle of gravitational pits and twisted warp-lines. Navigating there by anything but jump would be impossible. Not only that, the more time we took getting there, the more time the Scouts would have to get word to the station. If that happened, Cassandra would be beyond our grasp forever.

Valka and I stood in the chamber. The moment had finally come, though not by any circumstance we ever could have imagined. We would be powering the ship together. Masters and Grecca were in the bridge, monitoring the systems, but giving us a bit of privacy.

The other Scout ship held Robert and Shirley, also finally together and also making the best of the situation. Robert couldn't pilot the ship—couldn't handle a gun or help with the mission, either—but he could power it to come up behind us for another rendezvous at a random set of coordinates beyond sensor range of the research station.

I started by peeling the robe from Valka's body, exposing four breasts and a swollen belly.

She closed her eyes, bracing herself as if about to be struck.

"You're beautiful," I said, caressing one full breast and leaning in for a kiss.

She smiled. "You lie so sweetly."

"No lie," I said, bringing my hand up to her chin. "You would be beautiful to me no matter what shape you wore. I love you, Valka. I always will. Besides, you have four breasts. What's not to like?"

She pulled me in for another kiss, this time furiously passionate, and when we parted again, I could feel a tear wetting my cheek—hers or mine, I couldn't tell. She pulled the hem of my shirt up over my head and threw it aside, then removed my shorts.

"I love you, too," she said, and took my cock in one hand, stroking it lightly as it grew firm.

"How would you like to do this?" I asked, letting my hands roam over her body, as well.

"It'll work best from behind," she said, "but that can come later. You really don't mind what happened to me?"

"It hurts me terribly what they did to you." I knew her stomach wouldn't be so distended unless someone had fertilized her eggs. "Do you want to talk about it?"

"No," she said, bringing my hand up to her cheek. "I want you to make love to me. I want us to go out into the stars. I want the moment we have been waiting for, for so long. I want the moment we joined the Scouts for. Talk can come later."

I smiled, took her face between my hands, and kissed her again.

She broke off the kiss and laughed. "We need to get started, Challers!"

"I'm in no rush."

"Well, I am." She knelt and licked the underside of my cock, and a shudder ran up my spine.

"All right, okay, I get the point," I said, my voice starting to get hoarse with desire.

She giggled again, gave me another lick, and then put her lips around the head. She tickled the underside with her tongue, and for a moment, the thought sprang up that this was something she had done a hundred times with Masters. Rather than push it away, I accepted it, let it join my memories of Shirley and Grecca and all the things I had done without Valka. It was history, it was fact, and it was irrelevant to that moment.

Valka moved slowly, walking her lips forward along my shaft, gradually accepting my cock into her mouth and down her throat. The movement was so slow and subtle that I could barely tell it was happening at all. Her tongue, however, darted about inside her mouth with delightful speed, and the contrast added a wonderful dimension to the sensations. When she had taken it as far as I could expect her to go, she pushed on. I was hard-pressed to keep to my feet.

When I was fully hard, she tipped back onto her elbows and spread her legs. "Your turn, now."

I knelt over her and slid my hand down her round belly, slowly approaching her pussy. "Gladly."

While I teased the outer lips, promising entry but not quite giving it to her, I lowered my lips to one strawberry-pink nipple and pulled it between my lips.

She let out a contented *ahh* and stroked my hair, letting her body roll back down against the bed surface. I followed, kneeling at her side and supporting my body on one elbow.

"I can't stay on my back too long," she said. "It gets uncomfortable."

"Then let's make sure you're comfortable."

I rolled her onto her side and stroked her body, one hand roving over breasts and abdomen, the other concentrating on her pussy. Her skin seemed stretched, like it was under pressure, about to burst. She lifted one leg and pulled it up under her belly. I bent down to put my mouth to her pussy, and at first, I could only reach the lower part of her lips.

"Tease," she said and pulled her thigh up as high as she could.

That exposed more of her, which I eagerly took advantage of. As I licked and prodded, her leg relaxed a bit, pushing my face away from her vulva. She was in a little bit of a frustrating spot, never quite able to get beyond a certain plateau.

She whimpered in frustration and rolled onto her hands and knees. "Vack, Challers, just do me already! I'm ready, and I've been waiting for this too long!"

"Whatever you desire, my love."

I positioned myself behind her. This was it. This was the moment I had been waiting for all those painful days at the academy, the day I thought would never come. I pushed in. The sensation was exquisite.

We were doing it, we were really doing it! Yes, it felt wonderful to have my cock inside her. Yes, it was marvelous to be there with the woman I loved. Valka rolled her hips against me, engulfing me in slow, rhythmic pulses. She was so wet I could feel her fluids dripping down my thigh.

"Do it, Challers. Go ahead. Show me—vack! Fuck me across the stars!"

I chuckled. "Gladly, my love."

I started a gentle rhythm and she moaned slightly with each thrust. There were no more impediments. No more barriers. We were there.

Except—we weren't. I wanted more.

"I want to see your face," I said. "I want to look into your eyes as you come."

"All right."

She pushed up onto her knees, pulling away from me briefly. Then she guided me onto on my back, she straddled me, and slid my cock into her channel.

"There," she said, looking down at me. "Is that better?"

Our eyes met and the energy of the moment climbed another notch.

"Much better." I reached up for her lower set of breasts and gave them a gentle squeeze.

She rode me for a few turns, rising up on her strong legs, and then took my hand in hers. "Touch me down here," she said, and moved my hand downwards.

It was a bit awkward, but I was able to work my hand in underneath to touch her pussy lips. If she was wet before we switched positions, she was soaked after. My fingers were instantly covered with her fluids.

"Yes," she breathed, "like that."

I could feel little spasms starting to run through her. Pushing down with my legs, I met her from below, adding my thrusts to her movements. We were coming closer, circling our goal like satellites in decaying orbits.

And it happened again. I was falling into her eyes, falling in love all over again—only this time, instead of a long, slow, comfortable descent, it was a screaming, flaming, comet-like approach that made me glow with incandescence. A supernova went off inside me and I felt my body boil with desire. She was mine now, if only for this one moment, and that would be enough.

I could see it in her eyes, as well. Even though a sweat was breaking out on her forehead, even with orgasm just moments away, she kept her gaze fixed on me, on my eyes. The connection was there, stronger than with Grecca, stronger than with Shirley, so complete it terrified me. As much as I feared it, though, there was nothing I could do but let go and give myself to it.

Total acceptance. Total surrender. Total love.

We ceased to be Valka and Challers, went beyond being a fusion of the two, and found a state that transcended mere union. We weren't just one.

We were all.

The ship roared to life as she spasmed and gasped above me. I surrendered my body to the sensations, as well, and the noise and vibration suddenly carried an undertone I had never heard before—a throbbing harmonic in synchrony with the pounding of my heart. The transcendence of our union had been transformed into transcendence of the universe itself.

And then we were done. Valka collapsed beside me, breathing like she had just finished a round of calisthenics. The jump engines ground to a halt and I wondered whether we damaged them with our intensity. I turned my head and kissed her as the last of the vibrations died away.

Grecca's voice came over the intercom. "Congratulations. We're here."

Valka and I took turns getting quick rinses in the shower while Grecca spoke with the station's docking officer over the radio. She was still talking when we came out again and pulled on clothes that would fit our roles in the charade we were about to perform—a white Scout uniform for me, and colorful civilian dress for Valka.

"I know we're not a scheduled visit. I have authorization from Director Mozzarat. The project has hit a snag and you need to see what we've found. Just let us drop off our passenger, and we'll be on our way."

A man's voice came from the loudspeaker. "We're not equipped to handle prisoners. Clinical work is supposed to be handled at headquarters! So just turn around and . . ."

Another voice cut in. "Belay that. What's this 'snag?'"

Masters gasped. I looked over. He mouthed the words, "That's her."

"You know Director Mozzarat," said Grecca, crossing her fingers.

"Another one of his hunches. All right, I'm giving you clearance to dock. I'll need you to maintain custody of the prisoner, though. We really don't have the facilities."

"Understood." Grecca cut the connection and looked up at us from the control couch with a smile.

"Looks like we're in. Grab your gear and get ready to disembark."

Masters and I took helmets and pistols from the supply rack near the main hatch while Grecca mated the ship to the station's docking probe.

Grecca's voice came over the intercom while we prepped. "From the look of the power readings, they can't have more than twenty people on board, probably less."

"That's a good sign," I said.

Masters shot me a no-nonsense look. "If they decide to stop us, it'll be enough. Don't blow it."

"Don't worry, I won't."

We dropped down the ship's hatch and through the tube leading down into the station. We came out in a small chamber with spacesuits hanging on racks, clearly their EVA prep area.

A woman in a skin-tight red jumpsuit stood by another hatch leading further down into the station. "I am Research Director Cassandra Mallins. Would you please present your ID implants?"

Masters held out his hand and she passed a reader over it.

"Masters?" She raised an eyebrow. "Is that really you?"

He nodded. "Come on. We're here to rescue you."

She chuckled. "Rescue me? From what?"

"From this exile. This imprisonment."

"And go where?"

"We've got a contact with the Pirates."

She laughed. "Oh, Masters, you were always such a pawn." Her face turned to steel. "Computer, initiate full alert."

A siren blared and the hatch behind us clanged shut. A hissing sound filled the room.

"What? No! Cassandra, please! I'm trying to help you!"

"I'm sure you are." She smiled, but it brought no warmth to her face.

The gravity seemed like it was going funny, tilting from side to side. I blinked, trying to clear my vision.

Masters drew his pistol, but it hung from his hand. "You know what they're doing to people back there?"

"Of course I do; it was all my idea. Now be a good little pawn and go to sleep. I have work to do." She turned her back on him, stepped through the hatch, and closed it behind her. Her face, smiling, appeared behind the viewplate.

I sank to my knees. It was something in the air, some kind of gas. The room spun around me. Masters fumbled with his weapon, and the thought came to me that he was about to kill himself. I flung myself at the hatch behind us, desperate to get it open before I passed out entirely. The lock, of course, wouldn't open. I felt Valka collapse next to me, similarly affected. Dark edges crept inwards on the periphery of my vision.

Bang.

Masters stood, bracing himself against the wall with one hand, his pistol extended in the other. It must have been a supreme act of will to stand, because I was having trouble just keeping my eyes open. I turned my head to look where he was aiming and saw that the viewplate of the far door had shattered, destroyed by the armor-piercing ammunition in Masters's weapon.

Bang. Bang. He'd fired at the hatch's hinges and they exploded in showers of sparks. The hatch fell inwards, borne down by Cassandra's bloody body, and with it came a wave of fresh air.

Still feeling like there were weights tied to my limbs, I pulled myself back to my feet.

"Get her out of here," he said. "Any way you can. I'll cover." Masters stumbled to the ruined hatch and aimed his pistol down the hall.

"You'll hole the station," I gasped. "You'll die here!"

"Yes," he said. "I know. Tell Shirley . . . tell her I'm sorry." He disappeared down the corridor.

"Masters!" My voice echoed emptily.

Valka poked my ribs. "Pry up this access panel. We can get the hatch open."

I grabbed a likely looking tool from a nearby rack and worked frantically at the panel. I could hear gunshots, gradually becoming more distant. They terrified me, and at the same time, I knew that while they were happening, Masters was still alive. Finally, I forced the panel free of the wall, exposing a tangle of wires.

My ears popped and I found myself taking deeper breaths to get enough air. The pressure was dropping. As I had expected, all that gunfire had riddled the station with holes.

"There," said Valka, pointing to a junction of heavy cables. "That's the power to the magnetic locks."

I nodded, and aimed my weapon at the junction. I could feel the orgone collectors in the handle vibrating in response to the chaotic emotions surging through me. There would be more than enough power to do what was necessary. Two shots blew the cables apart, sending more air screaming out the holes. The hatch clanked open.

As we climbed back up the tube, my head cleared. A strong breeze of fresh air came from the Scout ship, sucked down through the station and out into the void. Grecca helped us up and I slammed my hand on the control to seal the ship.

"What about Masters and Cassandra?" she asked.

"They're not coming," I said. "She's dead, and he will be soon if he isn't already. We have to get out of here."

"Right. You two are in no state for the chamber. I'll handle that myself. Go up to the bridge and get us away."

Shaking with adrenaline, we staggered to the control couches and strapped ourselves in. I released the docking clamps and triggered the thrusters to put some distance between us and the station. The astronavigation computer already had the coordinates of Robert's rendezvous point. All that remained was to wait for Grecca, and we would be gone.

EPILOGUE

I arrived at my newly assigned "pod" with nothing but the uniform on my back. According to Robert, my share of the profits from bringing two Scout ships back to the Pirate headquarters was a hefty sum, though by no means did it make me a wealthy man. Still, I would have plenty of money for little luxuries.

Looking around at my pod, I decided it was a good thing. I would need some little luxuries. The room was tiny, with most of its space taken up by a reclining chair bolted to the center of the room, facing a large holographic viewscreen. Sanitary facilities were built into the wall on one side and there was a small food preparation area on the other. I stopped the door before it closed behind me.

I shuddered. "It looks like a prison."

Valka put her hand over mine. "It'll be okay, Challers. We haven't gone wrong trusting Robert yet. Go on, sit down. That's what that man said would get everything started up."

I sat down on the edge of the chair.

A pale, translucent holographic head appeared in the air in front of the screen. "Ward Challers Dizen, welcome to Port. This pod has now been keyed to your biosignature. What is your desire?"

"Food, I think."

I shifted in the chair, sliding against the backrest. It was comfortable, conforming to my shape. I felt around and found some controls on one side to make it change configuration.

"The kitchens are currently serving breakfast. Your choices are hot cereal, cold cereal, cheese omelet, and fruit and cheese plate. Side dish choices are fruit slices, toast with jam, fruit muffin, and honey muffin. Beverage choices are fruit juice, tea, water, and coffee."

"Cheese omelet, fruit muffin, and fruit juice, please."

"Your order has been placed, Ward Dizen. It will arrive in a few minutes at the delivery panel to your left."

"Can I order something for Valka?"

"Breakfast for a guest would cost five credits, Ward Dizen. I should advise you, however, that as she is a ward, she may receive her meal for free in her own pod."

"I'll splurge."

The head nodded. "Five credits deducted. Your remaining credit is forty-six thousand, five hundred, eighty-three."

I looked over my shoulder. "What would you like?"

"I should probably concentrate on the protein." She rubbed one hand over her swollen belly. "Omelet, fruit muffin, and tea, please."

"Your order has been placed, Ward Parl."

"Looks like they want us to stay in our pods," said Valka, moving to sit on the edge of my chair. I tried to scoot over, but there wasn't room. Valka shifted onto my lap.

I nuzzled her neck and laid a tender kiss just behind her ear. "Vacuum take 'em. I like you right here."

She giggled. "Do you think there'll be a place to keep my eggs? As far as I can tell, they're about ready to come."

"Let's find out." I turned to face the screen. "Um, computer?"

The face reappeared. "You may address me as 'Portcon,' Ward Challers Dizen."

"Right. Portcon. Is there a place on board for Valka to take care of her eggs? She's an Ovor, and she's going to be delivering soon."

"Matters of a medical nature are held under a privacy seal. I can tell you that our leaders make every effort to ensure that all wards are kept safe and healthy."

Valka shrugged. "I'll ask Portcon about it when I get into my own pod. I guess they'll want to do some kind of medical exam."

"That makes sense." I stroked her belly, running my hand up under her shirt.

"Looks like someone wants to make his own examination."

I chuckled. "Just want to make sure everything's where it belongs. We've been through a lot, after all."

She leaned in and nuzzled my neck. "And do I meet all the requirements?"

"I don't know." My hand drifted along the curve of her belly to stroke one round breast. Her nipple tightened under my touch. "I haven't made the examination yet."

Portcon's voice interrupted us. "Ward Dizen, your food is ready."

A small door opened in the food preparation area, revealing a tray stacked with covered bowls and utensils. A robotic arm appeared from under the chair, took hold of the tray, and brought it alongside the chair.

"How convenient," I said.

"I don't know about you," said Valka, "but I'm hungry. We had sex a little while ago, but all I've had to eat all day were those ration bars."

The food was good, if not up to the quality of what we had at headquarters. Without the extensive gardens and farm space, it would be hard to make that kind of variety available. While we ate, I couldn't stop thinking about our time onboard the Scout ship. The sex had been hurried and stressful, and I wanted to be able to take my time.

"Portcon, is there a place where Valka and I can have some quiet time with a little more space than these pods?"

"There are many activities on the boulevard level. What sort of amenities are you looking for?"

"Nothing unusual. A bed, maybe some food and drink?"

"Variable gravity," said Valka around a mouthful of egg. "I want variable gravity." She patted her belly.

I chuckled. "Yes, and variable gravity."

"The Warplight Hourly Hotel would be a good choice. Be advised, if you leave your pod, there will be an hourly life support charge to your account. In addition, the Warplight is one of the more expensive hotels."

"What's the rate?"

"The hourly life support charge is fifty credits per hour for each of you. The Warplight charges two hundred credits per hour."

"I think we can afford that."

Portcon displayed a route, and assured me that if we got lost, it would be available at any terminal to put us back on course.

The walk was quite an education. The narrow corridor that serviced the dozens of pods on our level led to an elevator that took us up to the boulevard, which evidently ran the entire kilometer's length of the topmost deck. It was at least thirty meters wide with trees and shrubs growing in two strips down the middle and illuminated by dim globes atop three-meter poles. Thirty meters above us, a transparent ceiling revealed a dark expanse of sky pricked here and there by stars. I knew it was real, rather than a projection, because the stars had the prismatic distortion of a warp field.

"We're under way," I said.

Valka followed my eyes upward. "It makes sense. They'd have to keep moving to stay ahead of the Fleet." She tugged my arm. "Come on. I want to get in some low gravity. My back is bothering me."

The boulevard was full of activity. Most folks wore fairly ordinary coveralls of the same sort you'd see on any station. But here and there, I saw men, women, and newgens wearing loose shirts and baggy trousers or skirts, along with shiny black boots and gloves. Each one had a nasty-looking pistol hanging from a heavy black belt. Everyone else was giving them plenty of room, so we made sure to stay out of their way, as well.

The Warplight Hourly Hotel wasn't far down the boulevard, which was a good thing. By the time we got there, Valka was getting sore. We stopped in the nicely decorated but small lobby only long enough to get registered at the desk and went immediately to our room.

The bed could have been taken from a Scout ship. The surface and controls were identical. The walls had a programmable holographic interface set to display a starscape complete with dazzling galaxies and nebulae. The bed looked like it was floating in the void.

Valka whistled. "They'd never get away with this back on the station."

The vista was more than a little unsettling. "No doubt. Mind if I pick something less disturbing?"

"Please. I already feel like I've given myself to the void just by coming here and joining the Pirates."

I picked a simple pattern of red curtains. It made the room look smaller, but after the endless void, it was welcome.

We stripped off our clothes and Valka laid down on her side in the center of the bed, letting out a relaxed sigh. I snuggled up behind her, folding one arm under my head and draping the other over her body.

"Can I take a little nap first?"

"Of course."

She yawned. "And maybe a shower afterward?"

"Absolutely. Portcon?"

The face didn't appear anywhere, but the computer's voice came softly from the console by the door. "Yes, Ward Dizen?"

"I'd like some soft music please. And wake us in a half an hour."

Music began playing, a simple, ethereal tune with a simple rhythm in the background. After a moment, I recognized the clicking beat as the sound a rotating neutron star makes when the radio signal is converted into sound waves. We had studied them in Astronavigation. How long had it been since I was in that class? It seemed like a lifetime ago.

Valka's breathing turned soft and regular. I lay next to her for a few minutes, just enjoying the fact that we were safe, fed, warm, and together. Nobody had us on their schedule, nobody had us on their watch list, and nobody had us in their sights.

We could just be us.

About the Author

A few years ago Nobilis Reed decided to start sharing the naughty little stories he scribbled out in hidden notebooks. To his surprise, people actually liked them! Now, he can't stop. The poor man is addicted. His wife, teenage children, and even the cats just look on this wretch of a man, hunched over his computer keyboard, and shake their heads. Clearly, there is no hope for him. The best that can be hoped for is to just make him as comfortable as his condition will allow.

Other Great Erotica Titles from Logical-Lust

The Cougar Book

Cougar women are smart. Cougar Women are sexy. Cougar women are *hot*.

Read this scintillating collection of Cougar stories edited by Jolie du Pré and featuring the best erotica writers around.

Includes an introduction by the original *Cougar* – Valerie Gibson.

$13.99 US, £9.99 UK, $6.99 eBook download

Swing! Adventures in Swinging by Today's Top Erotica Writers

Whether you are a swinger, think about swinging, or just interested in reading about it, *Swing!* has something for you!

Another acclaimed collection by Jolie du Pré and featuring the top erotica writers.

$14.99 US, £9.99 UK, $7.99 eBook download

The Award-Winning Kielan series

Time Currents, the second book in the Kielan short story series by Brenna Lyons, is the **2010 EPIC eBook Award Winner for Fantasy Erotic Romance.** You too can experience the Kielan phenomenon with *Time Currents* and *The Lady's Lowborn Lover,* with more series stories still to be released!

$1.99/$2.99 eBook downloads

Bittersweet

2010 EPIC Award Finalist.

Stories of tainted, bittersweet erotica, written in a literary, engaging, style by debut author Amber Hipple.

Not all love stories have happy endings. Be moved by the cycle of wanting to be wanted and the pain of wanting too much.

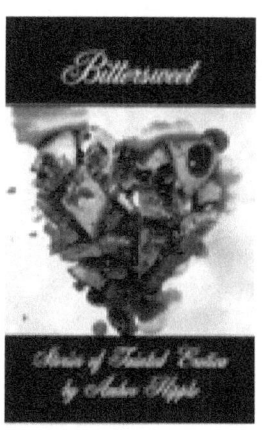

$7.99 US, £4.99 UK, $5.99 eBook download

Got Men?

Author G.A. Hauser takes the reality show phenomenon a step further in her original m/m erotica story, *Got Men?*

The set up for the big 'reveal' on the reality show Got Men? is more than just a simple decision. It's about taking a risk. The producers of the show want the subjects to take that chance, because to them, ratings mean everything.

$15.99 US, £8.99 UK, $5.99 eBook download

Future Perfect – A Collection of Fantastic Erotica

Speculative erotica at its best from author Helen E. H. Madden, from the adventures of a sexually obsessive superhero to the best orgasm you'll ever have – at the end of the universe.

Helen takes erotica to a whole new level in this astounding collection!

$11.99 US, £8.99 UK, $5.99 eBook download